Enjo...
"Haunt..."
Leta Hawk

ACKNOWLEDGEMENTS

To my family ~ Thank you for your continued love and support, for keeping me grounded and letting me dream.

To friends and fellow authors, too many to name them all, but especially J. Anne, Dianne, Joy, Kathleen, Kim, and Jennifer ~ Thank you for your friendship and support, for being lifeboats after the ship went down. I am so deeply grateful to each one of you for your advice, your kind words, and the occasional kicks in the pants as I struggled to find my way back to being a published author.

To Raven Blackburn, my cover designer extraordinaire ~ Thank you so much for bringing Kyrie to life. Your cover art is absolutely stunning; I am so happy that CampNaNo brought us together.

And most of all…

To Jesus, my Lord and Author of my Salvation ~ Thank you for birthing my writing dream. Thank you for helping me realize my dream. Thank you for breathing life back into my dream and into my stories, when I thought both had died. And thank you for your guidance as I rework the old stories and write new ones. May they be used for Your glory.

The night, though clear, shall frown,
And the stars shall not look down
From their high thrones in the Heaven
With light like hope to mortals given,
But their red orbs, without beam,
To thy weariness shall seem
As a burning and a fever
Which would cling to thee for ever.

Now are thoughts thou shalt not banish,
Now are visions ne'er to vanish;
From thy spirit shall they pass
No more, like dew-drop from the grass.

From "Spirits of the Dead"
by Edgar Allan Poe

CHAPTER ONE

My chair screeched in protest as I sat back, stretched, and rubbed my burning eyes before squinting at the clock on the wall—11:55 p.m. Still five minutes to go before the deadline. I turned my eyes back to the document I had been working on for the last few hours, hastily skimming the content one last time, even though there really wasn't time to add anything or make any more changes; what I had in front of me would have to do.

I quickly minimized the document and pulled up the Krazy Kountry Radio website. I clicked on the contest tab, entered my contact information, and attached my document. As I slid the cursor over to the Send button, a sudden surge of self-doubt washed over me. Who was I to think this silly story could compete with the hundreds of other entries they would likely receive? My hand jerked the mouse, sending the cursor to the red X at the top of the page. My finger poised over the button, ready to shut down the Internet and just forget about it. If I didn't enter, no one would know, right? *Wrong.* I sighed, knowing I'd never get away with that, at least not with JoEllyn and Aunt Julia. If I chickened out but told them I had entered, they'd know I was lying, and I would never hear the end of it. If I was honest and told them I'd chickened out, I'd still never hear the end of it. A part of me wished I'd never heard that radio announcement. . .

***

My friend JoEllyn and her boyfriend Brad were hosting one last cookout at his parents' house before they closed their pool for the season. Brad's ever-present radio was tuned to his favorite country station, the one that always had the most outrageous guests and the most over-the-top contests. This was the day they had promised to announce "the kraziest contest in Krazy Kountry Radio history." No one was really paying attention to the music, but when the DJ broke in at the end of a no-talk half hour, Brad suddenly dashed away from the grill, spatula in hand, to turn up the volume. "Everyone quiet," he shouted. "It's time."

The husky-voiced DJ excitedly announced, "Hey, hey, hey all you Kray-Kray-Krazy Kountry listeners, it's time for the contest announcement you've alllllll been waiting for."

"I hope this contest has a better grand prize than the last one," JoEllyn's coworker Angel drawled, tossing her burgundy hair out of her face and stuffing a dangerously-loaded tortilla chip into her mouth. "I mean really, who wants a hot pink pickup truck, even if it was a Forever '80s contest?"

I giggled and protested, "Hey, it was '80s Forever, and I happen to think that was a totally tubular ride, Ang." I didn't really, but I loved to yank her chain.

Brad frantically shushed us and turned the volume up even louder, glaring in our direction. The DJ continued, ". . . more exciting than a cornfield full of chainsaws or handing out candy to runny-nosed rugrats in overpriced polyester costumes, have we got a contest for you!" He went on to describe the Halloween Haunt Hunt Weekend contest, where three lucky winners would spend a weekend in mid-October doing a paranormal investigation of the Berkeley Mansion, a reputedly haunted Victorian house a few miles outside of town that I had dreamed of visiting since childhood. That house had always fascinated me, not only because of its spooky reputation, but also because of its sheer beauty.

JoEllyn's wide eyes met mine as she sat up excitedly, and I could tell that she was already planning to enter as many times as was allowed; she and Brad had their own paranormal investigation team—Ghosts and Beyond—and she always jumped at the chance to ghost hunt. However, the DJ's next words caused some of the excitement to leave her eyes. "But hold the phone; this won't be just any old call-in-and-win contest, no siree bob! You want this one, you're going to have to earn it!" I snorted into my iced tea; I could just imagine what kind of crazy stunts entrants would have to pull to "earn" a win. "In keeping with the spooky, paranormal investigation, Halloween theme of things, we want you cray-cray-crazies to tell us, in five hundred words or less, about your spookiest, scariest paranormal encounter."

It was my turn to sit up excitedly. I'd had quite a few paranormal experiences of my own, and I loved to write, especially ghost stories. I gnawed my lower lip as I contemplated entering, thinking I might actually have a shot at winning. Just when I thought my eyes couldn't bulge any larger, the DJ delivered the coup de grâce. "But wait, wait, wait! That's not all! Joining our panel of judges will be none other than Drac and Gabe Petery, founders of Petery Paranormal and stars of the hottest reality ghost show in the nation, *Project Boo-Seekers*." JoEllyn and I both stifled squeals as we sat on the edge of our seats waiting for details on how to enter. "But wait, wait, wait! That's *still* not all! Not only will Drac and Gabe be judging the essays—wait for it, wait for it—they will be *leading* the paranormal investigation at the Berkeley Mansion!"

JoEllyn and I both shrieked our excitement. I had been crushing on Gabe ever since I started watching the show five years ago. The idea that I might be able to win a contest and actually meet him and investigate with him was almost too much to bear. However, at that moment, my inner critic spoke up, informing me of the thousands of other people who would do just about anything for the chance to meet and investigate with Drac and Gabe. My excitement began to wane. Even though I knew I was a good writer, I knew I probably didn't stand a chance. I was sure that any number of others had had more intense and more interesting paranormal experiences than I'd had, and I was sure that one of those others would win. I immediately decided not to risk the disappointment; I wasn't going to enter.

JoEllyn caught the look in my eye and read it perfectly. "Oh, Kyr, you have to give it a shot." She set her iced tea down on the table with a thump. The sun reflected off the glittery polish on her perfectly-manicured nails as she listed the reasons why I should enter. "First, it's an essay contest, and you know you're a brilliant writer. Second, I know you've been trying to get up the nerve to go on your first paranormal investigation for over a year, so here's your chance. And third, you've been crushing on Gabe Petery for as long as you've been watching *Project Boo-Seekers*. How could you not enter?" When I responded with a doubtful half smile, she leaned towards me and brought out the big guns. "Come on, Kyr, with the exception of this cookout, you've done almost nothing but work yourself into the ground since you and Trevor split up. You spent that whole relationship letting him call the shots and bending over backwards to please him, and look where it got you; it's time for you to do something for *you*." She sat back and stated with finality, "You're not only going to enter this contest; you're going to win it and get out there and do something fun and exciting."

Leave it to JoEllyn to bring up my broken engagement. Even though it had been more than six months, the hurt of Trevor's betrayal was still fresh. I hated that he still had this hold over me. I hated that I still wondered what I could have done to make him stay. I also hated that my best friend would use him as leverage for her argument, but most of all, I hated that what she said was mostly true. Still, I had no intention of giving in, so I raised my chin, smiled sweetly, and retorted, "I don't have a *ghost* of a chance of winning this contest, Jo, so I'm calling the shots on this one and saving myself the disappointment of certain defeat by not entering."

I prepared to dig my heels in and counter the argument I was sure was about to begin, but to my surprise, she shrugged her shoulders and dropped the subject, going off to play the social butterfly. I eyed her suspiciously as she flitted among her guests, chatting, laughing, offering hors d'oeuvres, and refilling glasses, knowing she would never give up that easily. By the time Brad and his father were building a fire in the fire pit, she had disappeared into the house, and when she emerged almost a quarter hour later, there was a glint in her eye and a devious smile on her lips that suggested she was up to something. Not five minutes later, "Copacabana" started blaring from my hip. Grabbing my cell phone, I saw my Aunt Julia's number on the screen. JoEllyn smirked and fluttered her fingers in a wave, confirming my suspicion that she was responsible for this call. I curled my lip in a silent snarl as I shook my head at her and excused myself to answer my phone.

***

I snapped out of my reverie and glanced up at the clock again—11:58 p.m. *Well, it's now or never.* Taking a deep breath, I grabbed the mouse, slid the cursor down to the Send button, and clicked before I could change my mind. The loud outgoing-mail "Whoosh!" told me that my entry had been sent, with two minutes to spare. I quickly shut down the computer and headed off to bed, vowing to put the contest completely out of my mind so I wouldn't be overcome with disappointment when I didn't win. Of course, everyone knows what they say about the best laid plans . . .

Bright and early the next morning, as I was downing a bowl of cereal and a cup of extra-strong coffee, my phone rang. I rolled my eyes when JoEllyn's number popped up on the caller ID.

"Yes, JoEllyn, I sent in my entry," I mumbled through a mouthful of Cheerios, not even bothering with a greeting. Anticipating her second question, I quickly cut in, "And yes, I got it in before midnight." *Barely*, I added mentally.

"Good for you, Kyr! I'm proud of you," JoEllyn chirped, way too cheerily for as early as it was. "I know you were thinking about chickening out."

"Hey!" I protested, bringing my mug down with a thump and sloshing coffee onto the table. "Thanks for the vote of confidence."

JoEllyn's girlish laugh rang out as she apologized and then argued, "Be honest, Kyr. You were going to conveniently forget to enter, weren't you?" When I remained silent, she gloated, "See? I knew it!"

"All right, all right," I muttered. "Guilty as charged." I stabbed at my cereal with my spoon, trying to drown the last few Cheerios.

JoEllyn's voice softened as she relented, "I'm sorry for pushing you, Kyr, but with your talent, I really think you have a shot at this. You have a knack for putting things in writing, and you have had some creepy things happen to you." She giggled like a schoolgirl as she gushed, "Just think, in a few days, Drac and Gabe Petery are going to read *your* story! Isn't that exciting?"

I choked on a Cheerio as she reminded me of that fact. *Exciting isn't exactly the word I'd use.* My imagination began working overtime as I pictured their reaction to the story I'd sent in. I envisioned them rolling their eyes at my boring childhood encounter, laughing at my cowardly reaction to seeing a ghost, and mocking my belief that I'd even have a chance at winning. I couldn't wait to get to work, where no one would mention the contest and I could get my mind off of Drac and Gabe reading my pathetic account of a very bland paranormal encounter.

Wrong again. No sooner had I walked into the Franklindale Public Library, dropped my tote bag at my desk, and stuck my lunch in the break room fridge than Maureen, the head librarian, poked her head around the corner to ask, "Did you enter your ghost hunting contest?" Maureen wasn't big on anything paranormal, so she didn't press for details when I told her I had; she just smiled and said, "Good luck; I hope you win," before going back to her office.

I breathed a sigh of relief, hoping that would be the end of it, but no such luck. I was met with the same question when Lisa, the assistant librarian, and Henry, one of our volunteers, arrived a bit later. Henry, like Maureen, was satisfied with an affirmative answer, but Lisa, who was also an avid *Project Boo-Seekers* fan, asked me about the story I'd sent in, how many other entries I believed there were, what I thought my chances of winning were, and on and on. Even worse, she was so excited for me that she mentioned it to a few of our regular patrons, some of whom also bombarded me with questions. *Oh, the joys of a small town where nothing ever happens.*

I was happier than usual to head home that evening, looking forward to a quiet night at home with no mention of *Project Boo-Seekers*, contests, or my estimated chances of winning. Just as I walked through the door, my phone chirped, indicating a new text message. Knowing there was one camp I hadn't heard from yet, I knew before I checked that it was from Aunt Julia. I looked at my phone, then shook my head and laughed; it was indeed from Aunt Julia. I smiled indulgently at her refusal to use "text-speak," even while texting. "Kyrie, honey, this is your auntie. I just wanted to see how your week is going. Give me a call when you get in. Can't wait to hear from you. Love you."

Knowing the real reason she had texted, I chuckled to myself. *Well, Aunt Julia, you'll have to wait a bit longer. I'm starving.* I bustled around the kitchen, preparing a quick supper of pasta and salad, which I ate standing up as I thumbed through the mail. When I finished, I slid the dishes into the sink and picked up the phone to face Aunt Julia's barrage of questions.

"Did you want to make sure I didn't chicken out too?" I asked only half-jokingly when she answered on the third ring.

"Oh, Kyrie, you know I'd never do such a thing," Aunt Julia chided, trying her best to sound offended at my suggestion. After a moment of silence on my end, she admitted guiltily, "Oh, all right, dear. Yes, JoEllyn talked me into checking on you." Chuckling indulgently, she added, "Although I haven't the foggiest idea what earthly good it would do now that the contest is closed."

Despite my irritation, I couldn't help but laugh at Aunt Julia's clear logic. "Well, you know how adept she is at 'guilting' people, Aunt Julia," I replied. "Sometimes I swear she's in training to be a Jewish mother."

She laughed out loud. "Oh, Kyrie, you're such a *nix-nootz*." I couldn't help smiling at her choice of words. *Nix-nootz,* Pennsylvania Dutch slang for a little stinker, was her childhood nickname for me that she still used occasionally. "She just knows how easy it is to make you feel guilty, and she uses it to her advantage." I let out a short, rueful laugh; that was certainly the truth. I couldn't count the times someone had played the guilt card with me to get me to agree to do something I wasn't keen on doing. "So, I'm assuming you did enter the contest. What did you write about?"

I walked into the living room and flopped down on the big, worn, red-and-black-plaid recliner that had belonged to my father. As I leaned my head against the back of the chair and breathed in the faint traces of his cologne, I smiled. "I decided to write about the time I saw that ghost of an old woman at the foot of my bed." It was such a simple story, really, and I wasn't sure why I had chosen that particular incident. I had begun my account by stating that because it had happened when I was so young and I had recalled and questioned the incident so many times since then, I honestly wondered at times if I had only imagined it, as my parents always insisted. As I was writing last night, I had already felt sure that my simple account wouldn't have a chance; adding such a disclaimer would almost certainly knock my story out of the competition.

Aunt Julia's voice snapped me out of my reverie. "I've never forgotten that incident, Kyrie," she assured me. The day after it happened, my mother had mentioned it to her hurriedly and in a low voice while my father and my uncle chatted in another room; Daddy didn't believe in ghosts, and he frowned upon my mother indulging in my childish notions. "You know your father and I never saw eye-to-eye about the supernatural, and I know he always insisted that you had an overactive imagination, but the way you described that woman in such detail, I had no doubts that what you saw was real." I smiled at her confidence in my experience, and I couldn't help thinking that her continued surety was one of the things that kept me holding on to that memory. "I do hope you described what you saw in detail," she added.

A faint tingle raced across my scalp and made me shiver as I recalled the incident, but I responded simply, "I only had five hundred words to work with, but I included as much detail as I could."

"Well, I'm sure you did a wonderful job, Kyrie," she doted. "You have such a gift with words, and I would love to see you use it more than you do." I smiled warmly, basking in her praise. Writing was one of my guilty pleasures, and it was one of the few abilities that I felt confident in. Still, my inner critic kept insisting that my talent was probably not enough in this case. As if she could read my downwardly-spiraling thoughts, Aunt Julia assured me, "I have to agree with JoEllyn on this, Kyrie. I do think you have a clear chance of winning this contest. Your story may not be the scariest or the most intense, but I think those Petery boys will appreciate your honesty in the way you doubt the experience, even though it's so clearly etched in your memory." A little voice deep inside me whispered, *I hope you're right.*

Thankfully, everyone's interest in the contest seemed to ebb within a day or so, and my friends and acquaintances went back to their lives. At least until the day two weeks later when Quinn Cassel, the lunch hour DJ, was supposed to announce the winners. JoEllyn called first thing that morning to remind me to listen at lunchtime so that I wouldn't miss hearing my name. I rolled my eyes. *How can I miss what I'm sure they won't announce?* Aloud, I assured her several times that I would be listening, as long as I wasn't busy with a patron. When Lisa arrived for her shift at the library, she met me with a huge, childlike grin, squeezed my arm, and asked, "Today's the day, Kyr; how can you be so calm?" I just gave her a brief, tight-lipped smile and told her I was saving my enthusiasm for lunchtime.

Just then, Maureen came around the corner carrying an armload of old magazines. Overhearing Lisa's question, she raised an eyebrow at us and admonished, "I hope you two aren't going to let this contest interfere with your work today." Lisa's cheeks reddened, and she gave Maureen a guilty look before scurrying off to begin her work day. Maureen dropped her stern façade and winked at me. I could tell that despite her unflappable exterior, she was anticipating the announcement just as eagerly as Lisa. And JoEllyn. And Aunt Julia.

For all my attempts to put this contest out of my mind and pretend I didn't care about the results, I realized that I wanted to win in the worst way. I brought my hand to my stomach, trying to quell the swarm of butterflies that seemed to have taken up residence there. Adding to my nervousness was the knowledge that so many of my friends were truly pulling for me to win, not to mention the fact that JoEllyn and Aunt Julia seemed certain I was going to be among the winners Krazy Kountry Radio would announce in just a few hours. I wondered whose disappointment would be greater when I inevitably didn't win, mine or theirs.

Despite the steady flow of patrons that morning, the few hours before lunch seemed to crawl. At one point, during a lull in activity, I waited for Maureen to go into her office and for Lisa and Henry to be otherwise occupied, before grabbing a new battery from behind the circulation desk and sliding a chair over to the wall where the clock hung. I stood on the chair and quickly lifted the clock from its nail so I could replace the battery I was sure had died. Just as I slipped the clock back onto its nail, Maureen came out of her office and caught me. "Kyr, what on earth are you doing?"

Startled, I gasped and hastily jumped off the chair to face her. "I was just replacing the battery in the clock," I replied matter-of-factly. "It seemed to be running slow."

Maureen jammed her hands into her hips and cocked her head at me. "Now, Kyr," she began in her most motherly voice. "I assure you that clock is working fine; I only replaced that battery last Wednesday. I know you're excited about the contest, and we're all excited right along with you. The quickest way to make it to noon is to just stay busy as you have been doing."

Accepting her gentle reprimand, I decided to begin working on ideas for the children's Halloween party. Between searching online for games, crafts, and decorating ideas and creating posters for the event, I managed to keep my mind off the contest for the rest of the morning. In fact, I was so intent on my work that I completely lost track of time, till Lisa stuck her head in my office to squeal, "Kyr! Come on, hurry up! Henry's covering the circulation desk, and Maureen has her radio tuned to Krazy Kountry. They're about to make the announcement."

"Oh!" I exclaimed, quickly saving my work and jumping up to follow Lisa to Maureen's office. The swarm of butterflies returned to my stomach, and I noticed that my palms felt moist. I hoped that Quinn Cassel wouldn't drag out the announcement the way he usually did. I didn't think I could take the suspense.

The station was taking a commercial break when Lisa and I got to Maureen's office. After what seemed like an endless stream of ads for local businesses, miracle treatments for hair loss, and the first wave of local Halloween-themed events, Quinn Cassel finally came on the air. "Hey, hey, hey, all you Kray-Kray-Krazy Kountry listeners! Put down that pumpkin spice latte, turn up the volume, and tell the boss you're taking a krazy break. It's time to announce the winners of the biggest, spookiest, craziest contest in all of Krazy Kountry Radio history!"

"Oh, good heavens," Maureen chuckled, sitting back and crossing her arms. "Just a bit overboard, don't you think?"

I laughed and responded, "Well, they don't call it 'Krazy Kountry' for nothing. I only listen to this station when I'm with JoEllyn."

"Or entering *Project Boo-Seekers* contests," Lisa giggled, reaching over to turn up the volume.

". . . literally hundreds of entries, and I must say, you people have had some close encounters of the *cur-reepy* kind," Quinn was saying. "Over the past couple weeks, we've read about graveyard ghouls, wailing banshees, hooded demons in the woods, and even a handful of alien abductions." As he mentioned some of the stories they'd received, my heart sank. Those accounts had to have been more frightening and interesting to read about than the benign bedroom visitor from my childhood.

Maureen, always the skeptic, shook her head and exclaimed, "Alien abductions? I thought this was a ghost story contest."

"Maybe they were alien ghosts," I offered jokingly, trying to keep the feeling of impending disappointment out of my voice.

After several more minutes of chatting with co-hosts about ghosts, Halloween, and the Berkeley mansion, Quinn finally got down to business. With an obviously-contrived DJ laugh, he said, "Well, before every listener of Krazy Kountry begins storming the station in anticipation . . ."

"Hey, Quinn, you're a poet, and you didn't know it," one of his co-hosts cut in. "Maybe you should do a rap."

Another contrived DJ laugh. "Hey, yeah, I caught that, but I'm not a rapper, Mishon. Maybe our next contest could be a Krazy Kountry rap write . . ."

"Come on!" Lisa screeched, fighting the urge to throttle Maureen's radio. "Quit the chit-chat and announce the winners."

Maureen threw her head back and laughed. "Honestly, Lisa, the way you're acting, you'd think you had entered the contest instead of Kyr. Look at her; she's cool as a cucumber." I gave her a dubious smile. I was either a very convincing actress, or she was just that bad about reading people. The butterflies in my stomach had morphed into a flock of vultures, and I was silently thanking heaven that I hadn't had lunch yet.

"With such talented entrants, we had our work cut out for us, but our Krazy Kountry panel of judges finally came to agreement on two of our winners, and Drac and Gabe gave the final say on the third winner. So without further ado, let's announce our first winner.

Drum roll please . . ." Obviously, no one at the station had a drum, so someone rattled a can of peanuts before Quinn announced, "Our first winner is . . . Andy Belcher of Paxtang. His spine-chilling encounter with a sinister spirit while on vacation in New Orleans earns him our first spot."

Lisa gave me a pained look, obviously thinking the same thing I was: How could my story compete with something that exciting? She patted my shoulder reassuringly as Quinn continued, "Our next winner shared a childhood experience . . ." My breath caught in my throat, and I grasped Lisa's hand excitedly. ". . . of following a spectral light in the forest that led him to an abandoned house . . . a house that had completely disappeared by the time he returned with his parents the next day. Kyle Forney of New Oxford, congratulations!"

I let out a disappointed sigh. So much for getting my hopes up. Quinn said the third winner had been chosen by Drac and Gabe; I was certain that there was no chance they would choose mine. I looked towards the door, ready to just go back to work. Seeing the direction of my gaze, Maureen chided, "Come on, Kyr. There's still one winner to be announced. Don't give up yet." Her hazel eyes tried to encourage me, but I could see in them the lingering doubt that matched my own.

Quinn went on, "The account from our third winner stands out not only because Drac and Gabe personally chose it, but also because of its simplicity and lack of embellishment. Mishon, you and I had both read this story and enjoyed it, but we weren't convinced it was creepy enough to win."

"That's right, Quinn," Mishon replied. "While the description was excellent, and the author conveyed how frightened she was when it happened, she herself wrote that she wasn't sure if it had ever happened at all, or if it was just a dream." I gasped. Were they talking about *my* story? It certainly sounded like my story.

"We showed the story to Drac and Gabe, wanting them to read this very well-written piece, but we had a backup story that had the spooky factor we really wanted to see," Quinn explained. "Both Boo-Seekers read the story in question and our back-up choice, and hands down, they chose the simple childhood account."

Mishon added, "While they whole-heartedly enjoyed all the over-the-top scary stories we showed them, they both said this one stood out because of the author's inquisitive skepticism, her clear memory of a childhood occurrence, coupled with her desire to know what really happened, qualities they look for in potential paranormal investigators." I was hardly breathing at all at this point. They were definitely . . . they *had* to be . . . talking about my story.

Quinn agreed, and joked with Mishon for another minute before finally saying, "Well, I see my production manager giving me the hand motion to speed it up." That annoying DJ laugh again! "Our third and final winner, hand-chosen by Drac and Gabe Petery of Petery Paranormal and the hit show, *Project Boo-Seekers*—what an honor *that* is—is . . . Kye-ree Carter of Franklindale. Congratulations, Kye-ree!"

A loud, high-pitched squeal startled me, and then I realized that the squeal was mine. It hardly even registered that Quinn, like a lot of other people, had butchered my name; I was too elated to care at this moment. Lisa all but strangled me with a hug, and Maureen was clapping her hands delightedly when Henry came barreling around the corner, along with Phil, one of our regular patrons. "Kyr, did you win the contest?"

I was too excited to speak; I just nodded, squealed again, and bounced up and down on my chair, still hugging Lisa. How on earth was I going to get through the two weeks before investigating the Berkeley mansion and *meeting Gabe Petery*?

CHAPTER TWO

Throughout the rest of that day, I kept pinching myself to make sure I hadn't been dreaming. The smattering of bruises on my forearm was enough to remind me in the days that followed that I had indeed been wide awake when I heard the announcement. If the bruises weren't enough of a confirmation, I received phone calls from several people, including, of course, JoEllyn and Aunt Julia, who wanted to share my excitement. And to beg for autographs and photos. And to give me advice on everything from how to behave around celebrities (as if any of them had any actual experience with that) to how to dress for the investigation.

Thankfully, I found that I didn't have to worry about how to get through the next two weeks. October was one of my busiest months as Children's Librarian for Franklindale Public Library, with several reading programs done in conjunction with local elementary schools and the children's Halloween party at the end of the month. I had little free time to while away in anxious anticipation of my first ghost hunt.

Soon enough, the big day came. I left work early amid over-excited squeals from Lisa and well-wishes from Maureen and Henry and headed across the river to the Krazy Kountry radio station. I stopped at the front desk, and the receptionist walked me down the hall to a cozy waiting area. Of course, in my excitement, I had arrived a half hour early, so I sat on a red leather couch sipping extra-strong leftover coffee and nibbling on a granola bar from the snack machine while I waited for the others.

A short time later, the receptionist brought a young man down the hall and introduced us. This was Kyle of the disappearing house. I shook his hand, and he smiled amiably as he returned my greeting. He seemed younger than the graduate student he said he was, possibly because of his level of enthusiasm and the lock of blond hair that fell forward into his eyes. I sat down again as Kyle helped himself to a cup of coffee. I had to duck my head over my own coffee as I watched him dump six or seven sugar packets into his cup; I guessed that had something to do with his enthusiasm.

Not long afterward, the receptionist brought another young man down the hall, the third winner, Andy. Where Kyle was all friendliness and enthusiasm, Andy seemed aloof and hardened. His expression was steely, and he had the physical appearance of someone who spent a lot of time in the gym. His heavily-muscled arms and thick neck almost seemed to be chiseled out of stone. As he shook our hands, he didn't even crack a smile, but gave a curt nod to each of us. With introductions out of the way, we all sat down and waited to see what would happen next.

About fifteen minutes later, the receptionist and an older, heavyset man came back the hallway. "Sorry to keep you waiting," she began, handing each of us a clipboard. "These are liability waivers that each of you needs to sign." I felt a slight pang of uneasiness at the thought that we'd need to sign waivers for a ghost hunt, but I did my best to shake it off, telling myself it was likely just a technicality. Kyle, Andy, and I quickly read the forms, signed them, and handed them back to the receptionist. After verifying that we had all signed, she turned to the man standing next to her and said, "This is Randy. He'll take you out to the Berkeley mansion, where Quinn Cassel will conduct an interview with you, the Peterys, and the owner of the mansion. You'll be given further instructions and receive your paranormal investigation kit when you get to the mansion." She smiled, gave us a nod. "Good luck, be safe, and have fun."

Randy walked us out to the green and orange Krazy Kountry van. Andy, Kyle, and I loaded our weekend luggage into the back and then piled into the back seat. Randy started the van and then turned to ask gruffly, "Anyone care if I smoke?"

I fought the urge to wrinkle my nose in distaste, but since Andy and Kyle indicated that they didn't mind, I didn't want to be the only voice of dissent. Randy lit up a cigarette and took a few puffs before backing out and heading out of the parking lot on our half-hour trek to the mansion. I leaned my head against the side window and tried to catch a quick nap.

***

The van hit a pothole as it crawled slowly up the dirt-and-gravel driveway, jarring me out of a light doze. I looked out the side window and caught my first close-up view of the Berkeley mansion through the trees lining the drive. A gasp escaped my throat as I took in the stately three-story brick house. It was every bit as beautiful as I'd imagined it would be, but up close the signs of age in the structure were evident. Even in the approaching twilight, I could see the paint peeling on the white shutters that framed the windows, and some of the molding had come off around the front porch. A slight movement in the window of one of the turrets caught my eye, and I focused on the third floor, trying to see if someone was there. Although I saw no one, I had the feeling that an unseen presence watched us from the shadows. An involuntary shudder raced down my spine as I suddenly sensed a menacing air about the house. I wrinkled my nose and shook my head slightly, willing my imagination not to run away with me before I even set foot inside.

"Dude, look," Andy exclaimed, elbowing Kyle excitedly. "There's Drac and Gabe on the front porch." Finally, the guy showed some emotion.

I leaned forward in my seat to get a better look, biting my lip to keep from squealing like a fangirl. Drac and Gabe both stood with arms crossed, chatting with two other men. Drac's expression looked stern, even though he was smiling, and his muscles strained against his red T-shirt. Many of his mannerisms on the show reminded me of my father, and to my irritation I found myself hoping, as I had always done with my father, that I wouldn't screw up and be a disappointment. Pushing that thought away, I let my eyes drift to Gabe, the more laid-back of the two brothers, and I felt my pulse quicken. While everything about Drac was hard and chiseled, Gabe, while fit and somewhat muscular himself, seemed softer. The way his shaggy brown hair always fell into his brown eyes made him seem almost boyish, and his playful antics and quiet kindness on the show appealed to me. Just then, he threw back his head and laughed, and my stomach began fluttering.

As our driver parked the van and the three of us got out, I noticed for the first time the Krazy Kountry table set up at the side of the house beneath a large oak tree. Quinn Cassel, the midmorning DJ, was setting up microphones. The pleasant fluttering in my stomach turned into a sickening lurch. *Of course. The radio interview.* I had never been good at public speaking, and just the idea that thousands of Krazy Kountry listeners would hear every word that tumbled out of my mouth set my nerves on edge every bit as much as the impending ghost hunt.

Noticing our arrival, Quinn flipped a switch and announced, "The Krazy Kountry VIP van has just arrived with our lucky contest winners, Andy Belcher, Kyle Forney, and Ky . . . Kyr . . . Kye-ree Carter." I cringed as Quinn stumbled over and then mispronounced my name again. "In just a few minutes, we'll sit down and talk to them, and to Drac, Gabe, and the owner of the Berkeley mansion, Chuck Evans."

Quinn ripped off his headset and microphone and hurried over to us just as the Peterys and the other two men came down from the porch. One of the men stepped forward and introduced himself as Sean Cavanaugh, the station manager, and held his hand out to each of us. "Congratulations on winning the contest, Andy. Kyle. Kye-ree."

"Kyrie," I corrected bashfully as I shook his hand. "It kind of rhymes with 'eerie,' but with an 'ay' at the end. Or like the Mr. Mister song from the '80s."

Unfazed by their error, both Sean and Quinn apologized good-naturedly. Sean recovered right away and turned to the other man I didn't know. "Well, anyway. Kyrie, Andy, Kyle, this is Chuck Evans, the owner of the mansion you'll be investigating this weekend."

He stepped forward somewhat awkwardly and shook our hands. "I'm very pleased to meet you folks." He seemed almost as nervous as I felt.

As I shook his hand, I gushed, "Mr. Evans, I have admired your home since I was a child. I could see it from the road as we passed by on the way to my grandparents' house, and I always wanted to see it up close. I'm so excited to be here."

"Please, call me Chuck," he replied, beaming proudly. "And thank you for your kind words. The house has been in our family for generations."

Sean obviously wanted to keep things moving along. "And last but not least—Drac and Gabe Petery, these are the winners you helped select."

First Drac and then Gabe stepped forward and shook our hands. Andy and Kyle were at ease, as though they met celebrities every day. My hands shook as I greeted Drac, feeling small and fragile next to him, but I thought I held myself together well. When I turned to Gabe to shake his hand, his smile turned my knees to Jell-O, and my inner fangirl came out uninvited. A tiny squeak escaped, followed by a giggle, and all I could say was, "Hi, Gabe." *Real smooth, Kyr.* I cringed as he laughed and returned my greeting.

Sean indicated that it was almost time for the interview, so he got everyone seated at the table. Quinn gave us a brief rundown of the types of questions he'd be asking and how all the microphones worked. I breathed a sigh of relief when he said that for time's sake, they would not be taking questions from callers.

One of the radio crew held up his hand and announced, "Okay, Quinn. Going live in three, two, one . . ."

Quinn flipped a switch and began, "Good Thursday afternoon, Krazy Kountry. This is Quinn Cassel coming at you live from the haunted Berkeley mansion. I'm here with Drac and Gabe from the Paranormal Channel's hit show, *Project Boo-Seekers*."

Drac and Gabe both said, "Hello, Krazy Kountry."

"And our Halloween Haunt Hunt contest winners, Andy Belcher, Kyle Forney, and Kye—oops, sorry, Kyrie Carter," he continued.

We greeted the listeners. I wondered if JoEllyn was listening at work, and if she was actually getting any work done.

Finally, Quinn turned to Chuck, who was rolling a pencil between his fingers. Obviously I wasn't the only one who was nervous. "And, last but not least, we have Chuck Evans, owner of this beautiful Victorian mansion. Welcome, Chuck."

"Thank you," he responded, his voice cracking. He took a sip of water and continued, "Good afternoon, everyone."

Quinn explained a bit about the Halloween Haunt Hunt contest and how we had been chosen the winners. Then he turned to Chuck and began the interview. "Chuck, would you start by telling us about the Berkeley mansion? Who were the Berkeleys, and what is your relationship to them?"

"Well, Quinn," Chuck replied, "The house was built by my great-great-grandfather, Jedidiah Berkeley around 1870. The house was handed down to his only son, Jeremiah, and then to Jeremiah's daughter, Belle-Anne. Since Belle-Anne never had children, she left the house to my father, Charles Evans, Sr., and he passed it along to me after my mother died."

Quinn gazed appreciatively at the stately home. "So this house has been in your family for generations. Quite impressive!"

Chuck laughed. "Yes, that is correct. Most folks hand down paintings or silver; my family hands down a house."

We all laughed at his joke, and Quinn asked, "The burning question, Chuck, is why have you decided to call in a paranormal investigation team? What kinds of things have been happening here?"

Chuck responded, "I suppose a great deal of it sounds like your typical haunted house experiences: footsteps when I'm here alone, unfamiliar voices, seeing figures out of the corner of my eye." He paused for a moment, and I involuntarily glanced up at the attic window, which thankfully remained empty. "My ex-wife always claimed she felt threatened in one of the spare bedrooms."

Quinn gave a nod to the Petery brothers and asked, "Drac, Gabe, how did *Project Boo-Seekers* get involved?"

Drac rubbed his hand across his stubbly cheek and said thoughtfully, "Chuck had contacted us some time ago. Wasn't it while you were still married?" Chuck nodded. "Between our crazy filming schedule and his personal family obligations, we just couldn't arrange an investigation."

Gabe picked up there. "Then when your radio station called us to see if we would be willing to participate in your contest, Chuck's case came up as a possible location, and things just fell together from there."

Quinn talked to Drac and Gabe about their team and how they typically ran an investigation. Drac stressed their desire to do as much disproving as they could before they labeled anything haunted. Gabe focused more on their relationship with their clients, and how they wanted to remain sensitive and respectful of the clients' homes and experiences.

After chatting with Drac and Gabe, Quinn turned to the three of us. "We had almost 2,000 entries for the Halloween Haunt Hunt contest, and you three were chosen by our panel of judges: Drac and Gabe; Holly Jorgensen, our late-night DJ; Mishon Smith from our Weekend Whackos; and myself. How does it feel to be here?"

We all responded simultaneously that we were excited and honored and couldn't wait to begin the investigation. Kyle made everyone laugh by calling out, "Bring it, baby!"

Quinn asked, "Obviously, you've all had ghostly encounters at some point, but have any of you ever done any investigating?"

We all looked at each other for a moment, waiting to see who would speak first. Finally, Kyle spoke up. "I've been investigating since my freshman year of college, so about five years. I belong to the Paranormal Paratroopers group near Gettysburg. Shout-out to my peeps!"

Andy jumped in next. "I'm part of a paranormal group too, the Harrisburg Area Spirit Seekers—HASS for short. My friends and I started the group seven or eight years ago. We cover a lot of rural spots that other groups aren't familiar with."

Great, I thought as I listened to their responses. *I'm the only one going in with no experience in paranormal investigation*. My mind was still scrambling for how to answer without sounding like a dunce when Quinn turned to me and prompted, "How about you, Kyrie? Are you a seasoned investigator as well?"

"Well, no," I admitted, seeing no way around the truth. "My friend JoEllyn has her own paranormal group, and she has invited me to come along on investigations, but I've never taken her up on it." I swallowed hard and smiled as I finished, "This will be my first investigation." I didn't mention the fact that I often did behind-the-scenes research for the group. While Brad and JoEllyn always insisted that my contribution was invaluable, in light of Andy and Kyle's actual investigative experience, I didn't feel that my role with Ghosts and Beyond was worth mentioning.

I immediately regretted my admission when Andy laughed and turned to Kyle to comment in a stage whisper, "Oh yeah, a newbie!" Quinn and Kyle laughed too, and Drac and Gabe exchanged an indecipherable look. I glared at Andy. I had taken almost an instant dislike to him when I met him, and the more I was around him, the stronger that dislike became.

Quinn turned to me again. "But living so close to Gettysburg, I'm sure you've taken advantage of the many ghost tours, right?"

Feeling my cheeks flushing, I shook my head and responded, "No, I've never had the opportunity to do that either." That wasn't exactly true, but I didn't want to have to explain my personal distaste for tourist-centered ghost hunts to all of Krazy Kountry. I rolled my eyes as Andy and Kyle nudged each other, snickering and obviously making snarky remarks. I sighed miserably. *This could be a long weekend.*

I noticed both Drac and Gabe watching them through narrowed eyes. Gabe jumped to my defense. "Quinn, if I may jump in here, ghost tours are entertaining and very popular in some places, but it's important to remember that an actual paranormal investigation is much different than a ghost tour." I breathed a sigh of relief as Gabe warned people against going on a ghost tour or watching a few paranormal reality shows and then thinking they could pull off an investigation. He mentioned the things the audiences didn't see, such as years of studying and learning under others who were more experienced. "A lot more goes into investigating than what you see on TV, and a lot can go wrong if you don't know what you're doing," he finished.

As Quinn directed another question to Chuck, I mouthed a thank-you to Gabe for getting me off the hook. He gave me a smile and a friendly wink, making my stomach do somersaults once more.

Soon—though not soon enough for me—the interview was over. Quinn announced, "We'll chat with Drac and Gabe, as well as with our contest winners, after this weekend's investigation . . . if they survive." He cued up some spooky music and gave an impression of a Vincent Price laugh that was only slightly less annoying than his contrived DJ laugh.

Everyone laughed at his joke, and I joined in, until Andy said loudly, "Shhh you'll scare the newbie." I clenched my jaw and glared in his direction, wondering if he would be this big a jerk for the entire weekend.

As the Krazy Kountry crew was tearing down and packing up the broadcasting equipment, the rest of us milled around for a bit. Andy and Kyle were obviously trading investigation stories. As I observed their conversation, I got the sense that Kyle was a tech guy, while Andy came across as intensely skeptical, questioning much of what Kyle said. I turned my attention to Drac and Gabe, who stood with Chuck, apparently discussing the layout of the house and where they could set up equipment. Chuck pointed towards the third floor, saying something about the attic. My eyes were drawn once more to the turret window, and I caught the slightest movement of the curtains. My breath caught as I stared intently at the window, trying to see who or what might have moved them.

As I watched the turret window, I suddenly heard a voice right next to me ask, "You all right?" I jumped and let out a startled yelp, grasping my chest before I saw it was only Gabe. He laid a reassuring hand on my shoulder and apologized, "I didn't mean to startle you." His brows came together in concern as he repeated, "Are you all right? You look like you've seen a ghost."

He laughed at his own joke, and I looked up and found myself staring into his eyes. On TV, his brown eyes looked almost black, but in person and up close, they were the deep golden brown of a strong cup of tea. I was a coffee drinker, but I couldn't help thinking that I'd gladly trade my cup of joe for a cup of Lipton if it reminded me of Gabe's eyes. I suddenly remembered that I hadn't responded to his question—what had he asked again? Oh, right. I stammered, "No . . . I mean, no, I haven't seen a ghost." Had I? I really didn't want him thinking I was going to believe everything was a ghost. "I'm all right. I was just . . ." I motioned awkwardly at the house. "I was just admiring the house. I love Victorians; I lived in one for a few years as a child...." I realized I was babbling like an idiot and clamped my mouth shut, lowering my head to look up at him through my bangs.

Gabe smiled warmly at me and then turned slightly to gaze up at the house himself. "It *is* an awesome house," he said, a faraway look in his eyes. "It's definitely showing its age in places, but it has so much character. Just think of the things this house has seen over the years." An icy chill ran down my spine, and my surroundings dimmed for a moment at his words. Before I could begin to wonder what that meant, Gabe's next words jarred me back to reality. "My wife and I live in a small Cape Cod right now. There's one Victorian house just outside of Endicott, New York, that we've had our eye on for years. If it ever comes on the market . . . "

I only half-listened to him as his words sank in. His wife. Of course, he was married; he had mentioned his wife on the show several times. As he continued talking about his dream house, I studied his face, mentally touching his soft, dark brown hair and wishing I could trace his strong, square jawline with my finger. Why couldn't I find someone as wonderful as he was?

I was still gazing up at Gabe when headlights shone in my eyes for a moment and the sound of a car coming up the gravel driveway caught everyone's attention. Andy and Kyle stopped talking and curiously watched the car approaching, likely thinking, as I was, that Drac and Gabe had arranged for another team member from the show to join us. Drac excused himself to Chuck and called out to Gabe, "Leave it to Spook to show up in time to miss the interview."

"Did you expect anything less?" Gabe joked in return.

Spook? The name didn't ring a bell, so obviously it wasn't someone from the show. I watched with interest as a dark blue, older model car pulled in behind the *Project Boo-Seekers* van. My mind conjured up all kinds of images of what a man named Spook might look like, most of them involving multiple piercings, numerous tattoos, and a shaved head. My eyes widened with surprise—and I have to admit, pleasure—as the car door opened and a tall, ruggedly-handsome man got out. He tossed his shoulder-length dark brown hair out of his eyes and grinned broadly at Drac and Gabe. A strange, intense electricity raced through my body as his deep voice called out, "I just passed the Krazy Kountry van; don't tell me I missed the interview!"

Gabe laughed and strode quickly towards him. "We told you four o'clock sharp, Spook. You get the wrong time zone again?" The two men hugged briefly, slapping each other hard on the back. "Glad you could make it down here, bro."

"I wouldn't miss it," Spook replied, glancing up at the house with the same appreciative expression that Gabe had worn moments ago.

"You wouldn't miss the investigation, but you *would* miss the interview," Drac said as he came up behind Spook, giving him a shove and putting him in a headlock so he could roughly mess up his hair. "I see you're still in need of a haircut."

The rest of us laughed as Spook wrestled out of Drac's hold and finger-combed his hair. "You're just jealous of my hair because you don't have any of your own," he retorted, slapping the large bald spot on top of Drac's head. "And you know I don't do filming or interviews; that's your gig."

When they were done with their rough-housing reunion, Drac introduced Spook to Chuck. "Chuck, this is Spook Steele, the colleague we told you would be joining us for the weekend. He works with us on cases from time to time." He glanced at Spook and raised an eyebrow. "When we're not filming, of course."

"Of course." Chuck laughed, picking up on the inside joke. "I'm so pleased you could join the investigation."

"Same here," Spook said, taking in the house and the surrounding property. "From what Drac told me, you have quite a bit going on here at the mansion."

After they had chatted for a minute, Gabe took over the rest of the introductions. "Spook, this is our fresh meat—I mean, new recruits—I mean, the Krazy Kountry contest winners. This is Kyle Forney." Kyle high-fived Spook, and the two spoke briefly about some of the equipment we would be using. "And this is Andy Belcher."

Andy stepped forward to shake Spook's hand and glanced at me. "Hey, man, don't listen to Gabe; Kyrie is the only fresh meat here. Kyle and I know what we're doing."

I gaped at Andy, seething inwardly at his barb. Either this guy had a problem with my inexperience, or he just enjoyed picking on me. Before I could even think how to respond to him, Gabe laid a protective arm across my shoulders and forced a laugh. "Come on, Andy; give the girl a break, huh? Everyone has to start somewhere, right?" I usually preferred to defend myself, but since it was Gabe Petery who was sticking up for me, I wasn't about to complain. Gabe gave me a wink before turning to Spook. "And this is Kyrie Carter, the newbie."

I felt my cheeks flushing as I giggled and gave Gabe a nudge. Coming from him, being a newbie didn't sound so awful. I glanced up at Spook and extended my hand to him. "Nice to meet you."

For just the briefest moment, Spook's eyes widened as he looked down at me, but then in a split second, the open friendliness in his expression vanished. Instead of shaking my hand, he jammed his hands in his pockets and glowered down at me. His voice dripped with disdain as he nodded curtly and growled, "Ms. Carter," before turning to Drac to ask, "What do you want me to do first?"

An uncomfortable silence settled over the group. I felt as though someone had doused me with a bucket of water and left me standing there soaking wet. Everyone's eyes were on Spook—no, *Steele*, if he wanted to play that game—and me. Even Andy seemed taken aback; his annoying smugness was nothing next to the frigid brush-off Steele had just given me.

After exchanging a bewildered glance with Gabe, Drac snapped out of his shock and cleared his throat uncomfortably. "We've already got a few cameras set up inside," he said. "Grab the other two equipment cases from the van and bring them inside." While Steele headed towards the van, Drac started slowly towards the house, casting a curious glance over his shoulder at Gabe.

Gabe stared at Steele's retreating back for a moment before turning to me with a shrug. "I don't even know what to say, Kyr," he apologized in a low voice. "He can be stand-offish, but I've never seen him so . . . abrasive."

I tried to brush it off. "Maybe I remind him of someone he doesn't like." *Or maybe he ate some rotten road kill on the way.*

"Maybe," Gabe replied doubtfully. He glanced at Andy and Kyle and changed the subject. "Why don't you three follow me, and you can help finish with setup?"

The other two followed Gabe right away, but I held back for a moment, staring at Steele as he wrestled the large cases out of the van. For just a moment, he caught my eye, and the cold hardness returned as he narrowed his eyes at me. Refusing to look away first, I raised my chin slightly to meet his gaze. Finally, he curled his lip at me and headed towards the house with the equipment.

CHAPTER THREE

After the radio crew had completely cleared out and Chuck had gone to a neighbor's house for the night, the property seemed almost eerily quiet. Drac and Gabe gathered us on the front porch of the mansion to go over some general rules and safety precautions and to fill us in on the specific claims. "First and foremost," Drac began, meeting each of our eyes with a serious gaze. "We want to be clear that even though you three are here because you won a contest, this is not fun and games. This is a real investigation, and you will be treated as investigators-in-training here to learn the ropes."

Out of the corner of my eye, I saw Andy roll his eyes and shake his head slightly. Obviously he felt that Drac's lecture was intended for a "newbie" and not for a seasoned investigator such as he was. I turned to meet his eyes directly, refusing to let his superior attitude get to me. I held his gaze until he curled his lip at me and looked away.

As I turned my attention back to Drac, I noticed Steele watching me through narrowed eyes, his mouth a hard line. I may not have allowed Andy to intimidate me, but this Steele character was a different story. I quickly looked down at my notebook and jotted down something Drac had said. When I glanced up again seconds later, I saw Steele leaning over to whisper something to Gabe, who glanced at Andy and then at me and shrugged. I pretended I hadn't noticed, but I felt my cheeks growing warm. I was sensing definite animosity, both from Steele and from Andy, and I didn't like it.

After Drac finished going over the rules and lecturing about safety and respect for the client, Gabe took over to tell us about the activity reported by the client. "As Chuck said during the radio interview, most of the activity is of the typical haunted house variety." As Gabe quickly ran down the specific claims—hearing footsteps while he was alone in the house, disembodied voices, shadows seen out of the corner of his eye—I jotted them in my notebook. It sounded as though most of the activity was occurring in the basement, the attic, and a couple second-floor bedrooms, with one lone claim of activity in the small family graveyard out back. "It's important to note," Gabe added, "that Chuck has recently started renovating the basement, and not surprisingly, the activity has increased and intensified." When he finished, he looked around at each of us to ask, "Any questions?"

Something Chuck had said during the interview suddenly came to mind, and as I scanned my notes, I realized that Gabe hadn't mentioned it when he went over the claims. He must have noticed something in my expression because he broke into my thoughts to ask, "Kyr, you seem perplexed. Do you have something to add?"

My eyes shot up to meet his, and he smiled and nodded encouragingly. I replied, "Chuck mentioned his ex-wife feeling . . . threatened . . . in one of the bedrooms. Do we need to be concerned about that?" Too late, I realized that my question made it sound as though I were afraid of whomever or whatever was in the house. As I might have expected, Andy and Kyle didn't miss the slight quaver in my voice. Kyle nudged Andy and began humming what I assumed was music from some horror movie. Apparently Steele found it amusing; he tried to hide a smirk as he quickly ducked behind Drac.

Gabe tried to hide his own amusement at their antics, but his eyes sparkled as he answered my question seriously. "I don't think you—we—have anything to worry about. His ex-wife seems to be the only one who reported that feeling." He narrowed his eyes and brought his hand up to his chin, thinking. "Although now that you mention it, I would be interested to see if another woman might have the same experience in that room." I wasn't sure if he was serious or not, but I had a feeling I would find out before the night was over.

We all pitched in to finish setting up for the investigation. Since I had no experience with mounting cameras or placing voice recorders, REM pods and other equipment, Steele gave me a brief, impatient crash course in equipment setup, which was given so quickly that I doubted I'd remember much of it. After setup was complete, we were ready to begin investigating. Drac informed us that we would be working in three teams, and we would rotate partners throughout the night and over the course of the weekend.

For the first round, the teams would consist of Andy and Steele, Kyle and Gabe, and Drac and myself. I was disappointed that I wouldn't have Gabe for a partner first, but I was relieved that at least I wouldn't have to deal with Steele.

Just before we went "lights out," Gabe pulled me aside for a moment. "Hey, Newbie, you seem pretty nervous. Are you okay?"

I was about to deny it, not wanting to let on how scared I really was, but when I saw the genuine concern in his eyes, I admitted, "I guess I am. Nervous, I mean. And a little overwhelmed." I shrugged and bit my lip. "I'm not sure I'm cut out for this." I looked away miserably, my mind spinning with whatever I had seen at the attic window, Chuck's ex-wife's feeling of being threatened in the back bedroom, and the others' attitude towards my lack of experience. I had been so excited for my first ghost hunt, and now I was almost too afraid to even go inside the house.

Gabe leaned against the porch railing and asked, "First time nerves?" When I nodded, he chuckled and gave me a good-natured shake. "Well, let me give you some friendly advice. First of all, you can't let those guys get to you. I know Andy has a big ego, and Spook . . ." His expression changed, and he looked perplexed. "Okay, I have no idea what Spook's deal is tonight . . . but anyway . . ." He smiled again. "The point is, we all like picking on a newbie. And since you're the token female on this investigation, they're probably going to go both barrels on you, just to see if you can take it, so you'd best man up if you want to be taken seriously."

I gave him a smile, knowing that even though he was making a joke, he was also being serious. Oddly enough, his admonition did reassure me somewhat. "Oh, I can handle those guys. I have three older brothers, so I'm used to being picked on. I'm more worried about . . ." I involuntarily glanced up at the attic and again felt a slight chill. I pressed my lips together, not wanting to say any more.

Gabe narrowed his eyes at me and then glanced up towards the attic himself, as though he sensed there was something I wasn't telling him. Instead of pursuing it, he simply assured me, "You'll be fine, Kyr. Once you get in there and start investigating, you'll catch on pretty quickly." He gave my shoulder a little squeeze. "In any case, you're in good hands."

As Gabe winked at me and turned to head inside, I bit my lip and smiled in spite of my nervousness, though not because I felt more confident. Just standing next to my celebrity crush made me feel like a teenager, and as I felt the blood suddenly rush to my face, I was grateful for the deepening twilight on the porch so that he wouldn't notice. As I started off to find Drac, I noticed Steele standing at the far end of the porch, watching me. Something in his eyes made my knees suddenly go weak, but before I even had a chance to wonder at my reaction, his expression hardened, and he glared at me. Not wanting him to think he could intimidate me, I narrowed my eyes dismissively at him and went off in search of Drac.

As luck would have it, the first place Drac wanted to investigate was the attic, which did nothing to allay my nervousness. Although Drac was good-natured and patient with the newbie, I still felt insecure around him, and as we climbed the steep staircase to the third floor, I sincerely hoped that nothing would happen to frighten me into making a fool of myself. His voice snapped me out of my reverie. "Chuck says he hears the sound of someone walking in the attic quite frequently, but when he checks, there's no one up here," he reminded me. "Apparently there have also been occasional sightings of a Civil War soldier peering out the window."

So it wasn't my imagination, I thought. It didn't help knowing that others had seen something in the attic window, and I hoped that that something wasn't waiting for us at the top of the stairs. In any case, I was glad Drac was going first.

Once in the attic, we sat down in chairs on opposite sides of the room, Drac with a thermal imaging camera and digital voice recorder, and me with just a digital voice recorder. As my eyes adjusted to the darkness, I noticed there were stacks of boxes and miscellaneous other items scattered around, which resulted in a lot of shadows. I glanced around nervously, hoping none of the shadows moved of their own accord. I heard rather than saw Drac turn towards me to say, "Let's get 'er started."

We both switched on the voice recorders, and Drac panned across the room with the thermal camera and began, "Drac and Kyrie, in the Berkeley mansion attic." He paused for a moment and continued, "Is there anyone here with us? We're not here to bother you; we just want to talk to you."

A few seconds later, I said, "We heard that people have seen your face at the window. Are you looking for someone?" The room was quiet except for the sound of our breathing and the soft moan of the wind outside. I noticed the temperature was beginning to drop, but I wasn't sure if it was paranormal or just because it was getting colder outside.

Drac shifted in his chair and commented, "It's feeling a bit chilly over here; how about you?"

"It's definitely colder all of a sudden, but I do hear the wind picking up," I replied, shivering. "Do you think we should check for drafts?"

Drac focused the thermal in a few spots and then encouraged, "Good call, Kyr. There are cold spots around all the windows, as well as along the outer wall. I'm guessing it's not well insulated up here." He turned towards me and added, "I wanted to see if you'd try to find a reason for the temperature change, or if you'd just assume it was paranormal."

Drac's praise encouraged me somewhat, and I felt myself relax. Maybe Gabe was right; maybe I would get the hang of investigating. A moment later, we heard what sounded like footsteps coming up the attic stairs. Drac whispered, "Did you hear that?"

"Yeah," I replied, tensing up again. We both sat listening for the sound again, but it seemed to stop about halfway up. I was glad I wasn't alone in the attic.

Finally, Drac asked, "You want to check it out, or do you want me to go?"

Hoping I sounded braver than I felt, I said, "I'll go." I crept toward the stairs, trying not to knock anything over and listening carefully for any sound that might betray the presence of someone or something. I shined my flashlight down the dark stairwell and said, "Hello? Is there someone down here?" I didn't know if I wanted an answer or not, but there was none. I descended slowly to the second floor and shined my flashlight up and down the hallway, watching for any signs of movement among the shadows. After checking things out thoroughly, I went back to the attic. "No one there," I told Drac. "Anything more up here?"

"Nothing," he replied. "It's been completely quiet. Your footsteps coming up the stairs sounded exactly like the sound we heard up here, though. I'm sure we caught that on the voice recorder; we'll have to see if that's what Chuck hears."

We sat in the attic for quite a while longer, trying different things to communicate with the spirit, but the room remained quiet. Soon, Drac called Gabe on the walkie-talkie. "Hey, Gabe? You ready to switch up teams?"

Gabe radioed back, "Yeah, Drac, sounds good. Meet you back at Center Command." Center Command had been set up in the back of the Petery Paranormal van, which was parked in the turn-around near the front of the house.

A few minutes later, we met back at Center Command to share experiences and plan the next move. Andy and Steele had been in the basement, where they heard disembodied voices and footsteps coming from the very back part of the old coal cellar, and Drac and I shared our lone experience in the attic. Gabe and Kyle had been watching the monitors at Center Command, and Gabe said, "The stationary camera in the family graveyard picked up a mist or something about ten or fifteen minutes ago, so I'd like to get someone out there and check that out. Spook, you up for that?"

Spook agreed, and Kyle's eyes lit up, and he asked excitedly, "Dude, can I come with you? I've never investigated in a graveyard."

A few minutes later, Steele and Kyle bundled up and headed out back to the small fenced-in plot. Drac and Andy settled in at Center Command, and Gabe and I headed for the second floor to check out the activity in the bedrooms. Obviously, my earlier hunch had been correct; Gabe was planning to see if the "token female" would have an experience similar to Chuck's ex-wife's in the back bedroom. As we slowly ascended the stairs, Gabe turned to ask, "So, are you feeling more confident now that you've started investigating?"

I hesitated for a moment before answering, "A little bit, I guess."

"But you're still nervous?" Gabe responded, pausing on the stair above me.

I didn't want to admit it to him, but I said, "I guess I wasn't prepared for how creepy it is to sit in a dark room waiting for something to talk to you."

I heard the smile in Gabe's voice as he reassured me, "Well, don't worry, Kyr. We've never lost an investigator." He turned to continue up the stairs, but suddenly glanced over his shoulder to say gravely, "Except that one guy a couple years ago..." My eyes widened, and I felt the color drain from my face before he laughed and reached back to nudge my shoulder. "Relax, I'm just kidding!" I wasn't sure whether I wanted to slug him or laugh along with him.

Gabe suggested we start in the master bedroom where Chuck often heard voices and occasionally saw shadows move out of the corner of his eye. Gabe handed me a K-II meter, saying, "The first thing I want to do in here is take some EMF readings. This is an old house, and I'm sure some of the wiring hasn't been replaced for ages." I began moving around the room with the K-II meter while Gabe watched. After a moment, he crossed the room and took my hand in his. "You want to move the meter more slowly like this, so you don't get any false spikes." I tried to focus on his instruction, but my mind kept screaming, *Gabe Petery is touching me! Gabe Petery is touching me!*

We didn't get any unusual readings, so we sat down to try to make contact with whatever spirits might be present. Gabe asked for the spirit's name and if it could give us a sign of its presence. For a moment, there was silence, but then we heard a muffled bang from the bedroom next door. Gabe and I looked at each other and asked simultaneously, "Did you hear that?"

We dashed into the next bedroom and shined our flashlights around the room to see if anything was out of place, but we found nothing. Gabe even yanked the closet door open to look inside, but he only found linens and extra pillows, nothing that would have made a loud sound. I made sure my voice recorder was switched on and requested, "If that was you, could you make another noise to let us know you're here?"

As if on cue, we heard another bang, this time from the master bedroom. "What the Sam Hill?" Gabe muttered as we ran back to the master bedroom. Again, we shined our flashlights around, but found nothing out of place that might have caused a bang.

We looked at each other again. "What, do we have a smart-aleck spirit on our hands?"

Gabe laughed. "It would seem so." He continued, "Okay, you've got our attention. Do you just want to play, or do you have a message for someone?"

Once again, we heard a bang come from the other room. We shook our heads and laughed. Then Gabe suggested we separate to see if one of us could corner the spirit. Gabe stayed in the master bedroom and, as I suspected he would, suggested I head to the other bedroom. I was a bit leery of the possibility of being alone with a ghost, but I tried to convince myself that we didn't seem to be dealing with a malicious spirit. I had my flashlight, a digital voice recorder, and a video camera that Gabe handed me at the last moment. I decided to set it up on the vanity to capture as much of the room as possible.

I sat down on the bed and tried provoking the spirit. "Okay, you've been playing hide and seek with us; now how about you show yourself. My name is Kyr; I'm here, and Gabe is in the other room. Quit playing games and let one of us see you."

No sooner had I said that than the room became drastically colder. Goosebumps rose on my skin, and I began to tremble, although I couldn't tell if it was from the cold or from fear. Trying not to let my voice betray my feelings, I said, "Come on, you'll have to do better than that!"

Just then, Gabe's voice came over the walkie-talkie, startling me. "Gabe to Kyr, it's pretty quiet over here. You getting anything over there?"

I replied, "Yeah, the room got ice cold as soon as I started provoking—" Before I could finish, the bedroom door slammed shut, and my flashlight flickered and went out, leaving me in complete darkness.

"What the hell was that?" Gabe asked.

Trying not to panic, I radioed back, "The door just slammed shut, and my flashlight went out. What do I do?"

Gabe must have sensed the fear in my voice. "Just stay calm, and keep trying to communicate. I'll be there in a second."

I stood up and made my way towards the door, asking the spirit if it had a reason for being there, why it stayed in the house. A moment later, I heard Gabe rattling the doorknob. "I can't get the door open. Is it locked from your side?"

"I wouldn't think so," I said, beginning to feel more apprehensive. I tried the doorknob, to no avail. "I can't get it open either." I fumbled around, looking for any kind of lock. Finding none, I tried pulling as hard as I could on the door.

Suddenly, the room became even colder, and I felt the hairs on my neck stand up as I became aware of a presence behind me. I turned quickly and pressed up against the door, not really wanting to see who or what was there, but not wanting to be taken by surprise either. I wasn't ready for what I saw in the room with me. A shimmering mist had formed beside the bed and was beginning to take the shape of a person. In a matter of seconds a tall, angry-looking man stood before me and began moving towards me. My eyes widened in terror as I realized I was trapped in a locked room with a very unfriendly-looking spirit. I began pounding on the door, shouting, "Gabe! Get me out! There's something here with me!"

Gabe was obviously concerned about what he couldn't see happening, but he tried to calm me. "Don't be afraid of it. See if you can communicate. I'll keep trying to get the door open."

I was so frightened that communicating with a spirit was the last thing on my mind. The spirit continued to move towards me, and it reached a menacing hand towards me. I stifled a scream, and then yelled, "Stay away! Stay away! Gabe, please get the door open!"

As I continued pounding on the door and imploring the spirit to leave me alone, I heard Gabe radio to Drac and Steele for help. The spirit loomed over me. I covered my head with my hands and pressed harder against the door. The last thing I remembered was screaming as I felt an icy blast go through my body; then everything went black.

When I woke up, I was on the floor in the hallway with Drac and Steele kneeling next to me. Drac said, "Gabe, she's coming around."

I was shivering uncontrollably and felt colder than I had ever remembered being, even though I was covered by a heavy blanket.

Gabe came closer and knelt down, slipping his arm under my shoulders to help me sit up before holding a glass of water to my lips. "Drink some of this, hon," he said gently.

After I drank some water, I asked hoarsely, "What the hell happened?"

Andy, who was standing on the top stair, leaning on the banister, said, "You freaked out, Newbie! We heard you scream all the way out at Center Command."

Well, that explained why my voice was hoarse. Drac glanced at Gabe, then with a glint in his eye, said, "You've definitely got a good set of lungs, girl." They all laughed at Drac's joke; I just pulled my knees up and hid my face in my arms. I couldn't believe this was happening. *I sure made a great first impression as a ghost hunter*, I thought.

Drac said, more seriously, "We were hoping you could tell us what happened."

I was silent for a moment, not wanting to think about it. Gabe said, "After you told me there was something in that room with you, I tried to get the door open, but it was locked. When you started panicking, I called Drac and Spook for help. Then you screamed, I heard something hit the floor—you, I suppose—and then the door flew open by itself. It was freakin' crazy!"

Steele continued, "By the time Drac and I got up here, Gabe had you out in the hallway and was trying to wake you up. What did you see in there?" Chancing a glance at him, I noticed that much of his earlier animosity was gone, and he just looked concerned.

I took a shaky breath and quickly told them all that had happened in those few minutes. I was seeing the ghost's angry eyes and his hand reaching towards me. It wasn't something I wanted to remember, and I felt myself beginning to panic again as I looked towards that room.

Gabe laid his hand on my shoulder and said, "You're okay now. Why don't we get you out of here? You think you can walk?"

I thought, *If it means getting out of here, I could grow wings and fly,* but I simply nodded my head. Gabe and Steele helped me get up and walk down the stairs and out of the mansion.

CHAPTER FOUR

I sat in the back of the Petery Paranormal van while Drac, Kyle, and Andy checked out the back bedroom. Gabe and Steele stood just outside the van, talking in whispers, which at that moment was fine with me; I could hardly look at either of them because I felt so foolish for losing my head. Even worse was the feeling that I'd lose my head all over again if I couldn't get the image of that angry ghost out of my mind. I shivered again and wrapped my arms around myself, trying to get warm and trying to shut my mind off. Gabe came inside and put his arm around me before asking, "Are you still cold?"

I nodded my head, still unable to look him in the eye. He gave me a little shake and joked, "So you got a little more than you bargained for on your first investigation?"

I heard Steele choke a laugh into a cough just outside the van, which didn't help. I couldn't speak, so I just nodded my head again. I knew Gabe was trying to lighten my mood, and I appreciated the attempt, but it just wasn't working; I was too upset.

Gabe moved so he was facing me and gently said, "Come on, talk to me. What's going on in your head?"

Trying not to break down, I took a deep breath and responded, "I'm trying to get that face out of my head. I've never been so scared in my life. I thought it was going to kill me." I glanced up and saw Steele poke his head around the side of the van. His expression was serious, but I could see a glimmer of amusement in his eyes.

I could hear the smile in Gabe's voice, too, as he answered, "I can understand how you might think that, but I don't think the entity was trying to hurt you."

"Well, it sure wasn't Casper the Friendly Ghost," I cried, suddenly irritated. "What was it trying to do?"

Gabe and Steele burst out laughing at my remark; then Gabe apologized and commented, "At least your sense of humor is still intact."

Steele stepped inside the van and sat down behind Gabe before interjecting, "Look, Carter, most of the time human spirits — and I'm sure that's what we're dealing with here — don't try to hurt people. It's hard to say what its intent was, but I'm sure it didn't mean you any harm."

Just then, Drac, Andy and Kyle came out of the house. I heard Drac tell Andy and Kyle to go ahead and take a break before he hurried out to the van carrying the video camera I had placed in the bedroom. He held it up and said, "This was set up in that bedroom — was it running while you were in there?"

Gabe looked at me quickly with an expression of excitement on his face. My eyes widened, realizing why he looked so excited: the entity's attack might be on that tape. I swallowed hard before answering, "Yeah, I turned it on before I started . . . provoking."

Gabe and Drac glanced at each other, and then at Steele, all three of them looking like kids in a candy store. Gabe said excitedly, "Man, it would be *sweet* if we caught that on video."

Drac added, "I can't wait to review this tape tomorrow!" I silently wondered if he'd even wait that long.

The three of them began discussing what had just happened upstairs; I really wasn't in the mood to relive it, so I quietly exited the van and sat down on a big rock by the driveway. I yanked my hood up and jammed my hands in my hoodie pockets, looking back towards the small, fenced-in family graveyard. Strangely, that seemed to be the one place on the Berkeley property that didn't give me the creeps, and I seriously considered taking a stroll up there, not sure I wanted to hear what they were talking about.

They must have noticed that I had slipped out, because the topic of conversation changed. My ears perked up as Drac lowered his voice to ask, "So, how is she?"

Gabe replied, "Physically, she's fine, but she's pretty shook-up." A piece of equipment creaked as someone leaned against it. "I just wanted to see if she'd have the same experience Chuck's ex-wife had in that room. I didn't expect anything as wild as what happened."

Drac chuckled and commented, "Especially when you initially seemed to have a playful spirit on your hands." After a moment of silence, he continued, "She had a pretty detailed description of what she saw in there. Chuck's ex-wife didn't see an apparition, did she?"

"No, not that he told us. He only said that she felt uneasy . . . threatened," Gabe replied. After a pause, he lowered his voice so that I had to strain to hear him. "You know, before we went inside to begin investigating, Kyr seemed to sense something. She kept looking up at the upstairs windows. You don't think she's . . ."

"Over-imaginative?" Steele interjected skeptically. "Making it up?"

I clenched my fists indignantly, fighting the urge to burst in there and slug him. What was his problem, anyway? Drac must have been wondering the same thing, because he shot back, "Spook, you've had a chip on your shoulder all night. What is your issue with her?"

Steele lowered his voice so that I couldn't hear everything he said. I did, however, manage to catch enough words to figure out his overall opinion of me: "Fan-girl...Gabe...wannabe..."

Gabe forced a laugh and jumped to my defense. "Spook, I think you're making a big deal out of nothing. How is Kyr any more a 'fan-girl' or a 'wannabe' than anyone else who entered this contest?" He laughed genuinely and added, "Admit it; she's nowhere near as bad as some of the women we've encountered."

Drac chuckled at Gabe's remark, and I wondered what experiences they'd had for him to make that statement. Drac added, "Besides, at least she was honest about not having any experience with investigating. Honestly, I almost prefer her inexperience over . . ." I guessed that he was motioning towards Andy on the porch.

"That's another thing that's bothering me," Steele growled. "I don't think it was a good idea bringing contest winners into a location we really know nothing about. We don't know yet what we're dealing with, and obviously newbie fan-girl out there has no business being here."

"Would you keep your voice down?" Drac hissed. "She *is* right outside, you know." *And I heard you loud and clear,* I thought. "Besides, you just accused her of being over-imaginative and making up what she saw up in that bedroom, and now you're implying there may be more here than we originally thought. Now, which is it?"

My irritation turned to apprehension as I waited for Steele to answer. After what seemed like an eternity, he responded weightily, "It's too soon to tell, but if—and that's a big if—Carter's experience was genuine, we might have more than a simple residual haunting." I felt the same prickly chill across my scalp that I had felt earlier as a sense of foreboding came over me. Steele finished, "In any case, I think she should sit out the rest of the night."

"Agreed," Drac and Gabe said together. I heard Drac stand up, and he said with more cheerfulness than I was certain he felt, "Let's round up the troops and get back at it, gang."

As Drac headed up towards the house to get Andy and Kyle, Gabe and Steele exchanged a glance before Gabe came over and sat down next to me on the rock. "How are you feeling, hon?"

I gave him a weak smile and responded, "I'm okay, just still a little freaked out." *More than a little. A lot more than a little.* I fought the urge to look up at the house, not wanting to give Gabe another reason to worry or Steele another reason to call me over-imaginative. Instead, I steeled myself and met Gabe's eyes before adding, "Maybe I should sit out for a bit."

Gabe's eyebrows shot up in surprise, and I thought he looked just the slightest bit guilty. I was certain that he suspected I had overheard their conversation, but he said nothing about it. Before he could respond, Steele laughed shortly at my comment, and both Gabe and I turned to look at him. As my eyes met his, I swear I felt a jolt of electricity pass between us before his expression hardened once more. Gabe's eyes darted quickly from Steele to me and back again before he declared, "I think you're right, Kyr. You should probably take a break. You can get some experience watching the monitors." Just as Steele smirked triumphantly, Gabe turned to him with a gleam in his eye and added, "Spook, you can stay here with her and show her the ropes."

My jaw dropped, and I gaped at Gabe. What was he doing? Surely, he had to know that Steele and I couldn't stand each other, and that I was already on the verge of throttling him. When I chanced a glance in Steele's direction, I noticed he was having the same reaction; if I hadn't been so irritated at that moment, I might have found it funny. Steele threw his arms out in frustration, and his mouth moved, but for a moment no words came out. Finally, he blurted out, "You're not serious…?"

Really? I thought, this time stifling a laugh. *That's the best Mr. Attitude can do?*

"I'm quite serious," Gabe replied. It was his turn to smirk triumphantly. "You're part of the Petery Paranormal family, and you're capable of being professional, right?" Steele's look of disgusted defeat was priceless. Gabe clapped him on the shoulder. "Good. You can show Newbie the ropes." He grinned at Steele, winked at me, and walked over to join Drac, leaving Steele and me to stare after him. Steele curled his lip at me before he turned and climbed back in the back of the van.

Fifteen minutes later, Steele and I sat grudgingly together watching the monitors in the back of the van while the others investigated. Drac and Kyle were in the back bedroom trying to make contact with my unfriendly ghost, while Gabe and Andy tried their luck in the attic. The minutes seemed to drag as we stared steely-eyed and silent at the monitors. I was surprised at how difficult it was to stay focused on the monitors when everything was quiet. I found myself fighting the urge to fidget or to close my eyes or look away for a moment, but I knew if I did, I might miss something. *At least I'm not tempted to chit-chat with Steele,* I thought ruefully.

Steele sat forward in his chair, zeroing in on one of the monitors. "What the hell was that?" he muttered, then turned his head slightly towards me without taking his eyes off the screen. "Did you see that flash of light in the graveyard?"

I leaned over to gaze at the graveyard monitor. "No," I responded. "I was watching the second-floor cameras."

Steele curled his lip at me and growled, "You need to learn how to watch more than one monitor, Carter." My jaw dropped at his rudeness, but before I could respond, he grabbed his walkie. "Spook to Drac and Gabe, do you copy?"

Drac responded right away. "Yeah, bro. What do you need?"

A second later, Gabe replied, "Copy. What's up?"

Still focusing on the graveyard monitor, Steele reported, "I just saw a bright flash of light on the graveyard monitor. Did anyone shine a flashlight out the window in that direction?"

Drac confirmed that neither he nor Andy had been anywhere near the window with their flashlights, and Gabe and Kyle were at the front of the house and couldn't even see the graveyard.

A sudden bright spot on the monitor caught my attention, and I exclaimed, "There it is again. That's not a flashlight." Without thinking, I leapt out of my chair, jumped out of the van and headed for the graveyard.

"Carter, what do you think you're doing?" Steele yelled after me. "Get back here!"

I ignored him, determined to find out what was lurking there. Hearing footsteps behind me, I assumed Steele was following me, but I wasn't going to take the time to look. I reached the waist-high wrought iron fence and easily vaulted over it instead of going around to the other side and struggling with the gate. Once inside, I paused to note the position of the stationary camera and then walked slowly around the tree to the spot where I thought the flash had been. As I looked around trying to see if we might have seen headlights reflecting off the tree, Steele finally made it through the gate and stormed over to where I stood. "Carter, what the blazes do you think you're doing?" he spat, looking at me incredulously.

I turned to face him and involuntarily took a step back when I saw the fire in his eyes. Drawing myself up as tall as I could, I replied, "I'm investigating. What do you think?"

Before he could catch himself, I saw a glimmer of amusement in his eyes as he quickly pursed his lips to hide a smile. With some difficulty, he responded sternly, "I thought you were sitting out the rest of the night."

"Maybe I changed my mind," I retorted, hoping I sounded more confident than I felt. I turned back towards the tree and looked up into the branches, and then over to the house, and finally across the yard to the housing development just beyond the property.

Steele leaned against the tree with his arms crossed, alternately watching me and looking up at the tree as though he sensed something. At one point, our eyes met, and we asked at the same time, "Any ideas?" We both laughed uncomfortably, and Steele said, "I think it's pretty obvious we didn't see a flashlight, even if they did shine one out the window. Any other ideas?"

The only other rational explanation I could think of didn't seem very likely either. Still, I wanted to say something so I didn't look like a complete...newbie. Motioning towards the housing development with my head, I asked, "What are the chances we saw headlights from a car coming from over there?"

Steele glanced over in the direction I had indicated, and his brows came together skeptically. I lowered my eyes and braced myself for a critical comment and was shocked when he gave me the benefit of the doubt. "I suppose we could test that theory." He radioed up to Drac to let him know what we were planning to do and then told me to stand by the stationary camera and watch through the flip screen while he drove through the development with the high beams on.

After he'd gone and I was alone in the graveyard, I began to feel apprehensive. I glanced over at the house, which loomed ominously in the moonlight, its windows like black eyes watching my every move. Knowing that the others were inside investigating did little to alleviate my growing sense of uneasiness. I inhaled deeply and slowly breathed out, telling myself I had read too many ghost stories. I turned my attention back to the graveyard, the same graveyard that earlier had seemed to be the least creepy place on the property. Now I wasn't so sure. Steele started his car, and as I heard the gravel crunching as he drove slowly down the driveway, I snuggled down into my hoodie to ward off the deepening chill.

A minute went by, and Steele's voice came over the walkie, making me yelp. "Carter, you ready? I'm turning in to the development right now."

I grabbed my walkie off my belt and replied, "Ready when you are." I kept my eyes towards the development, and when I saw the headlights from his car round the corner, I leaned over to focus on the flip screen.

"Okay," Steele radioed. "I'm going to make one pass with the low beams on, swing around in the cul de sac, and then come back around with the high beams on."

"Copy that," I replied. As he drove down the street, I saw the tree, the gravestones and the fence illuminate slightly, but it was obvious even through the small flip screen that I was seeing headlights.

He stopped the car in the cul de sac and radioed me again. "How did that look?"

"Nothing like what we saw on the monitor," I responded, discouraged that my idea hadn't panned out. "Even through the camera, I can tell I'm seeing headlights. Do you still want to give it a shot with the high beams?"

Steele was silent for a moment before he answered somewhat doubtfully, "Let me swing around, and we'll give it a shot."

As Steele turned the car around, the graveyard was plunged into darkness once more. I blinked a few times, waiting for my eyes to adjust, and focused on the flip screen again. My breath caught as a shadow quickly darted behind the tree. I stared unblinking at the screen for a moment before I slowly raised my eyes to look directly at the tree. Seeing nothing, I glanced back down at the screen. For a moment, everything was as it had been, but then the shadow moved from behind the tree. I stood up quickly, my eyes on the tree. This time, I saw the shadow duck back behind the tree. My scalp prickled, and my pulse pounded in my ears as I stepped to the side to see who or what was playing with me. As I brought my foot down, dry leaves crunched loudly. I pulled out my flashlight and shined it around underneath the tree. Dry leaves covered the ground there as well, and I realized that if I were dealing with a flesh and blood person, I would have heard footsteps in those leaves. I reached down to switch on my voice recorder and said, low, "Hello? Is there someone here who would like to talk to me?"

Almost immediately, my walkie crackled loudly, and Steele said, "Okay, Carter, I'm ready to come down through with the high beams." At the sound of his voice, I almost jumped out of my skin. I closed my eyes for a second to calm myself, and when I opened them again, the shadow was gone. Something was still in the graveyard with me, though; I could feel its presence, and it wasn't friendly. My breath came in short, shallow gasps as my eyes darted frantically around, trying to see what I could sense lurking in the shadows. Steele's voice came again. "Carter? Do you copy?"

I knew I needed to grab my walkie and respond, but I was frozen with fear. In my mind, I was a child again, reliving the night I had awakened to find an elderly woman at the foot of my bed, staring at me with cold, lifeless eyes. Now, as then, I wanted to run, I wanted to scream, I wanted to hide, but I couldn't. My feet were rooted to the ground as firmly as the tree in front of me. I felt as though if I moved, I would draw attention to myself. Logically, I knew that was crazy. Whatever was here was already aware of my presence. Steele's voice, urgent now, came again. "Carter! Answer me! What's going on?"

I mustered the courage to take a tentative step backwards, wanting nothing more than to get out of that graveyard. No sooner had I taken one step, and then another, than the shadow figure reappeared, this time in front of the tree, and it seemed to be advancing towards me.

Suddenly, a different voice came over my walkie. "Kyr, are you all right? What's happening?" *Gabe!*

The sound of his voice jarred me enough that I was able to make a grab for my walkie. "Gabe! Steele! There's something here . . ." The shadow figure started towards me again. I took a few more hasty steps backward, catching my foot on a tree root as I did. I fell sprawling, crying out as I landed hard on my back. My walkie and the voice recorder went flying, and my flashlight bounced off my chin and went out. I scrambled backwards towards the wrought iron fence, thinking that if I could just get to the other side of it, I could get away from the entity. Both Gabe and Steele radioed that they were on their way; I knew they'd never reach me in time.

I made it to the fence and tried to stand, but my traitorous legs refused to work. As the shadow moved closer, it became darker and more solid till I could hardly see through it. All the hairs on my neck stood up as terror rose in my throat, almost choking me. I pressed so hard against the fence that the iron bars dug into my back. I pushed myself as quickly as I could along the fence, trying to get away from the shadow that kept coming closer and closer. "Stay away!" I shouted, feeling somewhat foolish for giving an order to a shapeless black mass. As if it had heard me and was deliberately defying me, it came even closer, looming over me menacingly. The air around me became dramatically colder, but at the same time thicker and heavier, making it hard to breathe. The shadow seemed to envelop me, but just as I cried out and threw my arms up in front of me to defend myself, there was a bright flash of light.

Before I had a chance to think, a pair of strong hands grabbed me from behind and yanked me roughly to my feet. Keeping my eyes screwed shut, I screamed and struggled and flailed my arms till my fist made contact with something. A man's voice grunted and swore, and I was free for a moment before another set of hands grabbed me and gave me a shake. "Kyr! It's all right. It's me, Gabe."

My eyes shot open, and Gabe's concerned face was right in front of me. When he saw that I recognized him, he smiled tentatively, and I threw myself into his arms with relief. "Oh, Gabe! Thank goodness it's you!" He held me tightly for a second till I remembered that I had hit something . . . or someone. I pushed away from him, asking in a panic, "Then who did I. . .?" I turned and saw Steele glaring coldly at me and gingerly wiping blood from his swollen lip.

"I'm so touched by your concern, Carter," he joked irritably. "Remind me to wear armor the next time I try to rescue you. You've got a mean left hook."

My jaw dropped as I gaped at him in mortification. I glanced down at my left hand, and even in the moonlight I could tell it was beginning to swell. I tried to stammer an apology, but Steele threw his hand up to cut me off, turning and walking away.

A choking sound made me turn quickly towards Gabe. His arms were crossed, and one hand covered his mouth, but it was obvious he was laughing over what had just happened.

Before I could say anything, another voice called out, "Gabe! Hey, Gabe!" Drac was running towards us, followed by Andy and Kyle. Seeing Gabe's amusement, he stopped short, glancing curiously between Gabe and me. "What the hell is so funny?" he asked. "The way it sounded over the walkie, Kyr was being attacked by a hellhound or something. I come out here, and you're laughing your fool head off." He stopped and looked around. "And where's Spook?"

Gabe started laughing again and pointed towards the far side of the graveyard, where Steele stood with his back towards us, hands on his hips. He must have heard Drac's voice, because he turned and stalked back towards us. As Drac caught sight of Steele's bloodied lip, Steele glared at me and growled, "The only hell hound in this graveyard is Carter." I couldn't tell if his comment was made in jest or in anger. "Her left hook is the most dangerous thing here."

Drac shook his head, still confused; Gabe chuckled and joked, "Spook got in the way of Kyr's left fist." Then remembering what had brought him outside in the first place, he became serious. "Something out here really spooked her," he said. "Just as Spook and I got here, there was a flash of light . . ." He turned to Spook and me. "Is that what you saw on the monitors?"

I said nothing at first, since I'd had my arms up in front of my face and hadn't actually seen the light straight on. Seeing that I wasn't going to answer, Steele spoke up, "It was exactly what we saw on the monitors, except that when we saw it, it was close to that tree over there." He looked straight at me. "This time it was by the fence, close to where Carter was cowering."

Steele gave me a smirk as I narrowed my eyes at him and made a fist at him. Suddenly his words registered. "Close to where I was . . ."

"Cowering," Steele finished for me, crossing his arms and smirking at me again.

Ignoring Steele, I looked at Gabe and explained, "The light — whatever it was — it chased away the shadow figure."

"Shadow figure?" Gabe asked, looking first at Drac and then at Steele. "I didn't see a shadow figure, did you, Spook?"

Steele glanced sharply at me and then replied, "No, all I saw was the light." To me, Steele said skeptically, "Are you sure you didn't see your own shadow?" He looked up. "The moon is pretty close to being full."

A combination of anger at his words and fear at the recollection of what I had seen made me tremble as I retorted indignantly, "I did not see my own shadow, Steele. Not unless my shadow can move independently and try to attack me."

"Attack you!" Drac and Gabe exclaimed at once, looking at each other with concern. Steele watched them incredulously, unable to believe they were taking me seriously. Drac looked around at the others and declared, "Okay, gang, I think we need to call it a night." Rubbing his goatee thoughtfully, he added, "There's something happening here, and we need to look at some of the evidence we've captured before we go any further with this investigation."

CHAPTER FIVE

As we tore down equipment and carried it out to the van, I did my best to avoid Steele, not wanting to deal with his smirking and his superior attitude, and still feeling guilty for giving him a fat lip. I also tried to avoid the others, who were pulling pranks and trying to scare each other. The last thing I needed was one of them jumping out of a closet to scare the daylights out of me; I was still very much on edge after my experiences. I was sure I'd never hear the end of it if I gave someone else a fat lip.

"Hey, Kyr," Drac called from the van as I headed back towards the house after loading up a pile of extension cords. "Can you grab the camera and the REM pod out of the attic?"

Great, I thought. *The attic.* But, not wanting them to think I was shirking my duties or that I was afraid, I called back, "I'm on it."

I dashed up the stairs to the second floor and paused on the landing, looking down the hall towards the back bedroom. Thankfully, Steele was taking down equipment in that room. There was no way I was going back in there tonight. Even now, I was certain I could sense negative energy radiating from that end of the hallway. Either that, or it was just knowing that Steele was down there. I gave myself a shake and headed in the other direction towards the attic stairs.

Compared to what I had felt on the second floor, the energy coming from the attic seemed downright friendly. I flipped the light switch and heard a loud pop. "Damn it," I muttered. "Of all times for a light bulb to blow." I let out a huff and reached in my back pocket for my flashlight. I groaned when I realized it wasn't there. *It must still be in the graveyard*, I thought.

Rolling my eyes, I stomped up the stairs, too tired to run all the way back out to the van and then all the way back up to the attic. I was sure there was enough moonlight coming through the window for me to tear down the equipment. I just hoped that nothing else would decide to show itself while I was up there alone.

The REM pod was easy enough to collect and set by the top of the stairs. Next, I found the camera in the corner by one of the far windows. I thought it was odd that it wasn't plugged in at the outlet right next to it, but I just shrugged and followed the extension cord to the back part of the attic where all the boxes and other junk were stacked. The floor boards creaked as I carefully picked my way back through the darkness. I found the outlet and unplugged the camera. As I stood up, I felt something brush across my face and hair. Wonderful. A spider web. As I frantically wiped at my face to get rid of the sticky web, I stepped backwards and bumped into a stack of boxes. Something toppled from the top of the stack, hit me on the head, and landed right in my hands. As soon as I saw what it was, I screamed and threw it down, and then turned and made a beeline for the stairs, not wanting to be in the same room as that thing.

Just as I reached the top of the stairs, I ran headlong into someone. "Carter, what the hell is wrong with you?" Great, it would just have to be Steele, wouldn't it? He grasped me by the shoulders, and I noticed that he was leaning backwards, obviously not wanting to be on the receiving end of my fist again.

I pulled away from him and leaned against the windowsill, still breathing heavily. I swept a straggling lock of hair out of my face and muttered, "Nothing. I'm fine, Steele." That wasn't exactly true. The energy in the room had suddenly changed, but I couldn't tell if it was there was a spirit present, or if was just because Steele had shown up.

Steele brought a foot up to the top step and leaned forward, propping one elbow on his knee and resting his other arm on the top of the banister. His expression was unreadable as he replied, "You don't sound fine." He raised himself up and glanced around the attic before asking, "What happened? Did you see something?" He came the rest of the way up the steps and began walking around slowly.

"No, I didn't," I insisted, trying to figure out how I could get him to leave before he figured out what had frightened me and made a joke of it.

He stopped pacing and turned to look at me. I tried to hold his gaze, but his eyes seemed to bore into me, making my knees tremble and my stomach do somersaults. What *was* wrong with me?

"Well, something made you scream like that," he declared. "Again." Obviously, he couldn't resist taking a jab at me.

At last I just decided to tell him a half-truth, hoping it would be enough. "It wasn't anything paranormal, Steele. I stumbled against some boxes, and...something...fell down and scared the daylights out of me. That's all."

I could hear the suppressed laughter in his voice as he continued walking towards the back of the attic. "If you say so, Carter. So what was it? A rubber spider? A plastic snake? A scary mask?" He kept listing things that he obviously believed would scare a woman, but I didn't respond. There was no way I would tell him what it was. Suddenly his foot hit something and sent it spinning across the floor. "What the...?"

Oh no, I thought. *That sounded like . . .*

Steele bent down to pick something up. When he stood up with a grin on his face that I could see even in the darkness all the way across the room, I felt my face flush as I fought the urge to run down the stairs and out of the house. "*This* is what scared the daylights out of you?" When I didn't answer him, he burst out laughing and said incredulously, "It is, isn't it? Really, Carter? You lost *your* head over a Styrofoam wig head?"

That was it; I'd had enough. I turned and started down the steps. I only got halfway down when I remembered why I had been up there to begin with, so I turned and stomped back up the stairs, grabbed the REM pod and stomped back down the stairs. I would have grabbed the camera and tripod, but I would have had to walk past *him*, so I left it for him to carry down.

I burst out the front door and stalked down the steps and out to the van where Drac and Gabe were loading up the equipment. Drac turned to me as I handed him the REM pod, and then he did a double take as he saw the expression on my face. "What's wrong?" he asked, handing off the REM pod to Gabe, who was now also looking at me curiously. "Where's the camera from the attic?"

"Nothing," I ground out shortly, my chest still heaving. "Steele has it."

Drac looked over his shoulder towards Steele, who was coming out of the house with the camera, tripod, and another large case. When he caught sight of me, he grinned like an idiot and then began laughing when I glared at him. Gabe leaned over to poke his head out of the van and say, "Aw, Spook, come on. Don't tell me you pranked poor Kyr. Hasn't she had enough for one night?"

Steele handed off equipment to Drac and Gabe and replied with a gleam in his eye, "I didn't have to. She pranked herself." Drac and Gabe exchanged a questioning look, and Andy and Kyle came closer to lean against the side of the van, also wondering what had happened. Steele looked around and, seeing that everything was in the van, asked, "So, are we ready to . . . *head* out?"

My eyes flashed as I glared at him, not missing his attempt at humor. I turned to climb in to the back seat of the van, but Steele stopped me. He held out my walkie-talkie and my flashlight. "I believe these are yours," he said seriously, but with that annoying gleam still in his eye. I was about to mutter a hasty thanks when he added, "I found them in the graveyard, over by the big . . . *head*stone."

"Steele, you're such a..." I couldn't even think of something bad enough to call him, so I got into the back seat and slammed the door.

Gabe chuckled and said simply, "Spook, honestly. . ."

"What?" Steele asked, feigning innocence. "I'm just having a little fun. No need to . . . *wig* out."

Drac and Gabe just shook their heads, still trying to figure out the joke. Drac slammed the rear doors, and he and Gabe climbed into the front seats. Andy and Kyle piled in the back seat on the other side of me, chatting excitedly as Drac started the van.

Just as Drac threw it in reverse, someone tapped on my window; I looked over to see Steele motioning for me to roll down my window. I glared at him for a second before I did. "What?" I asked shortly, trying and failing to give him a withering glance.

He leaned against the door and tried to look contrite. "It looks pretty crowded in there, Carter. There's room in my car if you'd like to ride with me."

He had to be kidding. Ride ten miles back to the hotel with *him*, listening to him crack lame jokes about me losing my head? "No thanks, Steele. I'd rather walk."

His face froze, and his eyes hardened. I got the feeling I had wounded his pride, but after his initial coldness towards me and then his relentless picking on me, I found it hard to care about his hurt feelings. I needn't have worried; he recovered quickly enough and leaned over to look at Andy and Kyle. "Hey, you guys want to ride with me?"

Kyle was closest to the door, so he replied, "Sure, Spook." He nudged Andy's shoulder. "You coming, dude?"

Andy glanced indifferently at me and then looked to Drac, who shrugged and said, "Suit yourself." Andy and Kyle headed towards Steele's car, jostling each other like a couple of high schoolers.

Steele shot me a superior look as he followed them. I turned away with mixed emotions. *At least I have Drac and Gabe—especially Gabe—all to myself.* Somehow, the consolation felt hollow, and I felt completely rejected. A nagging voice told me, *You rejected him first.* I sighed and raised my eyes to Drac and Gabe, who were watching the interaction between Steele and me with curious smirks. When Gabe noticed I was looking at them, he teased, "Aw, come on, Kyr. You don't want the honor of riding shotgun in the Spook-mobile?" When I returned his gaze irritably, he said softly, "You two got off on the wrong foot—his fault, I'll admit—but I think he was just trying to make peace between you."

"I guess," I replied, feeling like a petulant child. I wasn't ready to give him the benefit of the doubt just yet.

Drac caught my eye in the rear view mirror and laughed, "Spook is rough around the edges, and he likes to act tough, but he's a good guy when you get to know him." He gave a wave to Steele, Andy, and Kyle as he inched the van around Steele's car. Steele's eyes met mine, his expression still full of coldness, hurt, and . . . something else.

I was quiet for the ride back, while Drac and Gabe shared their experiences from the investigation and their theories about what we were dealing with. I had the feeling they wanted to ask about what I had seen in the bedroom and in the graveyard, but they spared me, at least for now.

When we got back to the hotel, Drac and Gabe gathered us together in the lobby and went over some quick instructions and the schedule for the next day's activities. They were going to walk us through an analysis in the early afternoon, and then after dinner, we'd head out for the next night's investigation. I was exhausted and emotionally spent, so it was hard for me to stay focused on their words. Even though I kept my head down and avoided meeting anyone's gaze, out of the corner of my eye, I saw Andy curl his lip at the prospect of being told how to analyze evidence. At one point, I felt someone's eyes on me. At first I ignored it, thinking my nerves were just getting to me. Finally, though, the feeling got so intense that I raised my eyes enough to peek through my bangs and saw Steele staring unabashedly at me. I tried unsuccessfully to read his expression before he looked away, wondering if he disliked me that much, or if there was something else bothering him.

Drac finally dismissed us, and while the others stayed to chat for a bit, I grabbed my duffel bag and headed for my room, not feeling much like socializing. Once I got to my room, however, I found that I didn't want to be alone either. As I lay in the dark waiting for sleep to come, I seemed to hear every sound around me and immediately recalled either the malicious spirit in the back bedroom or the shadow figure in the graveyard. I grabbed the remote and tried to find something on TV to take my mind off the night's events. Unfortunately, the only things I could find on TV at that hour were horror movies, cheesy infomercials, and stale sitcom reruns, so I gave up on that idea.

Finally, I gave up, got out of bed and yanked my hoodie on over my nightshirt. I grabbed my key and flipped on the bathroom light so I wouldn't return to a dark room, and then I headed down the corridor towards the lobby. The hotel was mostly quiet at this hour, although I could hear music coming from a couple rooms, and a door slammed on the floor above. I passed the front desk, where a young woman sat playing Spider Solitaire on the computer. She glanced at me, and I smiled as I continued through to the vending area. I stood looking disinterestedly at the vending machines. Besides the usual soda and snack machines, there was also a machine that dispensed toiletries and various personal items that guests may have forgotten. I let out a huff and headed slowly back towards the front desk, stopping to browse the tourist brochures. Having lived in the area all my life, I shook my head and wrinkled my nose at some of the attractions being advertised.

Eventually, I strolled over to the coffee station. *Yeah*, I thought. *Coffee at 2:30 a.m.; not a good idea, Kyr.* I figured I wasn't sleeping anyway, so I grabbed a cup and mixed regular and decaf together, and then added a liberal amount of creamer and a third of a packet of sugar. I stirred it and popped a lid on it, and was just about to leave when a voice right next to me said, "Do you always drink coffee in the middle of the night?"

I gasped loudly and almost dropped my coffee. When I saw it was only Gabe, I replied more irritably than I intended, "No, not always. Do you always sneak up on people and scare the daylights out of them?"

He laughed and gave my shoulder a nudge. "Touché. Sorry about that." He studied my face for a moment and then asked, "Can't sleep?" When I shook my head, he nodded towards my coffee and joked, "That won't help, you know."

I shrugged and smiled slightly. "I suppose not."

"Look," he said, motioning towards the vending area. "I'm just grabbing a couple sodas and then heading back to the room. Why don't you come over for a bit? We're just hanging out."

He caught my eye, and I felt my pulse quicken. *Gabe Petery just asked me to hang out with him!* I had the sudden girlish urge to call JoEllyn until I realized with a jolt that he had said, *"We're* hanging out."

"Who's 'we'?" I asked warily, not wanting to be in the same room with Andy and Kyle—especially Andy. Or Steele.

Gabe gave me an easy smile, which made my knees go weak, and chuckled, "Just Drac and me." His eyes twinkled mischievously as he added, "And Spook."

My shoulders slumped with disappointment. I was okay with Gabe and Drac; it was Steele I wasn't sure about. I hadn't forgotten the icy brush-off he'd given me when we met, and I sure wasn't going to forget the way he had picked on me and made fun of me in the attic. I was certain he had told the others that a Styrofoam wig head had scared the daylights out of me. "I don't know," I hedged. I really didn't want to hang out here in the lobby, but neither did I want to go back to my room alone.

Gabe sauntered back to the vending area while I leaned against the counter and slowly sipped my coffee. I heard him put money in the machine and pull sodas out several times. I laughed to myself, wondering if the three of them planned to sleep at all tonight. He came back carrying four cans of soda. I raised an eyebrow at him and gave him a crooked smile. He stopped in front of me to ask, "What's the verdict? You want to come hang out?" He knew I was balking because of Steele, and when I hesitated again, he mouthed, "Come on, come on." Finally, I relented, and he faked a cheer. "I'll make sure Spook goes easy on you," he promised.

"I'm going to hold you to that," I declared, wondering what I was getting myself into.

We headed down the corridor to Drac's room, and Gabe banged on the door with his elbow. Drac and Steele were laughing loudly at something inside. After a moment, Drac opened the door, his face red and tears at the corners of his eyes; I wondered what was so funny, but then had the thought that maybe I didn't want to know. As soon as Drac caught sight of me, he stopped laughing abruptly and raised an eyebrow at Gabe. Gabe grinned and announced, "Look who I found skulking about in the lobby!"

I responded sheepishly, "I was not skulking. I couldn't sleep, so I . . . was getting some coffee." No, that didn't sound stupid at all.

Drac laughed and commented comically, "Always helps me sleep." I gave him a bemused look, and he stepped back to let us step through the door. "*Velcome*," he said in a Dracula voice. "Do come in and stay *a-vile*."

As I came into the room, I glanced over and saw Steele in black lounge pants and an olive green T-shirt that perfectly complemented his brown eyes and chestnut brown hair. My eyes lingered on his profile and the way his muscles strained against his shirt. He was sitting in a chair by the table with his legs stretched out and feet propped up on the bed. He leaned back, taking a long swig of Mountain Dew from a bottle. When he caught sight of me, he choked and sat up quickly, coughing. Drac and Gabe glanced at him, and then exchanged a knowing look. Gabe joked in a Scottish accent, "I warned ye not to take such strong drink, Spook. Should I be heating ye some warm milk?"

I stifled a laugh, but Steele still heard it and looked towards me. His eyes seemed to ask, *What are you doing here*? but he said nothing to me. He swept his shoulder-length hair out of his face, but it flopped forward again into his eyes, which riveted my gaze to him. Again, I wondered what was wrong with me. Thankfully, he didn't notice, as he turned to Gabe and shot back, "I'll bet I could drink you both under the table." He took another sip of soda and made excuse, "It just went down the wrong pipe."

As Steele and Gabe continued to fire jests at each other, Drac pulled out a chair and motioned for me to sit between them as if he wanted me to act as a mediator to their friendly squabbles. I swallowed hard and sat down, feeling Steele's eyes on me, but refusing to look at him. Once we were all seated around the table, everyone went silent. *Way to go, Kyr. You show up and the party dies.* After several moments, I glanced first at Gabe, and then over at Drac, who were both regarding me seriously. Finally, Drac laughed, "Come on, Kyr, you look like you're headed for the gallows. Lighten up!"

I gave him a weak smile, then lowered my eyes again. This was even worse than the radio interview. At least then someone else asked questions that I simply had to answer. As I sat there clutching my coffee and trying to think of something interesting to say, I imagined that the others probably thought I was the most boring person they had ever met.

Just as I was trying to get up the nerve to excuse myself, Gabe leaned forward to ask, "So, Kyr, you survived your first night of ghost hunting. What do you think?"

I should have expected that question, but for some reason, it caught me off guard. I gave him a deer-in-the-headlights look for a moment before recovering enough to answer. "It's definitely more . . . intense than I thought it would be. JoEllyn always says— JoEllyn is the friend with her own investigation team—she says that most of the time it's like sitting in the dark talking to yourself. I didn't expect to be . . ." I almost said *attacked*. "I didn't expect to encounter such an aggressive spirit."

Drac and Gabe exchanged a grave look; obviously they had been thinking about the same thing and wondering how to broach the subject. I chanced a sidelong glance at Steele and found him watching Drac and Gabe. His eyes slid over to me, and as he held my gaze, I felt as though he could see all the way into my soul. I shivered and looked away as Drac said, "I'm sure you're aware that what happened tonight is not typical of what we usually experience on an investigation."

When I nodded, Gabe continued, "Chuck's claims didn't indicate anything even close to what you experienced either in the back bedroom or in the graveyard. I'd had a hunch that, as a woman, you might have more luck than the rest of at making contact in the back bedroom, but I never thought things would get so out of hand."

"Neither did I," I muttered, glancing up at Gabe, wondering why the spirit had chosen to be so aggressive with me.

Drac stroked his goatee thoughtfully, glancing first at Steele and then at Gabe. "Kyr, we know that whatever happened in the bedroom—and in the graveyard—really frightened you, and you probably don't want to think about it . . ." I suddenly realized where he was taking the conversation, and I felt my pulse quicken. My expression must have betrayed my increasing discomfort, because Drac looked over at Gabe, silently pleading with him to jump in.

Gabe laid his hand on my shoulder and continued for Drac. "Look, I think you know that we suspect there may be more going on at the Berkeley mansion than even Chuck is aware of. Since you're the only one who had any type of encounter in that room, we were hoping we could talk to you about what happened so we could possibly figure out what it wants." His eyes drifted first to Drac and then over to Steele, who was regarding me skeptically again.

I reluctantly agreed, and for the next few minutes, Gabe and I shared with Drac in more detail about our experiences when we were investigating the second floor. We told him about the spirit playing games with us, going back and forth between the two rooms, seemingly responding to requests to make noises for us. Gabe told him that was why we had decided to split up, to see if one of us could corner the spirit and make it show itself.

"It seems that tactic worked, maybe a little too well," Gabe joked, nudging me.

Drac chuckled, but I was having a hard time seeing any humor in the situation. Steele sat up and gave his two cents. "I assume that we all agree that we're dealing with two different spirits here. The one that was playing with you two and the one Carter *says* she saw are most likely two different spirits." His emphasis on the word *says* implied that he still believed I was either overreacting or making it up. His implication might have bothered me if my mind hadn't been consumed with a nagging question. Steele must have accurately read my face because he leaned forward to peer at me and asked gruffly, "What's on your mind, Carter? Something is obviously bothering you."

The direct question made me meet his eyes. Despite my anxiety, I felt defiance rise up in me at his tone. I wasn't sure I wanted to respond, sensing his skepticism. I was also hesitant to voice the thought that had been nagging me since Gabe and Steele had taken me out to the van back at the mansion. When I turned my gaze to Gabe, he urged gently, "It's okay, Kyr. Tell us what's bothering you. Let us help you process what happened."

Finally I relented. Looking pointedly at Steele, I challenged, "What if you're wrong? What if there *aren't* two different entities? What if it was the same entity, and it wanted to get me alone in that back bedroom?" Steele rolled his eyes and was about to protest, but I cut him off. "That spirit wanted me alone, Steele; you can't convince me otherwise. Why else wouldn't it show itself to both of us? Or just to Gabe?"

Sensing a confrontation, or at the least a breakdown on my part, Gabe jumped in almost immediately to try to calm me down. "Okay, Kyr, first you need to get the Hollywood scary movie images out of your mind. Like Spook told you earlier, I really don't think the intent was to hurt you, even if that's how it appeared."

Drac added, "In our experience, when people think a spirit is becoming aggressive or wants to hurt them, it usually just wants to get their attention to ask for help or to leave a message. That's likely what this spirit was doing, Kyr."

My eyes darted back and forth between them. Obviously they believed what they were telling me, and I had no doubt that what they were saying was indeed what they had experienced. But that still didn't account for what had happened to me. My eyes drifted over to Steele, who was thoughtfully watching our interaction. His expression told me that he was wavering between agreeing with Drac and Gabe's assessment of the situation and considering the possibility that this time might be different. I wished he'd open his mouth and say something, anything, although given his earlier opinion that I was either imagining things or making them up, I wasn't holding out for him to jump in and defend me. I shifted my gaze back to Gabe and asked again, "Fine, so Casper the not-so-friendly ghost has a message. Why did it have to show itself to me? Why not to Gabe? For heaven's sake, why not to Chuck? He lives there, so why not tell *him*?"

My breaths came in short, rapid gasps as I looked between Drac and Gabe, my eyes silently demanding an answer. A sudden touch on my shoulder sent a jolt through me. I jumped and turned towards Steele. As our eyes met, I froze; his strong hand grasped my shoulder gently yet firmly, and he held my gaze with an expression I had never seen before. A warm, tingling sensation began at my shoulder and spread throughout my body. I had the crazy urge to lean against his chest and let him hold me. His expression suddenly changed, and I feared for a moment that he had read my thoughts. We both looked away, and he snatched his hand back as though he had been burned. He cleared his throat and replied gruffly, "Carter, I don't think anyone can answer that right now. Maybe you're more . . . open . . . to spirits, or maybe that spirit senses some kind of a connection to you." He looked at Drac and Gabe, his eyes hard and determined. "The only way we might find out is for you to go in there tomorrow night and try to make contact again."

My eyes widened, and my pulse quickened as his words sank in. Gabe laid a hand on my back and leaned close to look into my eyes. "Maybe it's too soon to ask, but would you be willing to do that, for Chuck?" He glanced at Drac and Steele. "For us?"

As soon as Gabe posed that question, I saw the apparition's face in my mind. The angry, piercing eyes, the menacing scowl, the hand reaching towards me as it approached all seemed just as real as they had been a couple hours before. There was no way I wanted to return to that room, or even to the graveyard, but I also didn't want my first investigation to be a complete failure or for Drac and Gabe to think I was a coward. As I gazed into Gabe's Lipton-brown eyes, I wanted nothing more than to say, *Yes, Gabe, I'll do it; for you, I'll do it*—but I couldn't. I swallowed hard and dropped my eyes. "I don't think I can answer that right now."

I glanced over at Steele and saw a flash of disappointment and—was that disgust?—in his eyes. Drac was obviously also disappointed, but he reached over to lay his hand on my shoulder. "I think it's only fair that you should have some time to think about it." His eyes met Steele's seriously. "That was quite an experience to have your first time out."

I nodded and looked down at my coffee cup and then towards the door, ready to face the solitude of my room. Gabe caught Drac's eye, and then gave me a half smile and teased, "You're not planning on running out on us, are you?" I didn't know if he meant running out of the room or running out of the whole investigation. Both seemed like a good idea at that moment.

Drac laughed and agreed, "Don't run out on us, Kyr. Stick around and chat. You want a soda? We've got a few in the fridge, right, Gabe?"

I smiled as Gabe motioned towards the fridge and nodded enthusiastically. I joked, "Don't you have anything stronger?"

They all laughed, and Gabe responded, "Well, we would, but Spook here is such a lightweight, and we don't want him to get hold of anything stronger than that Mountain Dew he's nursing."

"Hey!" Steele protested, leaning across behind me to give Gabe a shove. Our eyes met again; this time there was no coldness or hostility in them. *He's actually quite handsome when he's not being antagonistic.* Once more, I wondered what I was thinking. I smiled hesitantly at him; maybe Gabe had been right. Maybe Steele had been trying to make peace earlier. I decided to give him another chance, so I agreed to stay for a bit.

For a while the conversation centered on general topics. Since I lived near the place we were investigating, I told them some of the interesting stories of the area, and they asked about popular tourist attractions. Of course, since it was close to Halloween, we got on the subject of Halloween events in the vicinity and eventually came around to local ghost stories I'd heard. As I finished telling them about the Seven Gates of Hell, I caught Steele giving me a quizzical look. I glanced at Drac and Gabe and realized they were giving me the same look. Suddenly self-conscious, I shrank down in my chair and asked, "What? Did I say something wrong?"

Steele raised an eyebrow and challenged, "For someone as frightened as you were by what happened tonight, you sure seem to like telling ghost stories."

I recalled his earlier accusation that I was over-imaginative, and I wondered if I'd just given him more reason to have that opinion. "Well, I do like ghost stories as long as I know they're not real." I swallowed hard, as my experiences at the Berkeley mansion crept into my thoughts once more. "Or not happening to me."

Drac leaned forward in his chair. "I take it that you were more scared than intrigued by the apparition you saw in your house?" Obviously, he was referring to the experience I had written about for the contest.

I shuddered and admitted, "You can say that again. Even if it was just an old woman, waking up to her standing at the foot of my bed staring at me was enough to freak me out."

Steele chuckled. "Really, Carter? You were afraid of an old woman? That's almost as bad as being afraid of—"

"Well, I was only four, Steele!" I defended, cutting him off before he could spill the beans about what had frightened me in the attic. "Besides, I didn't have someone like Petery Paranormal to turn to for help or to explain things to me."

Steele chuckled again as my face flushed. He began to say something, but then stopped to regard me thoughtfully. I squirmed under his gaze, having the distinct feeling I was being read. Suddenly, something clicked, and he asked, "This weekend isn't all fun and games for you, is it? You're here for something more."

Although he had posed a question, his words were definitive, as though he already knew the answer. I decided to lay my cards on the table. "Yes, there *is* more on the line than just a celebrity ghost hunt. I was hoping this weekend would give me something that would help me understand the things I experienced as a child, the things I experienced in college, the things that happened…after my dad died." A lump rose in my throat, threatening to choke me, and I drew a ragged breath.

"What happened after your dad died?" Startled, I jumped and whirled my head around to look at Gabe. I'd forgotten he was sitting on the other side of me until he spoke. His gentle brown eyes held the intensity I'd often seen on *Project Boo-Seekers*, and I knew he was genuinely interested in what I had to say.

I swallowed hard and returned his gaze before looking across at Drac and then back at Steele. I had never told anyone, not even JoEllyn or Aunt Julia, what had finally pushed my fascination with ghosts over the edge from a mere interest into the desire to study them and to investigate hauntings and the reasons behind them. True, it had partly been that first experience as a young child, as well as the other experiences I'd had, and yes, *Project Boo-Seekers* had opened my eyes to the possibility of actually investigating hauntings. But there was something more, and this was my chance to ask a question that had bothered me for several years. After a long moment of gathering courage, I answered their questions with one of my own. "Is it possible for someone who didn't believe in ghosts while they were alive to come back as a ghost after they die?"

The room fell dead silent as the three ghost hunters looked at one another, unsure of how to answer my question. Finally, Drac offered up a comment. "That's not a rhetorical question, is it?"

Unexpected tears blurred my vision as I shook my head, and I couldn't hide the desperation in my voice as I pressed, "Well, is it?"

Steele shifted in his seat and tentatively touched my arm. "Carter, I'm not sure that any of us has an answer. Why don't you tell us what happened?"

Part of me regretted posing the question I was now somewhat reluctant to explore. What if they gave an answer that completely invalidated the concepts about ghosts that I'd grown up hearing in church, even if I didn't wholeheartedly believe those concepts myself? What if their answer supported what my church taught? Still, if anyone would understand my need to reconcile my beliefs with my experiences, they would. "Not long after Daddy died, I noticed...things...happening around my place. Nothing scary, just things like...footsteps outside my bedroom door late at night, feeling as though someone were looking over my shoulder, that kind of thing." I absentmindedly pulled at a thread hanging from my hoodie. My voice shook as I continued. "I started thinking maybe it was Daddy when I caught whiffs of his aftershave, and once I thought I heard his voice downstairs. On the one hand, I wanted to believe it was him checking on me, telling me it was okay, but on the other hand, it didn't make sense, you know?"

"Because your dad didn't believe in ghosts." Gabe's soft voice soothed me, but Steele's intense gaze held mine, feeding me, strengthening me, even as it turned my insides to mush.

I forced myself to look at Gabe before answering. "He believed that when you die, your soul either goes to heaven or to hell. There's no in-between and no coming back to earth. Ever. Anything else you see that you think is a ghost is just a demon trying to deceive you." I didn't voice my fear and uncertainty over what my experience meant: Either Daddy and the pastors I'd grown up trusting with all my spiritual questions were wrong, or I'd been visited and deceived by a demon.

"Did you..." Steele's voice was almost as gentle as Gabe's now. "Did you ask your pastor about it? Maybe he could have given you some insight if you explained what happened."

I wrinkled my nose at him. Obviously he'd had a much different church experience than I'd had. "Believe me, after the last time I brought up the topics of ghosts in a church, there was no way I was going to ask my pastor if my father had made a post-mortem visit to me." Seeing the curious looks on their faces, I quickly recounted my experience at church the following Sunday when the pastor greeted the congregation in the name of the Father, and of the Son, and of the Holy Ghost. Naturally thinking of the apparition I'd seen only a few days before, I had said, loud enough for several people near us, as well as the pastor, to hear, "Daddy, is the Holy

Ghost like the ghost I saw in my bedroom?" The way my father's eyes had bulged out of his reddening face as he glared at me had frightened me even more than the apparition had, and I'd been scolded by both my father and the pastor for believing in such nonsense.

A choking sound made me look up at Steele. I could tell he was struggling to keep a straight face, but the playful gleam in his eyes made my breath catch. For a brief moment, I thought he was laughing at me, but something in his expression told me that his amusement was more likely in response to my description of my father's reaction to my childish outburst. The corners of my mouth twitched, and he lost his battle and laughed out loud, making me giggle in response. Suddenly, it wasn't quite so important to find the answer to my question. He suddenly noticed Drac and Gabe watching him, and his expression immediately became indifferent. Drac watched Steele a moment longer and then said to me, "Kyr, I think you know we'd really like to give you a definitive answer, but I just don't think we can, at least not right now."

My giddiness dissolved as his words sank in, and I shrugged. "I know. I guess I didn't really expect an answer; it's just one of those things that keeps gnawing at me, you know?"

Drac nodded and glanced at Gabe, who gave me a sympathetic smile. "And that's completely understandable, Kyr. To be honest, it's those unanswerable questions that keep most paranormal investigators searching for answers. We've all got that one experience that just pushed us over the edge from just wondering about what we'd experienced into trying to find out what we'd experienced." He opened his mouth to say something else, until he saw Drac sneak a glance at his watch. Taking the hint, he said, "We could sit here for hours telling you about how and why we got into the business, but it's getting late, and we should probably let you go and get some sleep. We need you well-rested for the analysis tomorrow. Come on; I'll walk you back to your room."

I grinned like a smitten schoolgirl and agreed. As we got up to go, Steele suddenly stood up as well and made an excuse. "It *is* getting late. I should probably leave too."

Drac exchanged a brief, amused glance with Gabe before getting to his feet to show us all out. At the door, he tugged on my braid and asked, "You think you'll be okay now?"

I nodded, certain I'd be able to put the night's unpleasant experiences behind me, at least for a few hours. My room was at the end of the corridor, and Steele's room was right next to mine, so I took a bit of comfort from that. We stopped at Steele's room first and waited as he unlocked the door. He bumped fists with Gabe and then turned to me. As he looked down at me, his expression suddenly softened, and I had the strangest feeling that if Gabe weren't standing right next to us, Steele might ask me to come inside. Even stranger still, I was actually entertaining the thought of accepting the invitation, telling myself that I merely wanted to continue the discussion we'd had in Drac's room.

Steele and I stood gazing at each other for several moments, until Gabe cleared his throat, interrupting my reverie. Steele gave his head a little shake as though he, too, needed to snap out of it, and then he leaned towards me with a wicked grin and whispered, "Good night, sleep tight, don't let the wig heads bite!"

"Steele!" I hissed, feeling my face grow hot. All the warm fuzzy feelings I'd just had flew right out the window, and I sputtered as I scrambled for a witty response. Suddenly I decided that he wasn't going to get the best of me. I took a deep breath, drew myself up as tall as I could, and smiled sweetly as I replied, "I'd rather deal with a biting wig head or a scary old-woman ghost than meet up with *you* in a dark attic."

Gabe guffawed loudly as Steele's eyes flew open wide at my retort. With a sassy toss of my head I turned and flounced down the hall towards my room. I only made it a few steps before I heard footsteps and a playful growl behind me. The next moment, Steele's arms were around my waist, and he began tickling me. I let out a squeal and began laughing uncontrollably as I tried to push his hands away.

Laughing at our antics, Gabe stepped in to pull Steele away from me. "Hey, Spook, take it easy. It is after 3 AM, you know. People are trying to sleep."

Steele released his hold on me, chuckling triumphantly. Making a "V" with his fingers, he pointed to his eyes and then to me as he backed away slowly and went to his door.

After Steele went into his room, Gabe and I continued down to my room. I unlocked the door, and he waited while I checked to make sure everything was the way I had left it. Satisfied that it was, I turned to him, unsure of what to say. His eyes were soft as he gave me a smile. He reassured me, "I'm sure you'll be okay, Kyr. Remember, Spook is right next door, and Drac and I are just a few doors down."

I nodded and smiled sheepishly. "I'm . . . sorry I lost my head tonight." I looked down at my sneakers, which were still caked with mud from the graveyard.

"Think nothing of it," Gabe replied, giving me a gentle shake. It was his turn to smile sheepishly. "Would it be crass of me to ask again if you'd be willing to go back into that bedroom tomorrow night?"

Suddenly feeling just a bit braver, I responded, "I guess I'm willing to give it a shot."

Gabe grinned broadly, making my stomach do somersaults. "Atta girl! I knew you'd come around!" He pulled me into an unexpected bear hug, which I more than willingly returned. As I leaned into him, inhaling the musky scent of his cologne, I had to remind myself sternly that he was happily married.

As we parted, I glanced briefly over his shoulder and could have sworn I saw Steele watching us from his doorway. He wore the same cold, hard expression I'd seen when Gabe introduced us hours before. By the time Gabe moved out of my line of vision and I could clearly see Steele's door, he was gone.

By the time I climbed into bed, I could hear the shower running in Steele's room. Had I just imagined what I just saw, or was he still playing Dr. Jekyll and Mr. Hyde? As I continued to puzzle over his behavior, the sound of running water soothed me, and as I took comfort in knowing that he was right next door, I soon fell asleep.

CHAPTER SIX

Despite the fact that I fell asleep easily, my sleep was littered with strange dreams, mostly broken images from inside the Berkeley mansion. I woke up around nine o'clock and lay there trying to make sense of my dreams. Finally, knowing I would be unable to get back to sleep, I threw back the covers and got out of bed. After a quick shower, I headed down to the lobby to grab some coffee and whatever breakfast fare the hotel offered. As I was leaving the lobby with a cup of coffee and a powdered donut, I ran into Drac and Gabe, who obviously had the same idea I had.

Drac grinned and said, "Well, you're up bright and early after a late night."

I raised an eyebrow at him. "Yeah, well, I could say the same about you."

They both chuckled, and Gabe asked, "Did you sleep well?"

Gabe's brown fleece pullover made him look like a big, huggable teddy bear, which made me have to fight the urge to snuggle up to him. I gulped and responded, "I wouldn't say that. But that's what they make caffeine for, right?"

Drac threw his head back and laughed, and Gabe shook his head and grinned. Then he cocked his head at me. "Are you ready for analysis in a few hours?"

I met his eyes anxiously as I considered the question. Was I ready? Sure, I was ready to analyze the evidence from the attic, the basement, and the master bedroom, but was I ready to go through the evidence from the bedroom where I'd encountered that spirit and from the graveyard where I'd seen the shadow figure? I wasn't so sure. Still, I wanted to make a good impression, so I put on a brave face. "Yeah, I'm ready."

Obviously I didn't sound very convincing to either of them because I saw them exchange one of their looks before Gabe said, "Look, I know you're not thrilled about reviewing that video, especially not with Andy and Kyle there." He quirked his eyebrow at Drac. "Kyle isn't so bad by himself, but I know Andy isn't the easiest person to work with."

I laughed ruefully at the way Gabe had so accurately assessed my feelings about both analysis and Andy, and I drummed my fingers nervously on my coffee cup, wondering where this conversation was headed. A second later, Drac jumped in, "We were hoping, if you're willing, that we could look at that part of the evidence before all of us get together, so you have some time to process anything we find without Andy and Kyle there making you uncomfortable."

Knowing how anxious they both were to get to that video, but at the same time unwilling to relive that experience, I chewed my lip and wrestled with what I should do. In the end, the desire to make a good impression won out. I took a deep breath and answered shakily, "Okay."

I couldn't help smiling briefly at the way their eyes lit up at my answer. Drac threw an arm around my shoulders, gave me a big childlike grin, and said, "Awesome! Let me and Gabe grab some breakfast, then we'll get the equipment set up and come get you."

As they hurried off towards the lobby, I swallowed hard, feeling as though I was about to go in for a root canal without any Novocain. I saw Gabe glance back at me and smile before saying something to Drac that made them both laugh. As I headed back to my room, I suddenly thought about Steele, and I wondered if he would be there.

A short while later, the three of us were sitting in front of a laptop in Drac's room. Just as Drac was about to start playing the video, there was a knock at the door. I tensed up, just knowing it was Steele. Drac motioned to Gabe to open the door.

As Gabe opened the door, Steele stuck his head in and asked cheerfully, "Anyone else in the mood for something better than stale donuts for breakfast?" His face froze when he saw me, and his expression immediately masked. *How does he do that?* His sharp eyes took in the open laptop and the equipment cases, and he raised an eyebrow at Drac and Gabe. "A little private analysis?" he asked peevishly, turning his eyes to me. I couldn't help wondering what had happened to the caring, even playful Steele who had briefly come out just a few hours before.

I looked away, not wanting to be under his scrutiny, and Gabe quickly jumped in, "We're just looking at the footage from the video camera Kyr placed in the back bedroom. Drac and I wanted to let her see whatever we caught before we all meet together this afternoon."

"I see."I could feel his eyes boring into me even though I wasn't looking in his direction. I clasped and unclasped my hands under the table as I glanced up at Drac. His jaw was set and his eyes hard as he looked sharply back at Steele.

The tension in the room was almost unbearable till Gabe pulled out a chair and chided good-naturedly, "Now, Spook, don't be jealous. We still love you too. Come on in and join us." He stood back and did a Vanna White imitation as he presented the chair for Steele.

Steele tried to glare at Gabe but couldn't keep the corners of his mouth from twitching at Gabe's antics. In the end, he relented and came over to sit next to me. Gabe sat on the other side of me, and Drac squeezed in between Steele and me to set up the clip. Drac looked to me and asked simply, "Ready?"

I took a deep breath and answered, "As ready as I'll ever be." As I glanced at Drac, I noticed out of the corner of my eye that Steele had that odd, indecipherable expression on his face again as he looked over at me.

As the video started, I felt Gabe's hand on my shoulder. I glanced at him, and he gave me a quick, encouraging smile; I returned a hesitant smile and turned my attention to the monitor.

The video started with an out-of-focus shot as I set up the video camera on the vanity and checked the shot. The three of us watched on the screen as I began my EVP session. As soon as I had told the spirit to show itself, we heard a voice quite close to the camera. I gasped and slid my chair back a few inches, as though doing so would keep the entity away from me. Drac and Gabe glanced at each other, and then at Steele, before Drac said, "I take it you didn't hear that voice at the time?"

My mouth had gone dry and I was unable to speak, so I just shook my head. As many times as I had seen this happen on *Project Boo-Seekers*, it unnerved me to realize that an unseen and unheard presence had been right next to me, communicating with me. Gabe jotted something down before rewinding and replaying that part of the video several times, trying to make out what the voice said. We had no success with that, so he suggested, "I made note of the time stamp; why don't we just listen for that on the voice recorder to see if it was picked up there? Let's move on."

The next part of the video showed me provoking the spirit. "Come on, you'll have to do better than that." Immediately after that, we heard the sound of Gabe's voice coming over the walkie-talkie, but the picture blacked out for a second, as though someone or something had walked in front of the camera. When the picture came back into focus, the door slammed shut. As we watched the next couple minutes of the video, I could feel the panic rising in my chest. I wanted to cover my eyes or look away so I wouldn't have to see what came next, but just as if I were watching a horror movie, I couldn't avert my eyes. As I watched myself tugging and pounding on the door, unsuccessfully trying to open it, I began trembling and breathing rapidly. The others leaned forward to watch closely, and I felt Gabe lay his hand reassuringly on my back. Last night I would have died of embarrassment if they had seen how scared I was during the investigation; at that particular moment, however, I didn't care.

"What the Sam Hill?" Gabe exclaimed suddenly, leaning forward to get a closer look at the monitor. Drac and Steele also leaned forward to see what was happening.

On the monitor, I saw the swirling, shimmering mist I had seen after the door slammed and locked. It was no less frightening seeing it on the monitor than it had been experiencing it firsthand, and I held my breath as I watched the mist begin to take the form of a person. While I fought the urge to bolt out of the room before it materialized completely, Drac, Gabe, and Steele were glued to the monitor, their faces aglow with excitement at the prospect of capturing a full-body apparition on video. Suddenly the monitor went black.

"What the frick happened?" Steele shouted, throwing his hands up in frustration.

Drac quickly checked the connections on the laptop. Finding nothing wrong, he muttered, "The camera must have shut off."

"Aw, I can't believe it," Gabe exclaimed, burying his face in his hands for a moment. "The spirit must have drained the battery to manifest itself."

Steele said nothing, but sat rhythmically thumping his fist on the arm of the chair.

The entire atmosphere of the room had changed. As excited as the others had been just moments before, that was how disappointed and deflated they now looked. "We were so close to catching an apparition on video," Gabe groaned, obviously devastated. "If only the camera had been plugged in . . ."

Steele suddenly turned to me and snapped, "Carter, I can't believe you didn't have the camera plugged in! I told you to always plug in the stationary cameras."

His words cut into me as I realized he was putting the blame on me for the loss of some compelling evidence. Even though technically it had been my fault, I recalled how hasty Steele had been in showing me how to set up the equipment. Suddenly angry, I shot back, "Maybe you did tell me that, Steele, but when you rush through training me how to do something I've *never done before*, what do you expect?"

Steele seemed a bit taken aback at my sharp answer, but the flash of uncertainty was gone in an instant and replaced once more by coldness and irritation. He replied with his typical air of superiority, "Well, forgive me, Ms. Newbie, but I didn't realize I was dealing with someone who had more fear and imagination than common sense. I would have thought that even a newbie fangirl would remember that spirits drain battery power to manifest, and would have set up accordingly."

A slap in the face would have hurt less than his accusation that I was lacking in common sense, not to mention his calling me a newbie fangirl again, this time to my face. Apparently my chagrin and hurt was obvious because Drac and Gabe both jumped to my defense. "Spook, that was really harsh. Chill out and give her a break, bro."

In the uncomfortable silence that followed, my eyes drifted to the disappointed faces of Drac and Gabe, and then to Steele's sulky face. Even though he was staring gloomily at the floor, with his hands jammed in his pockets, I could see a hint of remorse in his eyes. As I looked at the now-blank laptop monitor, I realized that although Steele's words had been harsh and unkind, they were also true; I had royally screwed up and cost the team a valuable piece of evidence. *Some ghost hunter you are*, I chastised myself miserably. *You can't even capture evidence when it manifests itself right in front of you.* Feeling like a complete failure, I wanted nothing more than to just run out of the room and out of the hotel, and to go back to my safe, predictable librarian job. I tried to swallow the lump that had risen in my throat as I ducked my head and wiped away a stray tear. I was determined not to let myself go to pieces, especially not in front of Steele.

Gabe was first to sit up and shake himself out of his funk. He seemed to notice my emotional state, because he nudged me and said cheerfully, "It's okay, Kyr. We all make mistakes as we're learning the ropes. At least you managed to capture the mist forming."

Drac leaned back in his chair and followed his younger brother's lead. "It is an impressive piece of evidence, even if we didn't actually capture the apparition."

They both raised an eyebrow in Steele's direction, waiting for him to chime in. For a moment, he returned their looks petulantly; then he sat up and grudgingly offered, "I suppose you're right. Maybe we can pull it together tonight when we get into that back bedroom."

Steele's words reminded me that I had agreed to return to the back bedroom tonight. *Tonight,* I thought. *Just a few hours from now.* I looked down and realized that my hands were trembling, so I quickly clasped them together, hoping no one had noticed. But Gabe had noticed. He glanced down at my hands and then into my eyes. Sensing how much I needed encouragement, he laid a hand on my shoulder and said softly, "You may not feel this way now, but I think you've got a lot of guts."

Steele looked at him as though he'd grown another head, but Drac laughed and agreed with Gabe. "Me and Gabe, we weren't too sure you wouldn't take off out of here overnight. But you're here, going over a video that I know you'd rather forget about. You may have been afraid, and I know you took some lumps." He paused and looked sharply at Steele, who looked away guiltily. "But you're still here. In my eyes, that proves you've got guts."

Unsure of whether they were telling the truth or just being nice to the newbie, I gave them a half-hearted smile before Gabe nudged me. "And I was really impressed that you agreed to go back in there tonight; I honestly didn't expect you to say yes." Obviously Steele had missed that part of the conversation, because his eyes met mine incredulously. "Of course, maybe you're reconsidering now..."

I looked at Gabe apologetically. Indeed I was reconsidering going back into that room, even though I knew that backing out would disappoint Drac and Gabe, as well as give Steele more reason to belittle me. Why would I want to put myself through that again? I just couldn't face that entity again, afraid that this time it might want to finish what it started. Just as I was about to tell Gabe the deal was off, I caught Steele looking at me. As our eyes met, I saw the unspoken challenge in his gaze. He thought I was going to back out. *Well, you're wrong, Steele. I'm going to prove I can do this.*

Turning to Gabe with a new burst of courage—or defiance— I said, "No, I'm not reconsidering. I'm going to go into that room again, and I'm going to find whomever or whatever I encountered last night."

Gabe laughed and gave Drac a shove. "Make way for Kyrie Carter, Supernatural Sleuth! I told you the girl had guts."

Drac laughed and shoved him back. "No, I told you."

As the two of them scuffled and argued good-naturedly, I stole a glance at Steele. He had his arms crossed in front of him and was giving me a skeptical half smile. Although I met his gaze evenly, something in his eyes made my pulse quicken. I abruptly looked away, wondering what it was about Steele that always got me flustered.

I left Drac's room with a renewed sense of purpose. Drac and Gabe seemed to have confidence in me, which gave my self-esteem a much-needed boost, and Steele, well, his prickly arrogance made me even more determined to prove myself. My next chance to do that would be at analysis. So after a quick lunch and an even quicker catnap, I met up with Andy and Kyle and headed to the small meeting room we were using for analysis. The equipment was already set up when we got there, and Gabe was putting in order the tapes from the video cameras and the voice recorders. The three of us sat down, notepads and pens in hand, and waited for Drac and Steele. After a minute they came in carrying bottles of water. Drac tossed one to Gabe and then looked at us and asked, "Ready to roll?"

We all replied that we were, so Drac and Gabe went through a quick explanation of what they did during an analysis, including jotting down notes and time signatures and trying to cross-reference video clips and voice recordings to get as clear a perspective as possible on each experience. Steele interjected his point of view from time to time, giving pointers about phenomena that was often mistaken for something paranormal but could often be proved otherwise. Drac stressed that first and foremost, our job was to disprove the claims, and only if we couldn't do that were we to even consider anything to be paranormal. I shot a quick glance at Andy and was a bit surprised that he wasn't rolling his eyes at the prospect of being taught how to analyze evidence.

At last we got down to the painstaking task of analyzing the data. Drac and Kyle looked at some of the video evidence from the basement while Steele and Andy tackled the audio from the basement. Gabe and I took audio from the basement. We put on headphones, and Gabe started the tape, and almost as soon as their EVP session began, Steele and Andy began experiencing activity. We heard Andy's voice begin, "My name is Andy, and this is Spook. Is there anyone here with us tonight?"

As soon as he had said that, we heard a faint, "Yessssssss," some distance from the recorder.

Andy asked in a loud whisper, "Spook, did you hear that?"

"Yeah, I heard it," Steele replied. "That was over here close to where I am." After a moment, there was a scraping sound, and Steele whispered, "Shhh. Shhh, what was that?"

So many sounds were on the tape that at first it was hard to tell what, if anything, was paranormal. However, having spent some time in my grandparents' coal cellar as a child, I was able to identify and dismiss the sounds of the furnace. Still, there were so many other sounds that neither of us could clearly identify that we had to run through the audio several times.

"Hey Gabe," Drac suddenly called out. "Come look at this!"

Gabe paused the audio, and we all gathered around Drac's laptop. Drac rewound the tape from the thermal imaging camera and began playing it. We saw the briefest image of what appeared to be a human form ducking behind a large shelf. Andy looked at Steele and exclaimed, "That's when we heard that really loud whisper, remember?"

"I remember," Steele said, scratching his stubbly cheek thoughtfully. "That was that same area where we saw a lot of shadow play."

Gabe made note of the time stamp so we could cross-reference it with the audio when we came to that point.

Over the next few hours, we worked through audio and video. The attic yielded hardly any evidence at all, only the footsteps Drac and I had heard and a few orbs that Steele dismissed as dust. The audio from the graveyard also yielded nothing but the sounds of nocturnal animals or typical sounds from the nearby housing developments.

When at last we were left with the evidence from the second floor bedrooms and the video evidence from the graveyard, Drac suggested we all take a short break before tackling it. As I was heading out of the room for the lobby, Drac stopped me and asked, "Are you going to be okay going through this evidence again?"

I bit my lip and thought for a second before answering, "I think so."

Gabe leaned against the doorframe and said, "I figure we'll let Drac and Kyle look at the video from the back bedroom, and you and I can stick to the audio. Spook wants to see the video from the graveyard, especially that part where you're there alone, so we'll leave that to him."

I understood that they were just trying to shield me from having to go through that experience again, but I couldn't help feeling a bit irritated. Sure, I was still unnerved by what had happened last night, and admittedly my courage and determination to go back into that room were wavering a bit, but since the worst part of the experience hadn't been caught on video, I was sure I could handle seeing it again.

After a short break, Gabe and I settled in to go through the audio evidence from the second floor bedrooms. There wasn't much to hear at first on the tape from Gabe's recorder; then we heard the bangs in response to our requests for a sign. After the second bang, when we had returned to the master bedroom and I had made the remark about the smart-alecky spirit, we heard Gabe's laugh, but there was also another sound. Gabe started, then glanced at me and asked, "Did you hear that?"

He didn't wait for an answer but quickly rewound the tape and played it again. We both put our hands over our headphones to hear better and listened closely. Sure enough, as Gabe laughed on the tape, we both heard a faint high-pitched voice that almost sounded like a laugh.

I gave Gabe a half smile and asked, "Did that sound like a laugh to you?"

He chuckled, nodded, and said, "Yeah, that's what it sounded like."

I jotted down the time stamp, and we moved on. As we continued listening, I kept that voice at the back of my mind, wondering if it could possibly belong to the spirit I had seen in the back bedroom. Somehow I doubted it.

We got to the part of the investigation where Gabe and I split up. We were still listening to the audio from Gabe's recorder, and we didn't hear anything else except for his voice and movements. He did capture our interaction as I dealt with the spirit in the other room. As we continued listening to the conversation, I began trembling. I felt Gabe move and glanced over at him. He was about to say something when Andy exclaimed, "Whoa, what was that?"

Steele slid backwards with a screech as he sat forward and responded excitedly, "That was the flash I saw on the monitors."

Gabe and I exchanged a look and then scooted over to Steele's laptop to squeeze in between him and Andy as he rewound the tape. Drac came over to stand behind us as Steele replayed the video. Everything was quiet, dark, and still on the stationary shot, when suddenly a bright light flashed somewhere up in the tree. After a couple minutes, there was another flash. Unfortunately, the source of the flash was just outside of the camera's direct view, so we couldn't see what caused it. "So far, that was the only time it happened," Steele mused, jotting something down.

"And it's not headlights?" Andy asked, obviously trying to debunk it.

Steele shook his head. "That's what Carter thought, too. We did a drive-by test, which will be coming up shortly on the video," he said, rewinding and replaying the video again. He hit pause at the moment the light flashed and studied the image. "I can't even tell where it originates. It's just a flash."

As Steele continued to puzzle over the mysterious light in the graveyard, the rest of us went back to analyzing. It wasn't long before Kyle let out a shout. Drac's expression told me that they had reached the part of the video where the entity had begun to manifest. Andy hurried over to watch and let out an exclamation of awe. Gabe paused the audio, and I closed my eyes and let out a slow breath, scribbling aimlessly on my notebook. The next moment, Kyle and Andy both shouted with disappointment, and I knew the screen had gone black. "What happened?" Kyle said.

"Most likely the entity drained the battery to manifest itself," Drac replied grimly.

"Drained the . . ." Andy cried, turning to glare at me. "Kyr, you didn't have the camera plugged in? How stupid can you—"

"Cut her a break!" Steele growled, swinging around so quickly that he knocked his notebook onto the floor. "She's just learning, you know. You have some learning to do yourself, about being a team player." Andy returned Steele's glare defiantly for a second before turning away guiltily.

When I was able to pick my jaw up from the floor, I shot Gabe a perplexed look. Hadn't Steele jumped down my throat over the same issue earlier? Why was he so eager to defend me now? *He's definitely a complex character.* Gabe smiled and winked at me, obviously amused by something.

We went back to work, listening to the tape from my recorder from the time I was alone in the back bedroom. At first, there was nothing but the sound of my voice and my movement around the room, but as I began asking the spirit to show itself, we heard the same voice we'd heard on the video. "There it is!" Gabe rewound the tape to listen again.

As he hit Play, I bent my head and closed my eyes so I could concentrate and try to figure out what the voice was saying. As I heard the voice again, I thought I could make out a word, but I wasn't sure. I asked Gabe to rewind it again. When he hit Play and we both listened once more, the words seemed to be clearer to me. I glanced uneasily at Gabe, wondering if he had heard anything close to what I heard. By the look on his face, I thought maybe he had. Eager to try something, I took my notepad and jotted down what I thought it said, not letting Gabe see it. He must have understood what I was doing, because he did the same. He took his headphones off; his voice was strange as he said, "Hey, Drac, come here for a sec."

Drac paused their video and came over. "What've we got?"

"This is that voice we heard on the video." Gabe said, rewinding the tape and hitting Play. "On the voice recorder we think we can make out some definite words. See if you can pick anything up."

Drac slipped the headphones on, and Gabe played the tape for him. Drac's eyebrows shot up, and he leaned forward on the table and asked, "Play it again?" Gabe did, and Drac listened again. "That didn't sound very friendly," he ventured, looking at me with furrowed brows.

Gabe asked, "What did you think it said?"

"It sounded like 'I'll show you,'" Drac replied grimly.

Gabe and I laid our notebooks on the table and sat looking at what we'd written. We had heard the same thing. I swallowed hard, wondering what the entity intended to show me. I shuddered as I realized that I might indeed find out later that night.

CHAPTER SEVEN

As we began setting up for the night's investigation, I was definitely on edge, even more so than I had been the previous night. I was very jumpy, and as I struggled to set up some equipment in the basement, it seemed that every noise and every shadow startled me. Once, as I was securing power cords for one of the cameras, Kyle came up behind me without me hearing him. I almost jumped out of my skin when he asked, "Do you need any help with that?"

Unable to keep the tremor out of my voice, I responded, "No thanks, I got it."

Kyle said, "Okay," giving me a strange look as he ducked out of the room and headed up the steps. After he left, I took a few deep breaths and turned to finish my task.

Just as I finished, I heard footsteps on the stairs. I looked up to see Steele coming towards me. I rolled my eyes and muttered epithets under my breath as I knelt down to double check my work, certain he was there to nitpick all my mistakes. As I worked, I felt his eyes on me. I tried to avoid looking at him, but at last I couldn't stand it anymore, and I met his gaze. The earlier spark of remorse was there, but he was struggling to keep it hidden beneath his cold façade. Knowing that we had to get past what had happened that morning in Drac's room, I swallowed my pride and said, "Look, I'm . . . sorry about last night. I really screwed up setting up that camera."

A moment of silence followed, and I wondered if he'd heard me. Just as I was about to repeat myself, he replied, "Yeah, that you did."

I glanced up at him, thinking he might be messing with me, but there was no humor in his dark eyes. *Okay, fine*, I thought, turning away again. *I suppose the blame is all on me.*

A low grunt made me look in his direction. Some of the coldness had left his face. "I . . . I'm sorry too. I shouldn't have snapped at you the way I did."

Well, that was progress, although I supposed I was still being held completely accountable. I pulled off a strip of duct tape.

"You had a right to be angry. I've seen enough of the show to know that I should have had backup with my camera."

Steele checked the focus on the camera I had just set up and made some adjustments before contradicting, "No, I shouldn't have said that either. I should have taken the time to show you how to do it properly and not assume you'd pick up the techniques from watching the show."

"But it was still—" I was interrupted by a voice on the stairs.

"Maybe you two should quit arguing over whose fault it was and finish setting up so we can investigate tonight." We both turned quickly to see Gabe standing halfway down the stairs, a stern look on his face. I lowered my gaze guiltily, but Gabe chuckled and asked, "Will you two be ready in half an hour?"

I nodded, and Steele responded, "I just need to check the focus on the camera, and we'll be ready to roll."

Steele and I finished up in the basement, and we headed back to Center Command with Gabe. When everyone was gathered together, Drac and Gabe went over the plan for the night. Drac said he wanted to hit all the rooms again, but he especially wanted to focus on the graveyard and the back bedroom, since we—I—had had the most intense experiences in those two places. I felt everyone's eyes on me when Drac mentioned the back bedroom, and I swallowed hard, thinking once again that I wasn't sure I wanted to go through with this.

Drac, Gabe, and Steele did a quick sweep of the house while Andy, Kyle, and I watched the monitors for any activity. When they returned, we split up into the same teams we had started off with last night. Drac had decided that Gabe and I would hold off going into the back bedroom until around the time I had encountered the spirit the night before to see if we could recreate last night's events. As Drac and Gabe finished laying out the night's schedule, Steele's jaw flexed repeatedly, and he folded his arms tensely in front of him. His eyes flashed angrily with whatever comment he fought to hold back. I found myself wondering what had him so worked up.

At last, we split up and began investigating. Drac and I headed for the basement. As we slowly descended the steep wooden stairs, Drac asked, "So how are you doing? Kyle mentioned that you seemed a little on edge."

I kept my eyes on the floor and responded, low, "I was hoping no one noticed."

"Look." Drac pulled me aside. "I know you're trying really hard to learn the ropes and not get overwhelmed with it all; we've noticed that." I swallowed hard, feeling a lecture coming on. "But you've got to be honest with us if you're feeling scared or overwhelmed or threatened. No one is going to put you in a corner and call you a failure."

"I know," I answered in a small voice, thinking I could name at least two people who might put me in that corner. "I'm sorry."

He leaned up against the wall, put a hand on my shoulder, and said, "None of us wants to see you go through a repeat of last night. You know . . ." He cocked an eyebrow and leaned close. "He didn't want to let on, but Gabe was pretty shook-up when he had to pull you out of that room."

I looked quickly at Drac. I hadn't realized that Gabe had been worried about what happened. He had taken such pains to calm my fears and cheer me up that the thought hadn't even crossed my mind that he had been concerned. "I didn't know it bothered him that much," I suddenly felt even worse about last night's events.

I could hear the smile in Drac's voice as he responded, "Gabe seems to have taken you under his wing; he feels really protective of you, like you're one of our little sisters."

In one sense, I was touched by Gabe's concern, not to mention thrilled at the idea that he cared about me, but in another sense I was a little irritated. I had spent my whole life being the baby of the family, the little sister who was always coddled and kept safe. One of the reasons I had agreed to enter this contest was to rise to a challenge and to prove to myself that I could do something out of my comfort zone. I gave the wall a frustrated kick. "Nothing's going to happen to me. I can take care of myself. Come on, let's get to it."

Drac chuckled and turned to lead the way to the back of the cellar. He said over his shoulder, "Don't be upset, Kyr. He knows you can take care of yourself; he just wants to be sure of it." He chuckled again and added, "And Gabe isn't the only one."

I stopped dead in my tracks. *What did he mean by that? Who else was worried about my safety?* I hurried after him to ask what he meant, but I only made it a few steps before he stopped short and hissed, "Did you hear that?"

I held my breath and listened hard. A second later, I heard the sound of shuffling in the back corner. Drac and I fixed our eyes on the spot where the sound had come from, trying to detect any movement. Drac shined his flashlight in that corner and around the room. I thought I saw movement just outside the flashlight's beam, so I slowly began moving in that direction. "Last night our friends talked to someone in this room. Was that you?"

We both listened intently for a response, but heard nothing. Drac swept the K-II meter around near the corner, asking, "Can you make the lights on this device light up to let us know you're here? It won't hurt you, but it can help you communicate with us."

While Drac continued to try to make contact with the K-II, I crossed the room to sit where the others had seen the figure last night. I started my voice recorder and tagged my location before asking, "Is there anyone here with us tonight?" I heard a slight rustling close beside me, and I shifted, shining my flashlight around, trying to find a source. "Hello? If that was you, can you come closer and speak into the device in my hand?"

I continued shining my flashlight around, still hearing rustling close to where I was sitting. Suddenly I heard scurrying at the wall next to me and saw something right outside the edge of the flashlight beam. When I finally caught the figure in my light, I squealed and jumped up away from the wall.

"What? What happened?" Drac asked. "Did you see something?"

I laughed shakily and answered, "Nothing paranormal, just a mouse." I brushed off the back off my jeans. "Sorry about that."

Just then, Drac's walkie crackled. "Gabe for Drac and Spook."

Drac fumbled at his belt for a moment and then answered, "Yeah, Gabe, what's up?"

Steele responded right after Drac. "Go for Spook."

"Just checking your locations," Gabe responded. "We're in the attic. Kyle said he glanced out the window and saw a light and some movement over in the graveyard. We were wondering if it was you."

My eyes widened as I turned to Drac. *The light!* And the shadow figure! Drac spoke into the walkie. "Wasn't us; we're in the basement."

Steele's voice came across next. "We're in the back bedroom. I'm looking out the window now; I don't see any—Wait. What the hell is that?" He was silent for a moment, and then: "Something is moving around out there. I'm going to check it out."

Without thinking, I grabbed my walkie and responded, "I'll meet you out there." I had a score to settle with that shadow figure. I only hoped it would still be there when Steele and I got there.

"Copy that," Gabe said.

Steele and I reached the back door of the mansion at the same time. As we hurried outside and around the back towards the graveyard, Steele gave me a stern look. "Just be careful," he warned unnecessarily. "We may be dealing with a living person, and some of them are more dangerous than the dead ones."

I bit my tongue and tried not to disagree with him. I was certain he thought I was over-exaggerating about what I'd seen last night, and the video evidence we'd managed to capture was inconclusive, but I was sure our spirit was quite dangerous in its own right. As we approached the small family graveyard, we slowed down and carefully looked around to see if we could determine whether Kyle had seen a person or if it might have been something paranormal. As carefully as we stepped through the grass, dry leaves still crunched and swished beneath our feet, and I thought again how the shadow figure last night had made no sound as it moved around. I doubted that a flesh-and-blood person could have gotten away so quickly without us seeing or hearing him. The moon was shining brightly even through the branches of the couple trees planted nearby, and we were able to tell that the graveyard was empty except for us.

We were almost to the wrought iron fence when Steele turned to me with a glint in his eye. "So, are you planning to leap the fence again, or are you going to use the gate this time?" I cocked my head to glare at him, but the mischief in his cocky grin made the corners of my mouth twitch traitorously as I responded by heading for the gate. Steele hurried forward, grasped my arm, and asked, "You sure you're okay out here?"

"I'm fine," I answered, returning his gaze steadily. "Graveyards don't bother me in the least." *Usually. Unless an aggressive entity who's out to get me shows up.*

Steele gave me a skeptical smirk before heading towards the older graves at the far end of the cemetery. He turned and faced the house, looking up at the attic and the back bedroom, getting his bearings. He pulled out his walkie and called for Gabe.

"Go for Gabe," he answered.

"We're in the cemetery over by the old graves," Steele said. "Have Kyle look out the window while I move around with my flashlight; see if that looks anything like what he saw."

"Copy that," Gabe responded.

Steele waited a moment, then Kyle's voice came over the walkie. "Okay, I'm ready."

He turned on his flashlight and walked around, shining it in different directions. "Any of that look like what you saw?"

After a moment of silence, Kyle responded, "It's kind of similar, except the light didn't change in intensity like it did when you shined it away from me, and it seemed to be higher up, almost like it was shining in that big tree by the fence."

"You say it was up in the tree?" Steele asked, moving back to look up at the tree.

"Yeah," Kyle said. "The light seemed to be up among the branches, like someone was up in the tree."

As Kyle described the light's position to Steele, I began walking around the tree, testing the branches and trying to figure out how to best get up into the tree. I managed to climb up a few branches and got quite a few feet off the ground before Steele realized where I was. "What the hell are you doing, Carter? Be careful up there!"

"Oh, quit worrying. I'm a tomboy," I grumbled. "Hand me your flashlight; I want to try something."

Steele handed me his light, which was bigger and brighter than mine, and I moved around in the tree as much as I could, shining the light in different angles. Steele caught onto what I was doing and asked Kyle, "Can you see Carter's light up in the tree? Is that what you saw?"

Kyle radioed back, "I can see it, but it's obscured by the branches. It's also obvious it's a person with a flashlight." He paused for a moment. "The light I saw . . . I don't know . . . I guess it seemed to hover outside the branches?"

I scooted out, testing my weight on the branches and said to Steele, "There's no way I can get out on these branches without them breaking."

"Well, then, don't do it, Carter," Steele replied gruffly. Then he radioed Kyle. "Thanks, Kyle. That's the best we can do."

Steele clipped his walkie back on his belt as I began climbing down the tree. Realizing that I couldn't both hold onto the flashlight and keep a solid grip on the branch as I scrambled down, I called to Steele. He hurried over, and I reached down to hand him the flashlight. Instead of taking the flashlight from me, he reached up to grab me roughly by the arm and almost effortlessly pluck me from the tree. As I slid off the branch and into his arms, our eyes met for a moment, and I was struck by the way the moonlight played on his face, softening his features. I caught the ghost of a smile on his lips before it was gone again. Clearing my throat to bring myself back to reality, I asked, "What do you make of it?"

He cleared his throat, too, and shook his head. "I don't know," he responded simply. "We certainly haven't debunked it. Yet." As he ran his hand slowly through his hair, I could tell he was still unwilling to call it paranormal.

Suddenly he turned to me and said strangely, "Something I just realized, last night the light was just random flashes that didn't move. What Kyle saw tonight was a steady light that hovered around the tree. I wonder what that means."

I returned his look before turning to gaze at the tree, puzzling over the mysterious light and wondering if it was in any way connected either to the entity in the back room or to the shadow figure I'd seen out here last night. We decided to hang around in the graveyard and do some EVP work to see if we could communicate with whoever or whatever had made that light.

During our session, the graveyard remained fairly quiet except for a slight breeze and the sounds coming from the housing development the next block over. Thankfully, I didn't see the shadow figure while we were there, although I still had a hunch that if I'd been there alone, things might have been different. After about an hour, Drac's voice came over the walkie, telling us it was time to switch up teams. Heading back to Center Command, I began to feel more apprehensive as I anticipated returning to the back bedroom. Steele, Drac, and Gabe briefly recounted experiences from the past hour or two, while I leaned against the van and gazed up at the house, wondering what the next hour would bring.

Gabe and I headed up to the second floor. I hadn't thought it would be possible for me to be more nervous than I had been the night before, but I was. As we ascended the stairs, Gabe turned to look at me several times. Finally he asked, "How are you doing? Nervous?"

I let out a sigh, looking past Gabe to the dark hallway at the top of the stairs, and admitted, "Yeah, pretty much."

Gabe reached back to nudge my shoulder and joked, "Well, just remember, we've never lost an investigator."

I managed to smile back at him before joking uneasily, "Well, leave it to me to be the first . . ."

Gabe stopped on the landing and grasped my shoulders. "Hey," he said as sternly as he could, "I don't want to hear you talk like that! You know, if this scares you too much, you don't have to do it."

I looked him squarely in the eyes, thinking about Andy's scorn towards me as the inexperienced newbie and Steele's superior attitude about—well, everything. A part of me did want to just pack it in and forget what was happening here, but I just couldn't. "No, Gabe. I *do* have to do this. Not only to try to answer my own questions about the paranormal, but also to prove I'm not a wuss."

Gabe chuckled and gave me a shake. I knew he probably thought I was being melodramatic, but there was no way he could understand how much it meant for me to face up to my fears and finish what I'd started here. "You don't have to beat yourself up, Newb. Being scared doesn't make you a wuss, or a bad person, or even a bad paranormal investigator. It makes you human." When I looked down at the floor and didn't answer, he continued, "Look, last night when that door opened, and I saw you on the floor and couldn't wake you up, I was pretty scared. I didn't know what to think."

I glanced up at him, feeling like a smitten teenager again, and I felt my face flushing. I swallowed hard and tried to keep my voice steady as I responded, "I'll be okay. I'm afraid, but I'll be okay."

He touched my cheek briefly. "I know you will, Kyr. Like Drac and I said, you've got a lot of guts!"

I fought the urge to throw myself into his arms and lay my head on his shoulder, but instead took a deep breath, trudged purposefully up the remaining stairs, and headed towards the back bedroom. When I got to the door, my resolve weakened a bit, and I turned towards Gabe, uncertain of what I should do next.

Gabe came down the hall to stand next to me and laid a hand on my shoulder. "The camera is set up on the dresser, just like you had it last night, except tonight Andy and Spook made sure it's plugged in. I'll be over in the master bedroom, just like last night, and Drac and Kyle will be watching the monitor in the van." He smiled at me and continued, "Just do your thing, and if you run into any trouble or start feeling really uncomfortable, either call me or just get out."

I nodded my head, but I was thinking, *What if I can't get out? What if the spirit locks me in, just like last night?*

Gabe must have read my thoughts, because he added, "Try to remember, a spirit feeds off your fear, so try not to let it scare you."

I nodded again, wondering how to not let the spirit scare me. I was beginning to feel overwhelmed and wished the night was over. *Well, it's now or never.* As I turned to go into the room, I looked over my shoulder at Gabe. He gave me an encouraging smile and headed down the hall towards the master bedroom. I heard him radio to Drac that I was going in, and Drac answered back that he was ready on the monitors.

I walked over to the dresser to double-check that the video camera was turned on before sitting on the bed and turning on my voice recorder as I had done the night before. My voice shook as I asked, "Is there anyone here who would like to speak with me?"

The room remained silent for the time being, which suited me fine. After a minute, I asked again, "Is there anyone in this room with me?"

I stood up and moved around the room, sweeping the room with my K-II and trying to sense if there was a presence in the room, but I felt nothing, no uneasy feelings, no cold spots, no K-II hits, nothing. I could hear Gabe's muffled voice in the other room as he, too, tried to make contact.

After another minute of silence, I decided to start provoking. "Come on, last night you sure weren't afraid to come out and play. What, did you use up all your nasty last night? Why don't you come out and talk to me?" I hoped I sounded braver than I felt.

A few more minutes went by, and I was just about to radio Drac or Gabe to see what I should do when I thought I felt a draft. I crossed quickly to the window to see if there was any wind blowing and coming in through a crack, but everything was tight. "Is that you?" I asked. "Is there something you'd like to say to me?"

The room grew steadily colder, and I started to shiver. I heard a low whisper, but I couldn't make out any words. "I thought I heard you, but you need to speak louder. Can you tell me your name?"

Suddenly, just like last night, the door slammed shut. *Oh great. Here we go again.*

Drac and Gabe both spoke into the walkies at once. "Are you okay in there? Do you need help?"

I radioed back, "The door slammed shut again, and the room is freezing, but I think I'm okay for now." I set the voice recorder down and walked as calmly as I could over to the door. I rattled the doorknob and yanked on it, but it was locked as it had been last night. A bit irritated, I called out, "Okay, so you can slam a door. I get that. You obviously don't want me to leave. Why don't you tell me what you want me to know? Do you need help?"

Just then, icy prickles spread across the back of my neck. I swallowed hard and spun around to see the same mist beginning to form over by the bed. I radioed Drac and with a shaky voice asked, "Drac, are you getting this?"

Drac's voice came over the walkie, "Yeah, I see it, Kyr. Just stay calm and try to—"

The walkie went dead.

"Drac? Gabe? *Gabe*?" I couldn't reach either of them by radio. I tried the door; it was still locked. Just as I had the previous night, I watched as the shimmering mist began to take the shape of a human. I unconsciously took a step backwards and pressed against the door. My eyes landed on the video camera on the dresser, and I said out loud, "Drac, I hope you're seeing this on the monitor. My walkie went dead—"

Before I could finish my statement, the video camera flew off the dresser and landed in the corner with a crash. I stared in shock at the camera and realized that we were indeed dealing with an intelligent spirit, one that did not want its presence documented. I tried to make a dash for the camera to see if it still worked and if I could capture on video whatever was about to happen. However, the entity seemed to have other intentions. It purposefully placed itself between me and the camera. My fear rose as the same angry-looking man clearly manifested in front of me.

The sudden rattling of the doorknob startled me, and I heard Gabe's voice outside, "Are you okay? What's happening? I can't get the door open."

I put my hand on the doorknob and tried in vain to open the door. I didn't even try to hide the fear in my voice as I answered, "He's here. He's here again."

"I know you're afraid," Gabe encouraged, trying to keep his voice low and calm, "but try to communicate. Try not to panic."

That's easier said than done. "Who are you?" I asked the spirit. "Why are you here?" For a moment, the spirit just stared at me, its eyes boring into me threateningly. My hands shook as I wrestled with the doorknob, and my pulse began pounding in my ears.

Suddenly, I recalled the voice we had captured last night; I opened my mouth to speak, but at first no sound came out. When the spirit reached its hand towards me and took a step towards me, I found my voice. "What did you mean, 'I'll show you'? What are you going to show me?"

If it were possible for the spirit to look at me more menacingly, it did. Suddenly, I felt a wave of pure malice and hatred surround me. The feeling was so intense that it almost smothered me as the entity came closer. Only an arm's length away, I sensed, rather than heard, a voice say, "I'll show you, worthless whore!"

I felt the same sense of terror and impending danger that I had felt last night as the spirit kept moving towards me. What did he want to show me, and why was he so angry? The air around me became thicker and heavier, and it became harder to breathe. A loud buzzing filled my ears, drowning out all other sounds, and tiny points of light danced in my vision. As my surroundings became blurry, I realized that the spirit was trying to overpower me. If I didn't fight back and regain control quickly, I would lose consciousness just as I had last night, and I had the feeling that tonight I wouldn't be as lucky.

I was only vaguely aware of Gabe's voice outside the door, but suddenly, there was another voice which reached inside me enough to jar me back to my senses. *Steele!* I recalled how upset Gabe had said he was when he found me on the ground unconscious, and I saw Steele's smirk as he wordlessly challenged me not to chicken out tonight. I was determined not to repeat last night. I shook my head to clear it, looked the spirit squarely in its eyes and shouted, "No! Leave me alone! You may have won last night, but not tonight! "

To my amazement, the spirit halted his advance and looked at me, almost as though I had startled him. Had my defiance broken his hold on me or only given him momentary pause? As my awareness of my surroundings returned, I heard Steele at the door calling my name and trying to get in. Strangely, the entity also seemed to hear him now, and he began fading away. Taking courage in that fact, I shouted again, "You're not wanted here! I don't want you here, and Chuck doesn't want you here. You need to *leave*!" The buzzing in my ears faded, and I became aware that the room had gone silent. Steele had ceased calling to me and pounding on the door, and I wondered what had happened to Gabe.

Angered by my words and taking advantage of my loss of focus the spirit started towards me again, his face contorted with rage as he took another step towards me. Refusing to lose the upper hand, I took a tentative step towards him, not sure what I would do when I came face to face with him. "You may have scared me last night, but I'm not scared now." I hoped he couldn't tell I was bluffing. "Just go away!"

A wordless yell filled the room, and a blast of icy cold air brought me to my knees as the door flew open. In the next instant, Steele charged in, handheld video camera drawn to capture visual evidence. Seeing the entity gone and me on the floor, he tossed aside the camera and hauled me to my feet, wrapping his strong arms around me.

For a moment, all the animosity between us vanished, and I leaned into him, drawing his strength and craving the warmth of his body. The spicy, woodsy scent of his cologne filled my nostrils and dulled my sense of reason, even as it brought me to my senses. I drew back to look at him, but the intensity in his deep brown eyes made me drop my gaze. My eyes locked on his lips, and I involuntarily moved closer. Before our lips could connect, Steele's fingers tangled roughly in my hair, and he pulled me tightly against him.

"Take it easy, Spook. She's not going anywhere," Gabe said with a chuckle. *Gabe!* Suddenly realizing what I had almost allowed to happen, I broke away from Steele and threw myself into Gabe's arms, mortified sobs wracking my body. He tentatively put his arms around me. "It's all right, Kyr. You're safe now."

Finally I calmed down enough to stifle my tears. As I pulled back to look up at Gabe, I saw that he wasn't looking at me. He was staring uneasily at something behind me. Lowering my head, I took a few steps backwards and spun around, suddenly afraid the spirit had returned. Instead, I saw Steele, his eyes hardened and glistening with a cold light that made me cower away from him. I almost leaned into Gabe, but something in Steele's gaze stopped me.

"Let's get her out of here," Steele said flatly, slipping an arm around me to support me. I tried to protest that I could walk on my own, but he ignored me. "Gabe, grab that video camera and Carter's voice recorder. I don't want anything happening to that evidence."

Gabe looked at Steele strangely for a moment before the corners of his mouth twitched, and he saluted. "I'm on it, Captain!"

Steele narrowed his eyes for a second before laughing shortly and turning to half-haul, half-help me down the stairs and out of the house.

CHAPTER EIGHT

Drac, Andy, and Kyle were waiting somewhat anxiously in the van when we exited the mansion. They had all gathered around the monitors while Gabe, Steele, and I were upstairs, so they had seen everything that had happened before the camera went flying. As Steele led me out to sit in the van, Andy and Kyle came tumbling out. Andy exclaimed, "Dude! That was seriously messed up!"

Kyle asked, "Are you okay? How did you manage to get out of that room?"

Drac jumped out of the van and burst between them, grasping both men's shoulders. "Guys, let her sit down for a minute and get her breath. She's pretty shook-up." After I climbed into the van and collapsed into a chair, with Steele right next to me, Drac pulled the tapes from both the video camera and the voice recorder. "That's two nights in a row that the same thing has happened," he said, looking at me grimly. "We need to get some more details from Chuck about his ex-wife's claims in that room."

"You bet," Gabe replied, crossing his arms and gazing at me with narrowed eyes. "He never said anything about these kinds of attacks."

Drac looked curiously at Steele sitting right next to me trying to warm me up, and then turned his eyes to Andy and Kyle, stroking his goatee. "So far Kyr is the only one who has experienced anything significant in that room. I wonder why that is."

Andy and Kyle exchanged a nervous glance before Andy ventured, "Do you think one of us should go up there?" I had to stifle a giggle; he was certainly acting less cocky and brave than he had last night.

Drac set his jaw thoughtfully before responding, "I think *someone* should go in there, but I don't know that I want either of you guys risking it. Gabe, maybe you should stay here with Kyr while Spook and I go up." Steele shot Drac a hard look; Drac threw his hands up as if in surrender and chuckled, "Or you could stay here and keep an eye on Kyr and the monitors while Gabe and I go up."

That satisfied him, but annoyed me a bit. Why did everyone think I needed someone to keep an eye on me?

Drac and Gabe soon set out for the second floor. I was a bit disappointed that Gabe wasn't staying with me, and without thinking, I gazed after him wistfully and sighed. A slight huff from Steele brought my attention to him, and my breath caught in my throat as I saw that he was gazing at me with the same cold, hard look he'd been giving me in the back bedroom. I looked away quickly, biting my lip and reaching up to tug nervously on my ponytail.

The four of us sat and watched the monitors while Drac and Gabe quickly swept the second floor with the K-II and the thermal. "No EMF spikes," Drac said. "All seems to be peaceful for now."

"Temperature is a steady seventy degrees, except right by the windows," Gabe added. "Let's get started." Drac retreated to the other bedroom, and Gabe began an EVP session. As with my experience, Gabe got no response when he asked the spirit to make its presence known. He soon began provoking, and I became more uneasy as I watched the monitor, afraid to see what might happen if and when the spirit decided to make an appearance.

I soon decided I couldn't watch anymore, so I got up and walked a little distance away from the van and sat down on a flat rock close to the driveway. I breathed in the chilly night air, looking over at the moon rising over the horizon and trying to steady my nerves. A sudden touch on my shoulder made me jump and squeal. When I turned quickly and saw Steele standing there with his hands thrown up in front of him, I snapped, "Would you guys stop sneaking up on me?"

Steele looked as startled, but chuckled as he took a step back. "Carter, take it easy. I didn't mean to scare you."

I walked away from him, leaned against the tree and mumbled, "I'm sorry. I just . . . I . . ."

Steele cautiously made his way over to where I stood. I felt him close behind me for a moment before he laid his hands tentatively on my shoulders. "It's okay, Carter. You're okay," he assured me uncertainly. Obviously he wasn't used to consoling frantic females. "You're outside, you're safe. Nothing is going to hurt you."

I spun around to look up at him for a moment. I wanted to believe him, but I couldn't; I didn't feel safe, not even out here. I thought about what I'd heard him say to Drac and Gabe last night. Feeling defeated, I admitted in a small voice, "I—you were right, Steele. I have no business being here." When I raised my eyes to look up at him through my bangs, his expression as he returned my gaze was a mixture of his usual arrogance and something that looked suspiciously like warmth. The intensity of his eyes drew me to him, and as he cocked his head to regard me, I felt the strangest urge to lean against him and let him hold me as he had upstairs, before I had thrown myself into Gabe's arms.

Steele's eyes softened, and his hands came up slowly to rest on my shoulders. My mouth went dry as he slowly stroked his thumbs across the top of my shoulder to my neck. I briefly glanced over at his hands and then raised my eyes to his to meet his gaze questioningly. As our eyes met, he seemed to snap out of his trance. He took his hands away as though he'd been burned, leaving me feeling off balance. "Look, Carter," he began uncertainly, running his hand through his hair. "I . . . I never should have said that. You—It took a lot of nerve to go in and face that entity tonight." He locked his eyes on some vague point over my head and continued, "You may be just a beginner, and you do have a lot to learn, but . . ."

"Hey, Spook," Andy called urgently. "Could you come here?"

Steele and I hurried back to the van and climbed inside to stand behind Andy and Kyle. "What's up, man?" Steele asked.

They were both silent for a moment, staring intently at the monitor. Gabe was still provoking, and he was getting more aggressive. With his eyes still on the screen, Andy quickly told us, "I heard a voice respond to Gabe, but he didn't seem to hear anything. Kyle and I just want you here if it happens again."

The four of us huddled around the monitors and watched. Gabe was sitting on the bed doing an EVP session. "So you're a tough guy, are you?" he challenged. "You think you're a badass, scaring a woman. Well, she showed you tonight, didn't she?"

Gabe was silent for a moment, waiting for a response, and the four of us distinctly heard a faint voice close to the microphone, although we couldn't make out what it said. It definitely wasn't the same voice I'd heard when the spirit was in the room with me. Steele pulled out his walkie. "Spook to Gabe, come in."

"Go for Gabe," he responded.

"Are you hearing anything in response to your questions?" Steele asked, leaning forward to watch the monitor intently.

Gabe paused for a moment as though listening, and then answered, "No, not a thing. The most I've gotten is a slight chill a few minutes ago."

"Copy that," Steele said. "Andy and Kyle thought they heard something respond to you, and we all just heard a voice as well. You say you didn't hear anything?"

Gabe was silent again, looking around the room, before responding, "No, I haven't heard anything."

"Copy that," Steele replied. He then radioed Drac. "Hey, Drac, you getting any activity over there?"

"*Negativo*, Spook," Drac responded. "I heard a few random taps, but there was no response when I asked the spirit to knock again if it was trying to communicate."

Drac and Gabe decided to switch up rooms to see if Drac might have better luck. We continued watching the monitors, hoping to capture something else. Drac jumped right in with provoking, trying to get any kind of response. "Come on," he growled. "Are you too much of a coward to show yourself to me? Are you only man enough to pick on a woman?"

As nervous as I was about the possibility of seeing something manifest for either Drac or Gabe, I was equally nervous that nothing would happen, which to me would mean one of two things: Either Steele was right and I was imagining what had happened to me, or the spirit was intentionally singling me out and attacking me. After a few more minutes of watching and waiting, I muttered petulantly under my breath, "I'll bet the bastard would come out if I went back up there."

I hadn't intended for anyone to hear me, but apparently Steele had. He turned to me with a stern expression and warned, "Don't even think about it, Carter."

As he turned back to the monitors, I let out a huff and rolled my eyes. As I half-heartedly watched the action—or rather, the lack of action—on the screens, I became aware of a strange urgency, as though there was somewhere I needed to be. I tried to shake it off as nerves, but the more I tried to ignore it, the stronger the feeling became.

As silently as I could, I slipped out of the van and walked towards the driveway. That didn't feel right, so I turned and took a couple steps towards the house, staring up at the dark windows and the paint-peeling shutters. I shook my head slightly; that wasn't it either. I closed my eyes to shut out everything else so I could concentrate on this game of hot-or-cold that something was playing with me. When I opened my eyes again, I knew where I needed to go. I took a few halting steps towards the graveyard and then stopped. There was no way I wanted to go up there alone.

In the next instant, Steele was next to me. "Carter, what are you doing out here?"

My eyes were trained on the graveyard, even though I saw nothing out of the ordinary there. "There's . . . something up there," I stammered.

Steele stood up straight and stared intently up the hill. "What is it?" he asked. "What did you see?"

"I didn't . . . see . . . anything," I responded, wondering what snide comment he'd have when I told him. "I just . . . have a feeling . . ." I glanced at him. "There's something up there."

Even in the dark, I could see the skepticism on his face. "You just *feel* there's something there?" he asked doubtfully.

Unable to answer him, I just nodded, then took a few more hesitant steps. Steele turned and hurried back towards the van. Apparently he wasn't going to waste his time on a hunch from an over-imaginative newbie. I took a deep breath and forced myself to walk slowly and purposefully up the hill.

The sound of footsteps made me turn. Steele was right behind me, carrying a voice recorder and a handheld video camera.

"You're not . . . going up there . . . alone," he said, out of breath. Apparently, I had been wrong. I looked at him, grateful for the company, yet doubtful I'd see anything if he were present. He pursed his lips and added irritably, "I'll stay back out of the way." He rubbed his still-swollen lip and added, half-jokingly, "Believe me, I will."

Now how did he know what I was thinking?

As we continued up the hill, the small cemetery loomed in front of us. With the moonlight shining in between the branches of the trees, making silhouettes of the handful of tombstones and the wrought iron fence, I couldn't help thinking the scene would make a perfect Halloween card. I glanced over at Steele, and he quirked an eyebrow at me. "Pretty Halloween-y, isn't it?" he joked. My eyebrows shot up. *He just did it again.*

When we reached the top of the hill, I paused just outside the gate, peering in among the graves to see if anything was there. Although I saw nothing, there was definitely a different energy this time. I took a deep breath and reached for the gate. Just as I unlatched it and was about to go through, I felt Steele's hand on my arm. He stepped up beside me to peer into the graveyard before looking at me squarely. He handed me the voice recorder. "You might want this," he quipped with a half smile. "I'll be outside the fence filming." He cleared his throat and laid a protective hand on my shoulder. "Don't try to prove anything, Carter. If you feel threatened, get out."

I nodded, took another deep breath, and entered the graveyard. A few steps in, I paused, waiting. Hearing and seeing nothing, I switched on my voice recorder. "Kyr in the Berkeley graveyard. Steele is outside the fence filming." I looked around at the tombstones and up into the tree, waiting for some sign or reason why I was standing in a graveyard in the middle of the night. Finally, I just said, "All right, you wanted me up here, right? What did you want to show me?" Silence. "If you have a message, you can speak into this device."

Steele and I investigated for about half an hour with no success. I walked around with my flashlight, reading aloud the names on the headstones, hoping for a response or a clue. Still nothing. Steele, too, walked around the perimeter of the graveyard, still puzzling over the light we had seen in the branches.

After about an hour, Drac's voice came over the walkies. "Hey, guys, I think it's time to wrap. It's been pretty dead for a while now."

While Andy, Kyle, Steele and I tore down and packed up the equipment, Drac and Gabe talked to Chuck about my experiences in the back bedroom the past two nights, as well as the strange goings-on in the graveyard, hoping he would be able to shed some light on who our belligerent, misogynist spirit might be.

Back at the hotel, we met briefly in the lobby, where Drac told us, "Looks like we're going to have to do some legwork to figure out who our entity might be. Chuck said neither he nor his ex-wife ever experienced that kind of attack, although his ex-wife flat-out refused to go into that room alone."

"Any ideas on where to look?" Kyle asked.

"A couple places to start would be the library, the town hall, or the historical society," I suggested, hoping to be able to dig into the research. "Although I doubt any of those places will be open on a Sunday."

"Our resident librarian has spoken," Gabe teased, grinning at me. Then he became serious. "But Chuck thinks we should also pay a visit to his father over at the Shady Grove Retirement Village. He said he could meet us there around lunchtime tomorrow. That will likely be our best bet for now."

Drac laughed, "Apparently his dad goes by the nickname 'Cherry Pit'; he said we'd probably hear the story of how he got that moniker. He sounds like a real trip."

I smiled too, thinking that talking to a man named Cherry Pit would be much more pleasant than dealing with an unfriendly ghost.

CHAPTER NINE

After a blissfully uneventful night of sleep, I awoke late in the morning. Remembering the day's agenda, I took a quick shower, dashed down to the lobby for some coffee and a stale bagel, and sat in one of the oversized sofas to wait for the others. I had just finished the last of my bagel and swallowed the lukewarm remains of my coffee when Andy and Kyle showed up, followed not a minute later by Drac and Gabe.

Just as Drac was about to give the day's agenda, Steele found his way into the lobby, carrying his ever-present Mountain Dew. "Nice of you to join us," Drac quipped with a mock-serious expression. Steele grinned and raised his soda in a toast. "Okay guys . . . and gals," Drac began. "We're going to do things a little differently today. Gabe and Kyr are going to head over to the Shady Grove Retirement Village to meet up with Chuck and talk to his dad, and then see about doing whatever other research needs to be done." Steele scowled in Gabe's direction, but said nothing. Gabe gave him a sheepish smile in return. If Drac noticed the brief interaction, he ignored it and continued, "Andy and Kyle, you guys are going to stay here with me and Spook, and we'll tackle evidence review."

Drac tossed the keys to Gabe, and we all headed out to the Petery Paranormal van. After all the equipment was unloaded and carried into the small meeting room, Gabe and I headed out to the van. It was strange seeing Gabe climbing into the driver's seat, and even stranger climbing into the front seat next to him. A sudden thought made me giggle as I fastened my seat belt. Gabe caught my poorly-hidden amusement. "What's so funny?"

Without thinking, I responded, "I just feel like my dad's old Irish setter, Ruby Mae. The way she used to get all excited riding up front with him."

Gabe gave me a funny look, and then started laughing so hard he had to lay his head against the steering wheel. I started giggling too, just watching him, but I felt my cheeks flushing as I realized how silly my remark must have sounded. He finally sat up and said, "I'm sorry, Kyr. I just got a picture of you sticking your head out the window as we're driving down the road." He started laughing again, and soon I was doubled over in laughter too as I pictured myself the same way, with my tongue hanging out like Ruby Mae's and my long red hair blowing helter-skelter in the wind.

A tap at the window made us stop short. Drac was standing there with his arms crossed and a mock-serious expression on his face. Gabe rolled down the window, and Drac admonished, "Shouldn't you two dorks be hitting the road?"

Gabe immediately put on a serious face (how he managed *that*, I don't know), saluted Drac, and answered, "Yes, sir! Right away, sir!"

Drac laughed, gave his brother a playful shove, and wagged his finger at me before Gabe rolled up the window and drove away, still chuckling. "So, you know where we're going, Ruby Mae?"

I started laughing again and responded, "Yeah, we go about ten miles up this road, out in the country."

We drove in silence a few minutes before Gabe said thoughtfully, "Irish setters are beautiful dogs. What happened to her after your dad died?"

I wasn't expecting a question about my family, so I bit my lip a second before answering, "My mom. . . was killed in a car accident not two years after Daddy died. My oldest brother Luther took Ruby Mae, but she was pretty old and died just a couple weeks later." As a lump rose in my throat, I thought, *You really didn't need to tell him all that, you ninny.*

Gabe's eyes widened, and I could tell he was embarrassed that he had brought the subject up. "I'm sorry, Kyr. I didn't know . . ."

I touched his shoulder and responded, "It's all right. How *could* you know? I'm sorry I mentioned it." I looked away uncomfortably and folded my hands in my lap. "It's just that I miss them so much sometimes."

"I'm sure you do." Gabe reached over to squeeze my hand. "I sometimes forget how blessed Drac and I are to still have our parents."

I cleared my throat and glanced out the window, suddenly feeling uncomfortable. After a moment, I pointed to a crossroads up ahead. "You'll want to make a left up here on Eloquence Ridge Road."

Gabe slowed down to turn, and he raised an eyebrow at me. "Eloquence Ridge Road?"

I shrugged and gave him a sheepish smile. "I'm sure there's quite a story behind the name, but I've never looked into it."

A mile further down the road, we turned on to Shady Grove Road and arrived at the retirement village. Gabe had a puzzled look on his face again, and I guessed he had observed that there was no shady grove anywhere nearby, just a half dozen saplings lining the parking lot like sentries. "Honest, there used to be a shady grove here," I told him. "Most of the trees were very old and came down in a really bad windstorm several years back."

"I'll take your word for it." Gabe chuckled as he backed the van into a parking space. "There's Chuck in the entryway."

After parking, we headed over to the entryway, pulling our coats tighter against the wind. Chuck shook Gabe's hand, and then mine, saying, "I hear my resident spook has been giving you a hard time."

His mention of the word "spook" brought Steele to mind. *The non-resident Spook has been hard to deal with too.* Aloud, I said, "He's certainly making me the center of his attention."

"Well, hopefully Pop will be able to give us some answers about what's going on at the mansion. If anyone knows the house's history, it's him."

The three of us walked into the cozy, well-lit lobby and went towards the reception desk. Behind the desk sat a stocky, middle-aged woman with small, dark-framed glasses and short strawberry-blond hair. Her nametag said "Rose," but her expression suggested she was more thorn than rose. She looked up when Chuck picked up the pen for the visitor's book. "Morning, Rose," Chuck greeted. "Cherry Pit behaving himself?"

Her face softened a bit when she recognized Chuck. "So far, Chuck, but it's still early. Once those Wheaties kick in, I expect we're in for the usual." She briefly glanced over towards Gabe and me and asked, "You bring some reinforcements today?"

Chuck suddenly seemed uneasy and replied shortly, "Oh, uh, yeah. With Pop, you never know, right?" He handed the pen to me, motioning for me to sign in quickly.

I signed the book and handed the pen to Gabe. He shot Chuck a curious glance and hurriedly signed the book before handing it back to Rose. She said to Chuck, "You know where to find him, Darlin'."

As Rose took the book to check off our names, Chuck ushered us—very urgently, I thought—down the hall. I was just about to ask what the rush was when I heard a loud, "Oh my goodness!" from the front desk. Chuck glanced apologetically at Gabe and explained, "I should have warned you. Rose is a huge *Project Boo-Seekers* fan. I knew if she recognized you we'd never get past the front desk." He glanced nervously over his shoulder as though afraid she had followed us. "I don't know how we'll get you out of here."

I thought I saw a faint blush tinge Gabe's cheeks as he glanced sideways at me and joked, "Yeah, the fame does kind of haunt us at times."

I made a face and rolled my eyes at his pun while he and Chuck laughed.

We came to the end of a corridor, turned the corner and stopped at Room 134, where Chuck paused and knocked on the half-open door before going in. "Hey, Pop, you up and at 'em?"

I peered around Chuck and caught a glimpse of a feeble-looking, white-haired man in a wheelchair staring out the window at a flower-filled garden with a large ornate fountain and several birdbaths. I almost felt sorry for our intrusion, and I hoped our visit wouldn't strain him too much. The old man's eyes lit up as he caught sight of Chuck, and then suddenly he didn't seem so feeble anymore. "Chucky! What a surprise! I wasn't expecting you till next weekend!"

Chuck stepped aside and motioned us in. "Well, I have some visitors for you, Pop." He introduced us, and the elder Mr. Evans shook our hands, beaming brightly and looking much younger than his ninety years.

"Well, well," Mr. Evans crowed. "It's not often I get to meet new folks here! No siree! So what brings you to see an old fart like me?"

I covered my mouth and bit my lip to stifle a giggle, and Gabe raised an eyebrow in surprise. Chuck seemed embarrassed and said, "Pop, for heaven's sake! No wonder you never meet anyone!" I could tell that the older Mr. Evans was not a prim and proper gentleman like his son. I took an instant liking to his irreverence.

Mr. Evans cackled and rocked back and forth in his wheelchair, "Ah, Chucky Boy, don't be so serious. An old man's gotta have some fun." He turned his attention to Gabe and me. He took my hand again and said, "You say your name is Kyrie, as in the *Kyrie eleison*?"

I felt myself blushing. Not many people made the connection of where my name came from, and I was always a little embarrassed having to explain why I had such an unusual name. I figured that the elder Mr. Evans wasn't likely to be familiar enough with '80s music for me to use my usual explanation, so I responded, "Yes, sir, that's right."

"How did you come to have that name? Your daddy a pastor?" His blue eyes had come to life, eagerly awaiting my story.

I half laughed and responded, "No, not officially. He always wanted to be, but my mom was kind of . . . a free spirit, I guess. She did go to church and knew a lot about the Bible, but she didn't want to be tied down being a pastor's wife, so Daddy settled for teaching Sunday school and serving as the Sunday School superintendent." I glanced at Mr. Evans, certain that my story was boring him, but he nodded expectantly, encouraging me to continue. "He insisted on all his kids' names being somehow church-related or biblical. My brothers are Luther, John-Wesley, and Graham—after Billy Graham. Mom wanted something a little more flowery and unique for me, so when she saw the word 'Kyrie' in the hymnal at my grandmother's church, she said it was perfect."

I shot Gabe a dirty look as I heard him chuckle. Mr. Evans found it humorous as well, and he laughed out loud. "Well, I like it! It suits you. Your parents must be something!"

I smiled wistfully, and I heard Gabe clear his throat. I answered quietly, "Yes, they certainly . . . were."

Chuck seemed to pick up that I didn't want to talk anymore about my parents. He jumped in, "Well, Pop, the reason they're here is, we—they want to know some history about the house."

Mr. Evans' sharp mind immediately grasped why Chuck was suddenly interested in the house's history. "You still having trouble with that damn ghost?"

"Well, things have been more . . . active . . . since I started fixing up the basement," Chuck responded. "So I decided to call in someone who could help."

"Wait a minute!" A light bulb had gone off in Mr. Evans' head. He wagged a finger at Gabe. "You're that spook-hunting fella that Rosie always talks about!" His words made a smile tug at my lips; he pronounced "spook" so that it rhymed with "book," as my dad and grandparents had. He crowed again, slapped a gnarled hand on his wheelchair, and said, "Imagine that! My old house is going to be on a TV show!"

"Actually, we're not filming this one," Gabe replied apologetically. "We just came in to check things out and . . . to train some new investigators." He winked at me and grinned.

"Oh." Mr. Evans seemed a bit deflated, and I sensed he might have wanted to use that for bragging rights. "Oh, well, that's probably for the best. Now that I think about it, I wouldn't want folks sneaking around the old place if they saw it on TV." He brightened up again as he remembered we wanted some information on the house's history. "So what do you need to know?"

Chuck and Gabe both looked at me to begin, but I bit my lip, shook my head and looked away. Gabe finally jumped in and explained, "We're specifically trying to figure out who or what is in the back bedroom." He quickly recounted my two experiences with the spirit. "We're trying to understand why Kyr is the only one being attacked in that room."

Mr. Evans had leaned over in his chair with his hand over his mouth as Gabe spoke. As he listened, he seemed to be searching his memory for an answer. When Gabe finished, Mr. Evans looked sharply at him and then at me before he spoke. "My dear, I believe you've had a run-in with my granddaddy, Jeremiah Berkeley. I never knew him, but my mama said he was one mean son of a . . ." He nodded towards me. "Begging your pardon, Miss. He had a mean streak that made an angry badger look sweet, and he didn't like women."

I gasped loudly and glanced at Gabe, who had been listening with a hand on his chin, but was now staring pointedly at Mr. Evans. "So he singled me out because I'm a woman? Why did he hate women so much?" I asked incredulously.

Mr. Evans' face lit up, and he sat up straighter in his chair. His face took on the appearance of a master storyteller as he began, "Jeremiah Berkeley was born into money. He was the only son of a very successful banker. His father, Jedidiah Berkeley, my Pappy, had built that house for Mammy Berkeley, and when they both passed on, the house naturally went to Jeremiah.

"Shortly after Pappy Berkeley passed away, Mammy began pushing Jeremiah to marry—she wanted a grandchild before she died, you know. Well, young Jeremiah was sweet on Abigail Stoltzfus, a farm girl from down the road, and he wanted to marry her. Mammy had other ideas. She had in mind a young lady of means, Rosanna Henninger, and Rosanna's parents agreed. Sure, sure, there were some arguments between Mammy and Jeremiah, but Jeremiah loved and respected his mama, so eventually he gave in and married Rosanna, roundabout 1897."

He paused in his story and began wheeling his wheelchair towards the small closet in his room. He slid the door open and craned his neck, looking for something. He pointed to the top shelf and said to Chuck, "Son, could you hand me down the family Bible?"

Chuck crossed to the closet and carefully brought down a thick, very old Bible held together by rubber bands and handed it gently to his father, whose hands shook as he took the rubber bands off and searched through the pages for something. At last he found what he was looking for, a sheet tucked in the middle of the Bible, filled with spidery scrawls. He pulled it out, adjusted his glasses, and looked over it for a moment while Chuck, Gabe, and I waited anxiously for him to continue.

Finally, as though he had remembered we were there, he looked up at us, beaming, and went on, "Well, there was no spark between Jeremiah and Rosanna, if you know what I mean, but they made a show of it for Mammy and for Nana and Pop-Pop Henninger. A grandson, George, arrived a year after they married," he said, pointing to the family tree. "Then a granddaughter, Belle-Anne, two years after that. Mammy was pleased, and it seemed to ease her mind, as she was becoming more and more sickly. Not long after Belle-Anne was born, Mammy passed away.

"Another daughter, Ruth, was born a couple years after that. Now, she died young; she was only ten or so. One thing about Jeremiah, he was faithful to Rosanna, even though he still carried the torch for Abigail. Now, Rosanna, she was another story. She was a looker, she was, and she knew it. She never stopped making eyes at other fellas, even after she was married."

Mr. Evans looked out the window for a moment, thinking. He seemed to be either upset or embarrassed about this part of his family tree, but he was determined to share it. He went on, "There was one fella she really seemed to like, a Benjamin . . . something. I can't recall his last name. Story was, he'd come around every time Jeremiah was out of town for business. Don't know how he never heard of it, but if he did know, he never let on. Anyway, there was another daughter, Evangeline, my mama, born in 1905, and it didn't take long till folks were talking that Jeremiah wasn't the father. Now whether Jeremiah ignored the talk out of pride, flat-out didn't believe it, or somehow never heard the rumors, no one really knows, but for the rest of Rosanna's life, he never treated her or my mama any different than the others . . . at least everyone thought."

He paused again, and I began to feel a prickle of foreboding. I knew this story was not going to end well. Chuck finally asked, "So when did Jeremiah turn mean? Sounds like he started off a peaceful man."

Mr. Evans nodded. "Well, he was. Till World War I, when things started to unravel for him. George, the only son, had set his cap for a local girl. I guess he'd been sweet on her since he was a boy, and he finally decided to declare his love."

"She turned him down?" asked Chuck.

Mr. Evans laughed ruefully. "More than turned him down. Laughed at him. Then made a joke of him to all her friends. Broke his heart and his pride. He ran off and joined the Army, got sent overseas to fight in the war. He figured he'd either win her heart by coming home a hero or he'd die trying."

Sensing where things were going, I asked, "He died trying?"

"Yeah, yeah," Mr. Evans answered. "He was killed in battle. That's when things really began to unravel for Jeremiah.

"Not long after George died, Rosanna took sick. No one knows if it was a real illness or just grief, but it wasn't long till she was quite ill. They brought in the doctor, and he gave her some medicine or tonic or something. She seemed to get a little better after that, but I guess her being so close to death there for a time made her feel guilty. One night while Jeremiah was tending her, she confessed everything. Told him about all her flirtations, and about Benjamin. She told Jeremiah that Benjamin was most likely Evangeline's father.

"He didn't yell, didn't raise his voice, but he turned real cold-like to her. He told her, 'You made a fool out of me. I'll show you, you worthless whore!' On the sly he stopped giving her medicine, wouldn't let the children in to see her, told them she was far too weak. He just let her die."

My blood had turned cold when he said those words. Gabe had left out the exact words the entity had said to me. Hearing those words from Mr. Evans, I was now certain we were dealing with Jeremiah Berkeley. I stole a glance at Gabe, and his concerned expression as he looked at me told me he was thinking the same thing.

"After that, Jeremiah seemed to take on a strong dislike for women. He refused to deal with any of the storekeepers' wives, said those 'jezebels' couldn't be trusted. He even had trouble trusting some of the men folk, especially when they tried to talk to his daughters. He all but kept Belle-Anne and Evangeline under lock and key, and he would never let them go out without him accompanying them. He didn't want them winding up like their mother. He even spoke ill of his own mother, saying she ruined his life making him marry Rosanna.

"Of course, my mama took the worst of his moods, called her a worthless wench and a jezebel; always said she looked like her mother and probably had her morals too. Oh, he never hit her, but she could never do anything right. He criticized her every move, made her miserable."

Chuck was shaking his head at these revelations. "Pop, that's awful! You never told me this."

"Didn't really want to," Mr. Evans answered. "Our family sure ain't no *Little House on the Prairie*. But with what's happening in that house, you need to know the truth. And I have to tell on my mama; she was no saint. She was sneaky in her own way. She had met my daddy at church, and they somehow managed to sneak around together enough to fall in love. He asked for Evangeline's hand in marriage, but Jeremiah said he wasn't paying for a wedding for a whore's daughter; he wasn't her daddy anyhow. Well, one night, he and Evangeline just eloped. Left a note, but never spoke to Jeremiah again."

He shook his head in resignation. "That just put Jeremiah over the edge. He became a recluse. Belle-Anne lived there with him, took care of him the rest of his days. She never married or had a family of her own. I guess she felt sorry for the bastard. Don't think I coulda done it."

"Pop, how do you know all this, if Grandma never spoke to him again?" Chuck wondered aloud. Gabe and I had been wondering the same thing.

"Well, Belle-Anne had been quite a writer in her day. Never published anything, but she kept a detailed diary of everything that happened. After Jeremiah died, the house was passed to her, as she was his only living relative. Since Belle-Anne never married, she willed the house to me, the only living heir, even though I was illegitimate and not really his. Just before she died, I received a letter from her telling me of the house. She told me her diary was hidden in the attic in a little cubby at the back. When your mother and I moved there, I found the diary and read it, and then put it right back. Probably still there."

I saw Gabe and Chuck exchange a look, and I figured Chuck would be looking for that cubby hole. It seemed that Mr. Evans' story had shed quite a bit of light on the house's activity.

"When did you start having paranormal activity in the house?" Gabe asked.

"Oh, almost right away," Mr. Evans replied. "Though nothing too much. My wife was never attacked like you, Kyrie. But then, she always felt that back bedroom was spooky-like. She wouldn't go in there alone. Ever."

"My ex-wife was the same way," Chuck added. "She said it was evil, like someone really wanted to hurt her when she was in there." He laughed ruefully, "Of course, maybe Jeremiah could sense what kind of person she turned out to be."

Gabe and I both shifted uncomfortably at this unexpected view into Chuck's life.

A knock at the door interrupted us. A nurse came in and said, "Mr. Evans, if you want some lunch, you'd better come get it now. We have your favorite today—ham loaf."

Mr. Evans gave an excited little jump in his wheelchair and said, "Hot dog! I'll be right there." He turned to Chuck to ask, "Chucky Boy, can I convince you and your friends to have lunch with me?"

Chuck agreed to stay right away. I glanced at Gabe and replied, "I'm game if you are."

Gabe shrugged and answered, "I can't say I've ever heard of ham loaf, but I'll try anything once."

We all went to the dining room and found an empty table. As we waited for our food, I took in the cheery décor: dark blue carpeting, cream-colored wallpaper with a fleur-de-lis pattern, and several paintings of the home in different seasons. Chuck pointed out a woman in a bright purple pantsuit waving at Mr. Evans from across the room. Mr. Evans waved back and whispered loudly to us, "That's Iris. She's my girlfriend."

Gabe and I laughed indulgently. Somehow, I could easily believe that the elder Mr. Evans would have a girlfriend. Chuck shook his head and said, "Pop, I thought June was your girlfriend."

Mr. Evans took a sip of coffee and retorted, "June was only here for rehab after her hip replacement. She's gone to live with her daughter and son-in-law down York way. I'm too old for long-distance love affairs."

We were all laughing merrily when our food arrived. Mr. Evans chortled delightedly with every bite of ham loaf. Even Gabe agreed it was delicious. After eating more than half his food, Mr. Evans asked, "Is there anything else you need to know about the house?"

Chuck and Gabe were satisfied, at least till they could find the hidden diary and see what information it held, but there was still something I was puzzling over. "Mr. Evans, did you ever have any experiences in the graveyard, like seeing shadows or lights near the big oak tree?"

Chuck turned to me with a curious expression; apparently Drac and Gabe hadn't shared that information with him yet. Mr. Evans sat back in his chair and dabbed his mouth thoughtfully with his napkin. "No, Kyrie, I can't say I ever did. I'd never been comfortable there, but then, who is comfortable in a graveyard? I assume Chucky has told you about the mist?" Gabe, Chuck, and I all indicated that he had. "Never seen it myself, but with everything else going on there, it wouldn't surprise me if the graveyard had some spooks as well."

After we had finished lunch and exhausted Mr. Evans' memories of the Berkeley mansion's history, Gabe and I decided it was time to head back to the hotel. As we headed out of the dining room, I suddenly recalled something Drac had mentioned, and I couldn't help asking, "Mr. Evans, how did you get the nickname Cherry Pit?"

Mr. Evans laughed gleefully, obviously tickled that someone wanted to know. "Well, believe it or not, I was quite a scamp in my younger days," he began, giving us all a chuckle. "I was a new recruit in the Army and was full of piss and vinegar. One day we had cherry pie for dessert at the mess hall. Now that was quite a treat, mind you, and I dug into the biggest piece of pie I could get my hands on. Well, next thing, I bit down on a cherry pit and broke my tooth off. Pissed me off so much that I didn't even think about it, I just spit that damn thing outta my mouth and across the room like we used to do when we were kids. Well, sir, that cherry pit hit the drill sergeant right smack in the eye. When he found out who did it, I earned the nickname Cherry Pit and a month on KP duty."

We were all doubled over with laughter by the time he finished his story. Before we headed out towards the lobby, Mr. Evans took my hand in his and said, "Kyrie, my dear, may I make two requests?"

"Of course, Mr. Evans," I replied softly.

He patted my hand and began, "First of all, I want you to be careful. Old Jeremiah was a mean one while he was alive, and it seems he still is. I don't want to see you get hurt."

I smiled and nodded. "I will." I glanced at Gabe. "I've got someone who has my back. What's your second request?"

He gave me a dashing grin. "I would be honored if you would come visit me. An old man gets pretty lonely always being in the same place with the same people."

My eyes misted over as I recalled visiting my grandparents in their later years and seeing how lonely they often were. I nodded and leaned over impulsively to kiss his cheek. "I would love to."

We headed out towards the lobby, and just as Chuck had feared, Rose was at the front desk, waiting to pounce. She made a fuss over Gabe, wanting pictures taken with him and an autograph, and begging him to stop back with Drac before they headed back to upstate New York. Just before we walked out the door, Rose grabbed him and planted a big, red-lipsticked kiss on his cheek. In a sense I thought it was the funniest thing I had ever seen when Gabe's face turned almost as red as the lipstick mark, but I also fought a wave of jealousy, wishing I were as gutsy as Rose. I sighed wistfully, lamenting the fact that the only man I had the nerve to kiss was a sweet old man like Mr. Evans.

In the parking lot, Gabe and Chuck talked about the diary hidden in the attic. He was certainly interested in looking for it, and he asked if Drac and Gabe wanted to accompany him, in case there was any activity when he found it. Gabe was certain Drac would like to be there, so they made plans to meet later in the afternoon.

Gabe and I got into the van. "Wow, that was some story," Gabe said, absently scrubbing at his cheek with a handkerchief. "Almost makes me feel sorry for the others, stuck reviewing evidence."

"I'll say," I answered shortly. I had too much on my mind to say more.

I was pretty quiet on the way back to the hotel, leaning my head against the window and thinking about Mr. Evans' story. Gabe noticed me brooding and asked, "Why so quiet? You tired?"

Shaking my head, I responded, "I was just thinking about Jeremiah Berkeley. That poor man! I feel so sorry for him."

"What?" Gabe exclaimed, laughing incredulously. "He—or rather his spirit—attacked you two nights in a row, and you feel sorry for him?"

I shrugged, smiling sheepishly. "I know, but can you blame him? To have been screwed out of marrying the woman he loved by his mother, wronged by his wife, and then having his . . . supposed daughter run off and never speak to him again—no wonder he came unhinged and learned to hate and distrust women!"

Gabe acknowledged, "I guess so, but to treat his daughters that way? It wasn't Evangeline's fault she was illegitimate. And to let his wife die to get even with her? There was no excuse for that! That was premeditated murder!"

I shifted uncomfortably at those words, not used to seeing this kind of anger from Gabe, but I had a sudden wave of compassion and understanding that urged me to defend Jeremiah. "I suppose you're right, but it's obvious you've never had someone you loved deeply betray you, nor ever felt like everyone but you was in charge of your life. Do you know what it's like having someone tell you what you can and can't do with your life, especially if you lose out on something you really wanted because someone else thought you 'weren't cut out for it'?" I knew I was babbling, but I couldn't stop. I felt like a can of soda that someone had shaken up and opened. "That's hard to live with, Gabe. At least these days you can see a counselor to help you work through issues like that.

Jeremiah didn't have that option. Yes, what he did was all kinds of wrong, but he had so much grief and heartache and anger inside that I'm sure he just snapped." I dashed angry tears from my eyes as I recalled my own hurts and lost opportunities.

Gabe pulled off to the side of the back country road we were on and looked squarely at me. "Why do I get the feeling you're speaking from experience?"

I closed my eyes against the hot tears rising again and said, "My father always made decisions for me, just like Jeremiah's mother did. They told me who to hang out with, where to go to college, what to study, what to believe. They shot down so many of my dreams because they were 'silly' or 'impractical.' I was the only girl, and the baby, so Daddy was stricter with me than he was with my brothers. He didn't want me screwing up like my older brother did by making stupid decisions. I didn't have the nerve to stand up to him, and I didn't want to disappoint him. I did whatever I could to earn his approval, and most of the time that meant pushing my own ambitions aside."

Gabe unbuckled his seat belt and slid closer to me, brushing back my hair and resting a hand on my shoulder. "Some things are starting to make sense now. Like why you're so determined to prove yourself to everyone."

I nodded and smiled through my tears. "This is something I've wanted to do for a long time but I was afraid to because . . ." I took a deep breath, pursed my lips, and admitted out loud for the first time, "I was afraid because I knew my dad wouldn't have approved." Gabe smiled understandingly, and I continued, "Besides, I guess I was also afraid of making a mess of things and disappointing you and Drac." I let out a huff and added grudgingly, "And Steele. But don't tell him I said that."

Gabe threw his head back and laughed, and I soon joined in. He gave me a shake and said seriously, "Kyr, you're far from being a disappointment. You came into this investigation without a shred of experience, stood up to some less-than-supportive teammates, got in almost over your head with our not-so-friendly entity, yet here you are, sticking to it and throwing yourself into finding the answers. We've had team members who were less committed than you're proving to be. You should be proud of yourself. You really are investigator material. I knew that when we read your contest entry." I flushed at his praise, and he gave me a shrewd look. "Now I'm going to put on my counselor's cap and give you some advice." I looked at him expectantly, sure I knew where he was headed. "Kyr, almost everyone wants to please their parents, make them proud. But you can't sacrifice your own hopes and dreams to avoid displeasing them, especially when . . ." His voice softened. "Especially when they're not around anymore. Your parents meant well, and they just wanted to protect you from getting hurt, but I'm sure they never meant to keep you from pursuing your dreams and being happy. You're a grown woman, Kyr, and this is your life, not theirs. You need to figure out what *you* want to do and get out there and give it your best shot, whether it's paranormal investigating, being a librarian, or flipping burgers at a greasy spoon." He slid back over, buckled up again, and started the engine. "Lecture over," he chuckled. "Now we'd better be getting back."

I sat silently for a moment, taking in everything he'd just said. I was a bit dumbfounded that even after everything I felt I'd screwed up, Gabe still encouraged me and praised me for things he thought I'd done right. His advice, too, seemed to hit home. Even though I'd heard the same words from JoEllyn, Aunt Julia, my boss Maureen, and even my ex-fiancé Trevor, somehow it carried more weight coming from someone I barely knew. Or maybe it was because he was my celebrity crush, and I was still enough of a "fangirl" to care what he thought. I shook my head, overwhelmed, by his words, by the story we'd just heard, by everything that had happened so far this weekend, but I felt I needed to say something.

"Gabe?" He glanced over at me, and I said simply, "Thanks."

He smiled, knowing that one word said a great deal. He reached over to give me a punch on the shoulder. "You're a very special woman, Kyr. You're going to make some man very happy someday." He leaned in and kissed me gently . . . on the forehead.

I remembered with some embarrassment—and disappointment—that Gabe was quite happily married to a beautiful wife, and I managed to answer, "You're pretty special yourself, Gabe. Your wife is a lucky woman."

CHAPTER TEN

The others were still working on evidence review when we got back to the hotel. Drac paused the audio he was listening to and took off his headphones expectantly when we came in. "How'd you two make out?" he asked.

Steele had looked up too, and his sharp eyes narrowed as they zeroed in on Gabe's cheek. "Funny you should say 'make out,' Drac," he said, smiling humorlessly. "Either Gabe started wearing makeup, or he got a little action." His eyes drifted to me as he quipped, "Did you find yourself a cougar, or was it someone a little younger?" My jaw dropped incredulously as I caught his insinuation.

Gabe's hand went immediately to his lipstick-stained cheek, and he blushed and replied sheepishly, "Oh, that. Yeah, well . . . It turns out the front desk receptionist is a rabid *Project Boo-Seekers* fan." When Drac sat back and crossed his arms with a smirk, Gabe taunted, "I wouldn't look so smug, bro. She wants to meet you, too." I recovered enough from my mortification at Steele's comment to giggle at Gabe's discomfort, and he glanced sideways at me to say, "Besides, Kyr was a pretty big hit with Mr. Evans. He wants to see her again."

Blushing, I responded, "Gabe is exaggerating. Anyway, I'd have to get past Iris."

Steele seemed to relax a bit, and Drac laughed and scolded, "I sent you two out to find information, not romance. So, did you have any luck?"

"Quite a bit, actually." Gabe excitedly rubbed his hands together. "And by the way, you and I need to meet Chuck at the mansion this afternoon. This case may be more involved than we first thought."

Gabe and I filled the others in on the story of Jeremiah Berkeley, his arranged marriage, his wife's unfaithfulness, the illegitimate daughter, and his deteriorating mental state that led to his hatred for women. Excitement flashed in Drac's eyes when we told him of the diary hidden in the attic, and he seemed eager to meet with Chuck to find it.

"What about you guys? Find any good evidence?" Gabe asked, looking at Andy and Kyle, who had stopped reviewing to listen to the story.

Drac's eyes lit up as he answered, "Did we ever! If only our entity hadn't gone Sean Penn on our video camera, we would have had some really compelling evidence to show Chuck."

Drac, Steele, Kyle, and Andy went through all the evidence they had that they had been unable to debunk. Andy played back some unintelligible whispers and footsteps from the basement, the same kinds of sounds they had captured the first night. He asked Drac, "Do you think there may be a residual haunt in that part of the basement? Except for that one response, a lot of the sounds we heard just seem to be random."

Drac scratched his head and thought for a moment before responding, "It's certainly a possibility, but I don't know that we can make that call just yet."

Steele played back the evidence they had gotten from the attic, several whispers and a shadowy figure moving in one corner. As he played back one particular audio clip, I gasped and felt my skin turn to gooseflesh, and Gabe moved in closer, asking, "Play that again, Spook?"

Steele rewound the tape and played it again. "Oh my . . . Did that say what I think it said?" I asked.

Gabe looked me in the eye and said, "Did you hear 'cubby'? I distinctly heard 'cubby.'"

"That's what I heard too," I said shakily, recalling what Mr. Evans had said about Belle-Anne's diary. I wondered if a spirit in the attic wanted to alert us to the hidden diary.

Steele stretched and clasped his hands behind his head, looking straight at Gabe and me. "That's what we thought we heard, but just the word 'cubby' didn't make any sense."

Gabe nodded and said, "Yeah, that's why good research is so crucial to an investigation. If we hadn't talked to Mr. Evans and gotten that piece of information, we'd be missing an important part of the story. We never would have found *that* information in a library or town hall."

I thought again about that diary and what other stories might be contained within it. How much of the Berkeley family history was preserved in that diary? Personal histories like this were fascinating to me, more so than any textbook history we had ever learned in school. Suddenly, one of the original claims Chuck had told us about sprang into my mind.

"Steele, could you play that clip one more time?" I asked, leaning in closer.

"Sure, no problem," he responded, rewinding the tape and playing it again.

I listened more closely to the EVP, then stood there staring at the monitor, thinking. Something bothered me about the EVP. Finally Drac said, "What's on your mind, Kyr? I can see the wheels turning in your head."

I shook my head and sighed before answering, "I don't know. The voice sounds female to me, which makes sense, since the diary is Belle-Anne's . . ."

"But?" Steele prompted when I didn't continue right away.

"But I keep coming back to Chuck's claims about the attic," I mused. "He said there was a Civil War soldier seen in the attic window. Where does that fit in?"

Everyone looked at everyone else for answers, but no one seemed to have any ideas just then. Finally Gabe suggested, "Well, let's see what else we've got. We can work on that mystery later."

"Did anything significant turn up in the graveyard?" I asked, recalling the odd feeling I'd had that someone or something wanted me there.

He shook his head. "We got absolutely nothing, except a glimpse of that light Kyle said he saw."

A glance at Kyle told me he was frustrated, knowing that what he'd seen was real and significant, but having no way to prove it. I knew the feeling. I was beginning to wonder if there was something we were missing in the graveyard. I had the thought that we needed to spend some time in the graveyard during the day; I wanted to get a better look at the tombstones to see who else was buried there and to see if we'd missed anything important. All at once, I had the urge to go back to the Berkeley mansion and investigate the graveyard while it was still light out.

Suddenly I noticed that everyone had stopped talking, and they were all looking at me curiously. "Kyr, when we listened to your EVP session in the graveyard, you said something about someone . . . wanting you there. What did you mean?"

My eyes drifted to Steele, who had turned to face me and was watching me with interest. With everyone's eyes on me, I felt trapped; what could I say that wouldn't make me sound like a complete freak? I knew Drac and Steele both suspected something, so I really couldn't just brush it off and say it was nothing. Finally, I swallowed hard and said, "I just . . . had a hunch there was something up there. I guess when I said that . . . I was just trying to provoke the spirit to communicate." Thinking to cover myself, I tried to joke, "Either I scared it away, or my hunch was wrong."

Steele shared a meaningful glance with Drac and Gabe, and then commented, "Obviously that's another mystery to address later." As he turned his eyes back to me, I wondered if he meant what was happening in the graveyard or why I felt that something wanted me there. For the time being, he didn't elaborate. Instead, he asked, "Are you ready to see what was captured in the back bedroom?"

I said nothing, but Gabe's eyes lit up, and he looked like a kid on Christmas morning as Andy got the video ready. While I felt I had a better understanding of Jeremiah Berkeley, the person, and wasn't so convinced anymore that his sole intent was to harm me, I was still sufficiently shaken by my encounters with Jeremiah Berkeley, the spirit, to be apprehensive about seeing this footage. I silently prayed that seeing this video wouldn't upset me the way it had the last time.

As Andy started the video, Gabe moved closer to me and put his hand on my shoulder. I glanced up at him, and he raised an eyebrow as if to ask how I was doing. I had a feeling he knew what I was thinking, so I gave him a quick nod and a smile and turned my attention to the monitor. He squeezed my shoulder and then moved back a step.

The video began with me asking questions and trying to make contact. As with the first night, things were quiet at first. Gabe and Drac both chuckled at my question, "What, did you use up all your nasty last night?" Steele turned around and smirked at me. Without taking my eyes off the monitor, I reached forward and gave his head a shove, making his hair fall forward into his face. My breath caught as he turned and grinned at me, flipping his hair out of his eyes, before turning back to the monitor.

"Watch right here," Drac suddenly said, reaching in front of me and pointing at the monitor. At the exact moment I had felt the draft, on the video a faint dark shadow appeared on one wall. I watched myself cross the room to the window, and the shadow seemed to darken and grow, although it did not move. I shook my head, wondering how I could have missed that happening. It looked so clear on the video. I was about to say something when Drac held up his hand for silence and then pointed to the monitor again. The whisper! "Could you play that again, Andy?"

Andy rewound the tape and hit Play again. His eyes darted back and forth between my face and the monitor. I listened closely to the whisper; it was a female voice. "Please don't do this," it pleaded.

Andy paused the tape again, and Gabe looked from Drac to Steele and then to me. "I heard, 'Please don't do this,'" he said.

I nodded and acknowledged, "Me too." Of course, my first thought was that this was Rosanna's voice. I wondered if we were hearing her plea for Jeremiah to have mercy on her . . . or on me.

Andy restarted the video, and we watched the scenario play out on the monitor, my request for the spirit to communicate followed by the door slamming shut. As I interacted with Drac, Gabe, and Steele on the walkies and crossed the room to the door, we saw on the monitor the same shadow along the same wall as before. It didn't seem to move with my movement, but remained stationary. When I asked the spirit if it needed help, we heard another faint whisper. Although Andy rewound and replayed the tape several times, none of us could make out what it might have said.

Kyle finally guessed, "It may be just a whimper or a sob. There don't seem to be any words, just a voice."

Drac and Gabe both nodded in agreement, and I ventured, "If that voice was Rosanna's, then that certainly could be the case, judging by what Mr. Evans told us about how Jeremiah treated her at the end." I shook my head sadly, remembering his story. "If I were her, I think I would be whimpering or crying too."

Andy asked, "The question is, is this an intelligent spirit interacting with you, or is it a residual spirit just playing out her last days?"

Always the voice of skepticism, Steele jumped in, "We have to be careful not to tie every little piece of evidence in with what Chuck's father told you. It's easy to make that assumption, but what if you're wrong?"

I wanted to protest that he was the one who was wrong. I had a hunch that we had just heard a portion of Rosanna's last days, if not her final moments, but given that my other hunch had proven false, I thought it wise to hold my tongue. Drac acknowledged, "Spook does have a point. Although we do have a reliable source concerning Berkeley family history, we can't just assume that a random voice is tied to that story. Right now, it *is* just speculation."

As Andy began the video again, I couldn't help thinking about how cold and cruel Jeremiah had been towards Rosanna in her last days, and it chilled me to the bone knowing how frightened she must have been of him, never knowing if he planned to let her die slowly or if he'd kill her one day in a fit of rage. As I saw in my mind once again the seething hatred in the spirit's eyes as it came towards me, I shuddered as I wondered which would be worse.

Drac leaned forward to show Gabe the mist beginning to form. "Now watch how the shadow on the wall fades away as the mist comes together." My eyes widened apprehensively as I tried to figure out whether the shadow was becoming the mist or if the mist was overpowering and banishing the shadow. I wasn't aware that I was trembling until I felt hands on my shoulders and heard Gabe's voice in my ear. "Are you okay, hon? You look pale."

Steele quickly rose from his chair and firmly guided me over to sit. "Carter, I'm not sure you should watch the rest of this."

I began to feel sick to my stomach thinking about the direction my thoughts kept going in, and I felt for a moment that he was right. Still, a part of me needed to know exactly what I had been fighting against. Taking a shaky breath, I replied, "I'm fine, Steele. I need to see this."

He regarded me doubtfully, but said nothing. As the video continued, I felt the same emotions I had felt when I watched the video from the first night, but I fought to hide my rising panic. Even though I knew it was coming, I still jumped and gasped loudly when the video camera flew from the dresser and abruptly stopped recording. What really unnerved me, however, was the fact that just before the camera went flying, as I was telling Drac, "I hope you're seeing this on the monitor," there was a blood-chilling, animal-like growl that overlapped my words, a growl I obviously had not heard at the time. I was thankful that no one asked Andy to replay it.

Gabe let out a low whistle and commented, "There's no doubt about it; we're dealing with an angry, intelligent spirit. Knocking over the camera was definitely a deliberate action."

"More likely, it didn't want anyone to see what it was going to do," I interrupted. "Mr. Evans did say that Jeremiah wouldn't let anyone else in Rosanna's room after she confessed her affairs to him. He didn't want anyone to know he was slowly killing her. He hated women; we know that. I can't help feeling that this spirit intended to do something to me and didn't want it documented."

Andy and Kyle shifted uneasily in their seats as I voiced my suspicions. I couldn't tell if they shared my suspicions or if they were just afraid I'd come unhinged. My sense of compassion for Jeremiah Berkeley was once again replaced by the fear that his spirit, for whatever reason, intended to do me harm. I knew Steele probably thought I was exaggerating or making it up, but the fact was, *he* wasn't the one who had been in that room, seeing the hatred in those eyes and feeling the intense negativity and animosity that surrounded me whenever he appeared.

Gabe leaned on the back of my chair and tried to calm my fears as he had the first night. "Now Kyr, don't get carried away with the Hollywood scary movie images again. We can't assume that the entity meant to harm you—" Something in his voice suggested he wasn't so sure of that anymore.

"Gabe, you said yourself that what Jeremiah Berkeley did to his wife was nothing short of premeditated murder," I argued loudly, feeling more frantic by the minute. "And you guys didn't see what happened after that camera went flying." I quickly told them how the spirit had stepped in between me and the camera to prevent me from going to pick it up. In my eyes, seeing the venom in the spirit's expression and feeling his intense animosity towards me as he rushed through my body and exited the room were enough to tell me he wasn't looking for a friendly conversation.

As much as I didn't want to lose it in front of everyone, my emotions swirled inside me like a hurricane, and I struggled to retain control. Everyone's eyes were on me, and I knew no one knew what to say. As calmly as I could under the circumstances, I got up, pushed past Drac, Steele, and Gabe, and walked out of the room. As soon as the door shut behind me, the floodgates opened, and I began sobbing. Not wanting anyone who might be in the lobby to see me blubbering like an idiot, I ducked into what used to be a phone booth and collapsed on the seat.

After a moment, my sobs subsided, but hiccups still racked my body. While I was still blinded by the tears that kept streaming from my eyes, I felt a hand on my shoulder. Thinking it was Gabe, I turned and leaned into him without looking up. His arms went around me and held me tightly for a moment. I could feel his strength and steadiness, and my breathing soon steadied. Somewhat reluctantly, I pulled back and looked up . . . right into Steele's smirking face.

He must have seen the embarrassment and disappointment in my face, because the smirk was immediately replaced by a frown. "Expecting someone else?" he asked irritably. When I ducked my head and turned away to wipe my tear-stained cheeks, he produced a handful of tissues. "Here, I think you need these." When I hesitated, he joked, "They're clean, I promise."

I gave him a watery smile without meeting his eyes, took the tissues, and buried my face in them. Steele squeezed into the phone booth and squatted down uncomfortably across from me. He laid a hand on my knee and said gently, "Look at me, Carter."

After a moment, I raised my eyes to peer at him through my bangs. *I must be a sight*, I thought, aware of my red-rimmed eyes, swollen nose and blotchy face. Steele gave me a crooked smile, and I saw him struggle to stifle a chuckle. He cleared his throat and tried to be serious. "What's on your mind, Carter?"

"You mean besides everything I blurted out in there?" I responded, feeling stupid. When he quirked an eyebrow and nodded, I lowered my eyes again, not knowing quite what to say. I had been so excited over winning this contest and getting to meet and investigate with Drac and Gabe. I hadn't expected to be so scared or to feel so inadequate, and I certainly hadn't expected the experience to get so far out of hand. What I thought would be a fun weekend and a check mark on my bucket list had turned into something that frightened me more than anything I had ever experienced before. I was a mess, a complete failure. "Gabe was wrong. JoEllyn should have come instead of me," I muttered, more to myself than to Steele.

"What was Gabe wrong about?" he asked, leaning his back against the wall and crossing his arms. "Why should JoEllyn have been here instead of you?" His expression told me that he had an idea what I would say, but he wanted me to say it out loud. *Probably just to make fun of me.*

Figuring I couldn't feel any worse than I already felt, I blurted out, "This weekend was supposed to be fun, a chance to do something I've wanted to do for a long time. But it's not fun anymore; it's downright terrifying. I'm in over my head, I don't know what's going on in that house, and I feel like a complete failure." I buried my face again, trying not to lose it all over again. Without thinking, I leaned forward to rest my head against Steele's chest. I still wished it were Gabe sitting across from me, but at that moment, I felt so much like a scared little girl that I didn't care who it was; I just wanted someone to keep me safe.

After a moment, Steele put his arms tentatively around me. He awkwardly whispered words of comfort, and I could tell it was something he wasn't used to doing. When I managed to get hold of myself again, he grasped my shoulders and pushed me away so he could look into my eyes. I started to apologize, but he cut me off.

"There's nothing to apologize for, Carter. Now, I don't know what Gabe said to you, but I have a pretty good idea. You've had a lot happen to you over the past couple days, more than a newbie usually has to deal with." I raised my eyes to his, and he gave me a lopsided smile before becoming serious again. "In all seriousness, I'd be willing to bet that even your JoEllyn would have a hard time sorting through this. Drac, Gabe, and I have been doing this for years, and we're still puzzled over some of the things that have happened." His expression suggested that he still thought I was making more of it than I should, but he said nothing more. He stood and helped me up, and we squeezed out of the phone booth. "All that being said, Newbie, you need to go back to your room and get some rest while we finish up."

Not wanting to look like a slacker or a coward, I began to protest, "There's not that much left to do, and I've already missed—"

Steele grasped my shoulders firmly and interrupted, "Carter, you need to take a break; Drac and Gabe even think so. You're overwhelmed, you're tired, and you need to chill." I clamped my mouth shut and glared at him, knowing he was right, but not wanting to give him the satisfaction of winning the argument. With a mischievous glint in his eye, he finished, "Besides, I have a hunch of my own that you want to tag along to the mansion with Drac and Gabe."

I gaped at him, bewildered, wondering how he had figured that out. He laughed and answered my unasked question, "You try so hard to hide what you're thinking, Carter, but sometimes you're an easy read." I blushed hotly, wondering what else he could read in my face.

Steele escorted me back to my room and ordered me to get some rest. "Drac and Gabe will stop by before they leave for the house."

Before I went into my room, I impulsively turned to Steele and asked, "Are you coming too?" Strangely, despite his arrogance and prickly personality, I felt secure in his presence, as though I knew I could trust him to keep me safe, a feeling I didn't want to admit to myself, let alone to him.

A look of surprise came across his face as though he hadn't expected that question. He smiled genuinely at me and replied, "I wouldn't miss it for the world."

The way my mind was racing, I was certain I wouldn't be able to rest at all, but not long after I lay down, my eyes drifted shut, and I fell into a deep exhausted sleep.

A strange noise in my room disturbed me, and I opened my eyes. The room was completely dark, and I wondered how long I had slept. I heard the noise again, and I sat up in bed. As I looked down, I realized I was wearing a long white nightgown with ruffled sleeves. *When did I change? And where did this nightgown come from?* When the noise came a third time, I asked, "Who's there?"

A shadow in the corner caught my eye, and when I realized what—or rather *who*—it was, I opened my mouth to scream. In an instant, the shadow crossed the room and a hand clamped tightly over my mouth. I stared, horrified, up at Jeremiah Berkeley, whose face was contorted with maniacal rage. I struggled against him, trying to get away, but he was too strong. He somehow managed to overpower me, lash my hands together and tie my arms above my head to the bedposts. *Bedposts?* My eyes darted around, and I realized that I was in the back bedroom of the Berkeley mansion. He spoke not a word, but his intentions were clear: He thought I was Rosanna, and he was going to kill me.

My eyes flitted back to Jeremiah's face. A thin line of spittle dribbled from his mouth as he opened it to speak. "I already killed you," he hissed in a crazed voice. "You should be dead already, you shameless whore. I'll make sure work of it this time, just like I did with your lover."

Lover? Benjamin Holtzman? So he *had* killed Benjamin! I could feel the pure hatred emanating from him, and I had never been so afraid in my life. He reached into his pocket and pulled out a handkerchief. A sickening smell reached my nose; the handkerchief had been soaked in something, and I suddenly knew with certainty that this was how Rosanna had died. He had smothered her using some kind of poison, and now he intended to do the same to me.

Just as he was about to cover my face with that handkerchief, a man's voice shouted, "No! Let her go!"

The spirit turned, and my heart surged when I saw who it was. "Gabe! He's going to kill me! Help me, please!"

Gabe had a look in his eyes that I had never seen before. He was angry, fighting angry. With fire in his eyes, he stared at Jeremiah. "You have no right to be here, Jeremiah Berkeley," he growled. "Kyr never did anything to you, yet you threaten her, attack her, and now you're trying to kill her? You're pathetic!"

Jeremiah spoke in a voice that sent chills down my spine. "She wronged me! That cheating witch wronged me! Made a fool of me, she did!" He turned venomous eyes to me. "I showed her before; I'll show her again. Damn women! Damn them all!"

He moved towards me again, handkerchief drawn. As frightened as I was, anger rose in my chest. I struggled against my bonds and shouted back at him, "Stop it! Just stop it!" He drew back as though startled by my response. "Just because one woman screwed you over doesn't make them all bad! If I'd killed every man that screwed me over, I'd burn in hell twenty times over."

Jeremiah's eyes adjusted as he looked somewhat uncertainly at me and back at Gabe. Suddenly, he seemed to realize that I was not Rosanna. His voice cracked. "I tried my damnedest to make it work. I loved my Abigail, but I wanted to make my mama happy. I never cheated on Rosanna, never looked at another woman, never even at Abigail." He looked more broken than angry as he spoke, and it became quite obvious how hurt he was by all that had happened.

"Jeremiah, I'm so sorry for what Rosanna did to you," I said softly. "It was wrong, and she knew it. I'm sure she would have made amends if you'd only let her."

Gabe interjected, "Jeremiah, your anger, your hatred, they destroyed the rest of your life; they destroyed Belle-Anne's life. You drove away Evangeline, and you missed getting to know your only grandchild. Jeremiah, it's your hatred that holds you here. Let it go; go to your rest."

"If only I could. If only I could . . ." Jeremiah sobbed, before disappearing.

Gabe and I stared in stupefied silence for a second before he came to his senses and quickly crossed the room. He sat down on the bed beside me, grasped my face in his hands and asked, "Kyr, are you all right?"

I nodded, suddenly hit with the realization of how close I'd come to suffering the same fate as Rosanna. Before I could say a word, Gabe leaned forward and kissed me, gently at first, and then deeply. Shocked, I returned his kiss, feeling torn. Kissing a celebrity I'd had a crush on for a few years was a rush, and he was definitely a wonderful kisser, but this was wrong; he was married. When he broke the kiss and pulled back, I whispered, "Gabe?"

He put a finger to my lips and murmured, "Shhh, don't talk," before he leaned in to kiss me again. Just as our lips met, he was hauled roughly away from me and thrown to the floor. Thinking at first that Jeremiah had returned, I screamed before realizing it was . . .

"Steele!" I shouted, afraid he would hurt Gabe.

He ignored me and yelled at Gabe. "You stay away from her! You're a married man!" He turned to me with fire in his eyes and came to stand over me. I let out a yelp and flinched, expecting him to strike me. When I felt his hands tugging on the ropes that held me, I opened my eyes and stared right into his. The passion I saw there stirred feelings inside me that I'd never known, not even with Trevor. "Besides," he growled, his hot breath against my neck. "This one needs someone who's man enough to handle her." His lips grazed my cheek, my neck, as he whispered in my ear, "Someone like me."

A part of me was angered by his arrogant words, but another part of me was set aflame by a heat that matched what I saw burning in his dark eyes. I could feel his lips on my ear, my neck, as he struggled to untie my bonds, and I closed my eyes and turned to him, willing him to kiss me. When he got me free, he scooped me up roughly and carried me out of the room. As we reached the doorway, I cast a bewildered look over his shoulder at Gabe, who was now standing by the bed, grinning slyly at us.

I jumped awake to the sound of someone knocking loudly on the door. I sat up quickly and glanced dazedly around. I looked at the clock; it was 4:18. Another loud knock sounded, and I got up and stumbled to the door, relieved to realize I was in my hotel room and fully dressed. I opened the door without looking to see who it was. When I saw Drac standing there, ready to knock again, I stared blankly at him.

He joked, "I was just beginning to think you'd finally had enough and taken off."

"I guess I fell asleep," I replied, still half-disoriented from my crazy dream.

"Well, it looks like you needed it," Drac said. "How are you doing?"

I reached up and shoved my hair out of my face, a bit disconcerted that I had obviously tossed around enough for my ponytail to come undone. I thought about everything that had happened that day, and about the disturbing dream I'd just had about Jeremiah. I finally responded, "I'm okay. I . . ." *Should I tell Drac about the dream? Should I tell him I wanted—no, needed—to go back to the mansion?*

As it turned out I didn't have to say anything about going with them to the mansion, because just then Gabe and Steele came down the hall together, laughing and joking about something. As soon as I caught sight of Gabe and then Steele, I felt my face grow red as I recalled what had happened with both of them in my dream. Thankfully, Gabe didn't notice my discomfort, but Steele took in my disheveled appearance and troubled expression and quirked an eyebrow at me. Giving me his usual smirk, he asked, "What's the verdict, Drac? Is she coming along?"

"I didn't ask her yet." Drac chuckled, turning back to me. "Well, what do you say? Are you up for another trip to the mansion?"

Gabe and Steele exchanged a conspiratorial glance, and I had a feeling that they'd had a hand in convincing Drac to let me accompany them. I just hoped this wouldn't turn into a disaster.

CHAPTER ELEVEN

I was quiet on the ride to the Berkeley mansion. Between my surging emotions over everything that had happened in the past few days and the crazy dream I'd just had, I wasn't up for conversation. I was especially unnerved over the part of the dream that involved Jeremiah Berkeley. How much of what I had dreamed about him was real, and how much was my imagination? And if it was real, how could I have known about any of that information?

Drac, Gabe, and Steele were chatting about various things, but I had too much on my mind to pay attention to their conversation. Drac's voice jarred me from my thoughts. "What do you think, Kyr?"

I abruptly turned my attention to Drac. I could see his eyes reflected in the rearview mirror, and Gabe was turned around looking at me with concern. "I'm sorry," I said, trying to sound casual. "I wasn't paying attention."

Steele stifled a laugh, and I turned to give him a dirty look. Drac chuckled, too. "We can see that. Anything you'd like to talk about?"

I considered that question. Did I want to tell them about the dream I'd had about Jeremiah Berkeley, or would they—especially Steele—think I was crazy, over-imaginative, or too emotionally tied up in this case? I finally decided to keep it to myself. "No, just . . . thinking."

Gabe continued to watch me doubtfully and reached back to lay a hand on my knee as he asked softly, "Hon, are you sure you want to go back into that house? Poor kid, you've had so much happen to you already."

I flinched at his touch, my face burning with embarrassment as images of him kissing me filled my mind, as well as irritation over his unnecessary concern. I replied, more harshly than necessary, "I'm fine, Gabe. Stop fussing over me!"

An expression of hurt flashed over his face and then was gone. He replied quietly, "Okay, just checking."

A sidelong glance at Steele showed that he, too, was surprised, and possibly a bit triumphant, over my reaction. Drac and Gabe exchanged a look, and I lowered my eyes and rubbed my forehead, feeling miserable for snapping at him. Once more, I considered telling them about my dream, but once more I dismissed the thought. I almost wished that Andy and Kyle were there, but because the case had taken this sudden turn and become more involved, Drac and Gabe had decided to put off the reveal planned to end our weekend ghost hunt. Since they couldn't stick around the extra day or so to work on things at the mansion, Drac had made arrangements with them and with Chuck and Quinn Cassel to meet the following week to do the follow-up interview. I lived only a few miles away and had a more flexible job schedule, so I was able to make the necessary arrangements to stay on. At the moment, however, I wished I could just leave and be done with it. Still, I knew that if I did, I wouldn't be able to rest easy. Whatever was happening here, I was fully involved now and had to see it through.

I was relieved when we finally pulled up to the mansion. The tree-lined driveway didn't look as creepy with the late afternoon sunshine coming through the trees. As I looked up at the stately brick home, it appeared so peaceful that it was hard to believe it was the same house where I had experienced some of the most frightening moments of my life. As we slowly ascended the stone stairs leading up to the porch, I glanced up at the windows, half-expecting to see a face peering from one of them. Thankfully, no eyes met mine, and I continued up to the porch.

Drac rang the doorbell, and as we waited for Chuck, I wandered over to the side of the porch, leaned over the railing and gazed up at the small graveyard, half-willing it to tell me what secrets it held. I didn't have much time to ponder, however, as Chuck came to the door and invited us in. Drac and Gabe both looked at me curiously, and Steele's eyes bored into me. I knew they were all thinking about my last EVP session in the graveyard.

Drac turned his attention to Chuck and asked, "Anything unusual happen since last night?"

Chuck shrugged his shoulders and replied, "Not really, no. I heard a few bumps upstairs after I got home, but nothing out of the ordinary."

Gabe joked, "You probably hear some noises so often you hardly think about them anymore."

Chuck smiled. "That's quite true."

We refused his offer of refreshments and decided to head right up to the attic. Drac and Steele carried small handheld cameras, and Gabe and I had digital voice recorders. Steele also had a K-II wedged in his back pocket. If anything happened while we searched for that diary, they were determined to capture it.

Chuck led the way upstairs. As we reached the second floor, I glanced down the hall towards the back bedroom. Even with the light shining through the windows at the rear of the house, it seemed dark to me. I felt a shudder go through my body, although I wasn't sure if I sensed a presence, or if the memory of my experiences there made me uncomfortable. Without realizing it, I had stopped to stare in trepidation down the hall. When I noticed the others watching me, I shook it off and quickly followed them. After a long, sober glance at me, Steele gazed down the hallway with narrowed eyes before following me.

As the five of us climbed to the third floor, the stairs creaked and popped as though announcing our arrival to anyone or anything that might be in the attic. Still, I felt more at ease in the attic than I had on the second floor, and I concluded that anything that might be in the attic was definitely more friendly and welcoming than Jeremiah Berkeley.

Once we had reached the top of the stairs, Drac glanced around at the stacks of boxes, bags, and piles of accumulated stuff, and asked, "So, do you know where this cubby is?"

Chuck scratched his head, looking this way and that. "I can't recall exactly whereabouts it is." He began inching around boxes and searching the inner walls for a door. "I barely took notice of it when I moved in, so I can't quite remember where it's at."

We all chipped in, moving boxes around to try to locate the door to the cubby. Only a single dim light bulb glowed from the ceiling, so it was difficult to see much. Suddenly, I heard what I thought was a loud whisper in one corner. I made my way around boxes towards that corner and started carefully sliding boxes away from the wall. Suddenly, something fell out of one of the boxes and clattered to the floor. I cursed under my breath and bent down to pick up what had fallen, hoping it hadn't broken. It looked like a picture in a frame. I picked it up and gently turned it over, relieved to see that the glass in the front was still intact. As I brushed some dust off and saw who was in the photo, my eyes widened in shock and horror. All at once, I fumbled the photo and let out a scream as I thrust it into the nearest box.

To my chagrin, everyone turned to see what had made me cry out. Seeing me standing there with eyes like saucers and breathing heavily, Drac chuckled. "What, did you find a spider? Or another mouse?"

Steele laughed aloud from the other side of the room and teased, "Or another wig head?" When I didn't react to his barb, he asked with concern, "Carter, what did you find?"

My eyes still locked on the photo, I managed to choke out, "It's a picture." I glanced up at Gabe. "Of him."

Drac and Gabe exchanged a look before they, along with Chuck and Steele, descended on me from their respective parts of the room. Chuck got there first. Taking the picture from the box, he studied it and nodded, and then showed it to Drac. "There he is, my great-grandfather, Jeremiah Berkeley, and his wife Rosanna."

First Gabe and then Steele came closer to peer over Drac's shoulder. After a moment, still trembling, but feeling braver with the others around me, I stepped in to look more closely at the picture, too. We gazed at it, I with unease, the others with interest. I had to admit that without the cold-blooded hatred in his eyes, Jeremiah was a handsome man, and he looked friendly enough. As I studied the faces in the photo, one detail made my heart leap into my throat, and I brought my hand up and bit down on my knuckle to keep from crying out again. I looked up at the others and realized they were all staring at me. Gabe finally asked, "Is this who you saw downstairs?"

Unable to speak, I nodded. At the moment, that wasn't what was bothering me most, and as my eyes went to Chuck and then to Steele, I could see that they had noticed the same thing. His face draining of color, Chuck asked Drac and Gabe, "Do you notice the same thing I do?"

They both stared at him and Steele curiously, before turning their attention back to the photo. Realization spread over their faces as it dawned on them that Chuck, Steele, and I had been focused not on Jeremiah's face, but on Rosanna's. As they raised their eyes to look at me, I saw uncharacteristic uneasiness in their expressions. Suddenly, one part of my dream made sense, the part where I had felt that Jeremiah thought I was Rosanna. While I was in no way a dead ringer for her, there was enough of a resemblance between us that an emotionally-distraught man could have mistaken me for her.

With new determination and a touch of urgency in his voice, Drac raised the video camera again and said in a businesslike tone, "Well, let's find that cubby, shall we?"

Chuck laid aside the photo, and he and the others turned back to moving boxes, but Steele stood looking at me quizzically, obviously wondering, as I was, how there could be such a strong resemblance between Rosanna and me. He reached over to pick up the picture and studied it for a long moment, shaking his head. I knew the wheels were turning in his mind, but he said nothing. I turned back to the wall where the boxes had been stacked and spied a small door that was only waist-high. Steele spotted it at the same time, and we both called out, "Here it is!"

Chuck hurried over and inched between Steele and me to get to the door. "Oh my," he exclaimed. "How curious!" He knelt down, turned the knob and pulled a few times. "It seems to be stuck," he said, wiping his hands on the back of his jeans.

Gabe replied, "No surprise there, if it hasn't been opened for decades." He, Gabe, and Steele shoved the boxes further from the wall so Chuck could get more leverage. He braced his feet against the wall and tugged harder. After a few more attempts, the door came roughly open with a loud creak of wood against wood. It was obvious that this door hadn't been opened since Mr. Evans had put the diary back in its place.

Chuck squeezed into the tiny door, and Drac and Gabe crowded around the doorway sweeping cobwebs out of the way and holding flashlights to illuminate the dark room. I stepped closer to peer between Drac and Gabe. The first thing I noticed was that the ceiling was too low to allow Chuck to stand up straight. Still, while the cubby was small, it was larger than we'd expected it would be. Chuck's flashlight beam darted around the cubby looking for any sign of the diary. It should have been easy to find, as there were no boxes or stacks of clutter, but Chuck couldn't seem to locate it. Gabe eased his way in to see if he could see anything. Just as I was about to suggest that maybe Mr. Evans had moved the diary and forgotten about it, I heard someone behind me whisper, "Shelf."

I turned to Steele and asked quizzically, "What shelf?"

Drac turned to face me, and Steele gave me a curious look. "What are you talking about, Carter?"

Chuck and Gabe stuck their heads out of the cubby, and I replied, "I thought Steele . . . or someone . . . said something about a shelf."

Steele crossed his arms and responded skeptically, "I didn't say a word."

I looked at Drac questioningly, shaking my head. He returned my gaze for a long moment before asking Chuck and Gabe, "Is there any kind of shelf in there?"

They began shining their flashlights around on the walls, looking for anything that might resemble a shelf. Suddenly Gabe called out, "Here, hidden behind these rafters is a makeshift shelf." He stood on tiptoe to get his hand around it. "Got it!" he exclaimed, pulling down a small, leather-bound journal and handing it to Chuck.

Chuck blew off the dust and cobwebs and leafed gently through the aged, yellow pages. His eyes glistened in the flashlight beams as he said thickly, "Just think of all the family history this book holds!" He and Gabe exited the cubby, with Chuck cradling the journal as though it were a wonderful treasure.

As we all left the attic, I felt an overwhelming peace, knowing that we had found a significant piece of the Berkeley mansion puzzle. Still, although I couldn't explain it, there remained a nagging sense that we were still missing a major clue, and I wondered if Chuck's father had read the entire journal; if there might be more to the story than even he had discovered. When we got down to the second floor hallway, the uneasy feeling that I'd had earlier returned, this time even stronger than before. There was no doubt in my mind that the entity in the bedroom at the end of the hallway—Jeremiah Berkeley or not—knew we had found that journal and was now watching us menacingly. The darkness emanating from that room had intensified, and I began to sweat despite the growing chill. My breaths became shallow and rapid, and I stopped in my tracks and took a step backwards. Strong hands grasped my shoulders and pulled me close. I glanced back and saw Steele gazing down at me with concern.

Drac, Gabe, and Chuck had paused a few steps down and also noticed my distress. "Kyr, what's wrong?" Drac asked urgently. "You're white as a sheet."

The darkness at the end of the hallway suddenly vanished, and I shook my head and tried to pass it off as nothing, saying the heat in the attic had just gotten to me. I knew no one believed me, as the day was somewhat cool and the attic not hot at all, but I wouldn't tell them what I had sensed. First Drac and then Gabe looked up at Steele, and I saw curious concern pass between them. Gabe started up the steps to offer me a hand, but then backed away when Steele stepped forward and grasped my arm protectively, almost possessively, to usher me down the stairs. I glared defiantly up at him but didn't protest. I was oddly glad for his closeness, although I would never admit it. As we started down the stairs, he narrowed his eyes and stared down the hallway for a moment.

By the time we reached the first floor, the menacing feeling had disappeared, and the color had come back into my cheeks. I could breathe again, and the house felt almost friendly. We went into the kitchen, and Chuck brought mugs of hot apple cider before sitting down excitedly with the journal in front of him on the table. As I savored the tangy, spicy beverage, Chuck glanced up at me and asked with concern, "Are you all right now, Kyr? You looked quite ill upstairs."

I nodded, smiled weakly and assured him that I was fine. My eyes went to the journal in front of Chuck, and he took the hint to drop the subject. He opened the journal and began paging through it. While the rest of us sipped our cider, Chuck flipped through the part of the journal containing the family history that Mr. Evans had told us about, not really reading, but skimming through to see if his father had left anything out. He came to the end of what his father had told us, and there seemed to be nothing more. Frustration showed on Chuck's face as he looked up at us. He shook his head, rubbed his chin, and commented, "I was sure there would be something else . . ."

We all sat for a moment, not sure what to say. Like Chuck, I had been certain the journal would tell us something more, some key to what was happening at the Berkeley mansion. No sooner had I thought that than I felt cold creeping up my neck, knowing for certain that there *was* something more. I suggested innocently, "Why don't you go back further in the journal? Maybe there are more entries towards the back."

Steele looked at me sharply, then exchanged a look with Drac, but Chuck just shrugged and began paging through the journal once more. Sure enough, a little more than halfway back, there was more writing. He briefly looked up at me, his eyes asking how I had known that. I was glad he didn't voice the question, because I wouldn't have known what to answer. He turned his attention back to the journal and read aloud, "Daddy seems to have lost his mind. Mother's infidelity has angered him so much that I fear he will do something rash. He has sworn revenge on Mother and on Benjamin Holtzman for making a fool of him. I also fear for Evangeline—will he hurt her too?"

He turned another blank page and continued reading, "Mother has died. Daddy said she died in her sleep from the sickness. Truly, I don't know if I believe him. He does not seem sad at all. The look in his eyes frightens me." Chuck paused and glanced up at us uneasily. Drac and Gabe appeared interested, and they waited for him to continue. I swallowed hard and shivered, recalling Jeremiah's words in my dream. The next passage from the diary made my heart leap into my throat.

Chuck found an entry dated about a month after Rosanna's death. His eyes widened for a moment before he continued reading. "Benjamin Holtzman has disappeared. Some folks in town say he ran off when word got out that he had fathered a child with Mother.

Even his own parents said, 'Good riddance to him, bringing shame on our family.' I fear it is not that simple. Daddy acts so strange these days, always looking over his shoulder, jumping at every noise, and not wanting to leave the house. And he is so mean to Evangeline, and even to me."

Chuck looked up again and wondered aloud, "Why did she hide these entries at the back of the journal instead of putting them with the rest of the history? We almost missed them."

We all shifted uneasily, unsure of what to say. Drac ventured, "Maybe she wanted to record her thoughts about what was happening—just in case—but didn't want those thoughts to be so easily discovered in the event Jeremiah found this journal."

Gabe nodded and added, "I imagine she was afraid of her father finding out she had these suspicions. Can you imagine how he'd have reacted to an accusation?"

As Drac, Gabe, and Steele discussed possible explanations with Chuck, I sat and pondered the whole situation. What did these journal entries mean for the activity going on at the mansion? And what was it about the graveyard that wouldn't let me be? I glanced out the small kitchen window and realized I could see a portion of the graveyard from where we sat. The afternoon sun was getting lower, and I knew there soon wouldn't be enough light to investigate.

"Kyr, is something wrong? You look as though something is troubling you," Chuck asked, bringing my thoughts back to the small kitchen.

I flushed as I considered what to say. I couldn't keep these thoughts to myself much longer, but I was afraid that if I shared what was on my mind, Steele would again belittle me for acting like an over-imaginative newbie getting wrapped up in a ghost story. Still, I couldn't shake the feeling that there was something we were missing. At last I said tentatively, "I just feel like there's something more to the story. The light Andy saw in the graveyard, the male apparition in the attic, Benjamin's disappearance . . ." I shook my head, trying to make sense of it all. "Something just doesn't add up."

Everyone stared at me for a moment before Gabe asked, "Do you want to check out the graveyard again tonight? Maybe do some EVP work again?"

I shook my head, hoping they didn't think I was crazy. "No, not tonight. Now. While there's still light."

Drac, Gabe, and Steele exchanged meaningful glances, and Chuck replied, "Of course, you have my permission, but I don't think there's anything to see. I've never seen anything unusual when I've tended the grass up there."

Drac and Gabe seemed to reach a silent decision, and Drac turned to me with a piercing look. "Well, Kyr, if you want to investigate before dark, we'd better get moving. At best, we've got a half hour of light left."

As Drac and I got up, Chuck asked, "Do you need a shovel? Are you planning on digging?"

A shudder went through me at the very prospect of digging for anything in a graveyard, and I was surprised that Chuck suggested it so nonchalantly. Seeing the others regarding me expectantly, I responded, "No, I'm not planning on digging. To be honest, I really don't know what I'm looking for. I just sort of . . . have a hunch." Steele raised his eyebrows and gave me a skeptical look. I averted my eyes, waiting for the comment I was sure he was about to make. Surprisingly, Steele held his tongue, and Drac and I headed out to the graveyard, while Gabe and Steele stayed in the kitchen with Chuck to search through the journal again.

Despite the fact that Drac still intimidated me, I was glad that he was accompanying me, and not Gabe or Steele. Being around either of them at the moment was disconcerting. I was struck by the realization that Steele hadn't seemed at all bothered that I was heading out with Drac. I knew that if it would have been Gabe, he would have had red eyes and steam coming out of his ears, and I wondered why that was. For the hundredth time since I'd awakened from my nap, I found myself puzzling over my dream, but this time I focused on what had happened between Gabe, Steele, and me. Dreaming about kissing Gabe wasn't really a shocker, even if it had left me feeling guilty and uncomfortable. I knew it was wrong to have the thoughts I was having about a married man, but every time

I looked at him or heard his voice I felt the way I had in high school when I'd had a crush on one of the most popular guys in school.

And what about Steele? The way he'd been acting, I could make sense of his aggression towards Gabe in my dream, but what about the rest of it? Why had he said what he'd said about me, and why had I reacted the way I had? The mere suggestion that Steele and I might become romantically involved made my stomach turn. Even though Gabe was married, there was no question in my mind that he was definitely the type of man I wanted and needed, and not someone like Steele.

We had just reached the top of the little hill, when Drac stopped and turned to me. He looked at me sharply and said, "Okay, Kyr, it's time for you to come clean."

I looked back at him almost fearfully, wondering if he could tell what I was thinking about his brother. I responded uneasily, "What do you mean?"

Drac crossed his arms and raised his eyebrows before saying, "I mean the way you keep having these hunches about things, hearing voices that no one else is hearing, being the only one being attacked by Chuck's resident specter." *Not to mention my resemblance to Rosanna*. He continued, "You're sure you've never been here before, never heard any of the details surrounding the Berkeley mansion haunting or anything like that?"

"No," I insisted. "I don't know what's going on. All I know is what I thought was going to just be a fun weekend has turned into some crazy ride that I can't figure out how to get off of. I want to run away from this place and never come back, but there's something holding me here. Even if I do leave, I know I won't have any kind of peace till this whole . . . mess is resolved." I met his eyes almost defiantly, struggling to hold back tears. I thought again how much Drac reminded me of my dad. My dad, whom I was always afraid to stand up to. My dad, who always expected more than my best. *Damn,* I thought in frustration. *Forget Jeremiah Berkeley. I've got my own ghosts to exorcise.*

Drac took a step forward and grasped my shoulders. "Kyr," he said, more gently this time, "I'm not mad at you; I'm not yelling at you. I'm just trying to figure out what's happening. Me and Gabe have both noticed how involved you're getting in this case, and it's concerning both of us." He led me over to the tree I had climbed the other night trying to figure out what Andy had seen, and I felt a shiver go down my spine. He sat me down beside the tree and asked, "Kyr, do you think it's possible you're an empath, a sensitive?"

His words made me sick to my stomach. *An empath, a sensitive.* Daddy had called them mediums, and the best he could say about them was that they were going to hell. I recalled what I had told Gabe about being afraid that my father wouldn't have approved of me ghost hunting; what would he say if he knew his daughter might be one of those "nutcases"? I looked at Drac, shaking my head slowly. "I can't . . . I don't want to be . . . no . . ."

Drac put his arm around me and replied softly, "Kyr, it's okay. Being a sensitive isn't something you ask for, and it doesn't make you a bad person. You know . . ." It seemed that he was about to tell me something important but then changed his mind. "You're not the only sensitive we've ever encountered." I wondered what he meant by that, but before I could ask who he was referring to, he gave me a conspiratorial smile that reminded me of Gabe's and said, low, "I can tell you that you're probably one of the more level-headed ones we've ever dealt with."

I gave him a watery smile and wiped away a stray tear. "This isn't the first time I've . . . had hunches about things," I admitted. "But I've never been in a situation where it mattered so much."

Drac met my eyes and continued seriously, "Kyr, if you are a sensitive, we need to acknowledge that and help you take precautions to protect yourself." I was about to ask what he meant, but he stood quickly and held out a hand to help me up. "Well, I think we can talk about this later. Right now we need to have a look around the graveyard while we've still got light."

We walked around the graveyard, reading headstones and looking for anything that might give us a clue, but we really found nothing. The only thing that drew me was the tree. What was it about the tree? I looked up into the branches, trying to see if there might be anything carved into the bark. *That was probably a stupid idea; anything carved in the bark would likely be long gone by now.* After walking around the graveyard three times, Drac suggested we go back inside to see if Gabe and Chuck had found anything else. I reluctantly agreed, not wanting to leave till I had some kind of answer, but knowing that it would be dark soon anyway.

As we started back towards the house, Drac turned to me with a glint in his eye and asked, "So what's the deal with you, Gabe, and Spook?"

I felt my face flushing as I looked up at him and tried to ask casually, "What do you mean?"

Drac chuckled and crossed his arms in front of him. "Well, when we started this investigation, you and Gabe seemed to get along like a long lost brother and sister, and you and Spook could hardly stand being in the same room. Now you're all touchy with Gabe, and Spook seems to find excuses to partner up with you." He couldn't suppress a wide grin as he finished, "Not to mention the way Spook wants to knock Gabe's head off every time he gets near you." *So you've noticed that, too.*

I sighed guiltily, recalling how I'd snapped at Gabe in the van when he had no idea what was going on inside my head. I couldn't tell him exactly why I was suddenly so stand-offish with Gabe, and I really couldn't tell him *anything* without telling him about the dream I'd had. He was waiting for me to say *something,* so finally I sighed and said, "It's kind of a long story, and you're probably going to think I'm crazy . . ." I told him the part of my dream that involved Jeremiah—how I'd awakened to find him in my room, how he'd thought I was Rosanna come back to life, and how he'd planned to kill me.

Drac stood staring at me as he pieced things together in his mind. Finally, he responded, "Okay, that does explain some things, but I still don't understand why you're acting like you're mad at Gabe."

I lowered my head to concentrate on my sneakers as I muttered, "Gabe was in my dream." When Drac didn't respond, I looked up to see him grinning as though I'd just told him something amusing. Certain that I knew what he was thinking, I tried to cover, "He burst into the room just as Jeremiah was moving in to kill me. I guess he kind of . . . saved my life." Even though I was crushing on Gabe like a schoolgirl, those last three words left a bad taste in my mouth.

Obviously still amused, Drac chuckled. "And that bothers you."

Suddenly irritated again, I snapped, "I'd like to think I can take care of myself." I closed my eyes and rubbed my forehead. "I guess between my dream and what you said about Gabe wanting to protect me . . . I'm just . . . a little pissed off."

Drac threw his head back and laughed out loud. "Kyr, no one doubts that you can take care of yourself. Gabe—well, all of us, really—we've been concerned that you're in over your head. Don't hold it against us that we just don't want to see you get hurt."

I nodded and agreed that in that respect I was overreacting. My determination to prove myself to them was coming back stronger than ever, and I was determined to see this case through. As the sun slipped down below the trees, we headed back to the house to see what Gabe, Steele, and Chuck had found.

CHAPTER TWELVE

When Drac and I got back to the house, we found Chuck, Gabe, and Steele puzzling over the journal. They both looked up when we came in, and Chuck asked hopefully, "Did you find what you were looking for, Kyr?"

I sighed and responded, "Well, I wasn't even sure what I was looking for, but no, nothing jumped out at me." I didn't mention the feeling I had gotten when I sat down with Drac by the tree. I chanced a glance at Steele, who was regarding me with interest. Thankfully, he remained silent.

"What did you guys find?" Drac asked. "You look confused."

Chuck shook his head and flipped some pages back and forth before saying, "We're trying to figure out if these entries are significant. Listen to this." He flipped back a few pages and began reading, "'Daddy is acting so strangely. I fear that his mind has truly left him. He does so many odd things now, and it is hard for me to even converse with him. He goes to the basement several times a day, and I have come across him several times sweeping the dirt floor back by the coal bin. And he is so worried about having enough coal. Why, my goodness, it's not even autumn yet; we have plenty!'"

Drac chuckled and stretched his arms above his head, almost touching the ceiling fan as he did so. "Slight case of OCD, there, Jeremiah?"

Chuck gave him a crooked smile and continued, "'I have also seen him washing his hands so hard that the skin is rubbed raw. I tried to ask him about it, but he only answers that he must get it off. Must get what off? I can see nothing on his hands but his own blood from such hard scrubbing. When I told him he was bleeding, he became agitated at the sight of the blood and scrubbed even harder. Oh, heaven help me!'"

I shivered visibly, remembering my dream, and Drac looked at me, understanding my reaction. Without thinking, I muttered, "Out, out, damn spot."

Chuck and Gabe both eyed me curiously, and Steele raised an eyebrow. "What does Shakespeare have to do with anything?" Gabe asked, smiling.

Drac cleared his throat and raised an eyebrow at me; Steele caught the exchange and narrowed his eyes. I shook my head at Drac before answering, "Um, nothing, I guess. Just. . . thinking about Belle-Anne's suspicion that Jeremiah may have killed his wife. Maybe he did and was feeling guilty." I just couldn't bring myself to share the details of my dream, especially with the look Steele was giving me.

I could feel Drac's eyes on me, but I refused to look at him. I glanced at Chuck and Gabe; Chuck was staring thoughtfully into the distance, but Gabe was looking pointedly between Drac and me, and when he turned eyes to Steele and quirked an eyebrow, Steele nodded almost imperceptibly. Gabe started to say something, but Drac caught his eye and shook his head at him, so he remained silent.

"There's a bit more," Chuck finally said. "'I saw Daddy in the graveyard. He must be visiting Mama's grave. Does he feel some sadness at last over her passing? But his eyes are not sad; they look haunted. What haunts him so, I wonder? If he indeed feels remorse for the way he treated Mama, he doesn't show it. He is so angry and mean towards me and Evie that I fear he will strike us.'"

There was something about that entry that was significant, but what was it? Why was Jeremiah in the graveyard? Why did I feel so strongly that there was something in the graveyard? There seemed to be a mystery there that was a key to this haunting, but I didn't have a clue how to solve it. As I stood there chewing my thumb, I realized again that everyone's eyes were on me. Although no one said anything, I knew they were thinking about my request to investigate the graveyard.

Chuck cleared his throat uncomfortably. "There's one last entry, dated a month or so before Evangeline eloped." He looked up at Drac and over at Gabe before reading, "'I am worried for Evie. She hears a man's voice that no one else hears. It tells her to leave—but why? And she says she has seen a man peering from the attic window, but it wasn't Daddy. Is her mind leaving her, too?'"

The apparition in the attic! So Evangeline had been the first to see it. That had to be significant, but why? Steele was tapping his fingers on the table, apparently thinking along the same lines. He finally asked, "Chuck, have you actually seen the apparition in the attic yourself, or has it only been others who have seen it?"

Chuck seemed taken aback by Steele's question, and he was quiet for a moment, thinking. He let out a long breath and answered, "Truthfully, in all my adult life, I don't believe I have ever seen that apparition. I do know that Pop saw it a few times over the years, and I believe Mom saw it once." He rubbed his chin thoughtfully and continued, "Now that I think about it, I vaguely remember seeing it as a child—I couldn't have been more than five or six."

We listened as Chuck recounted what happened one rainy afternoon when he went up to the attic to play among the boxes, since he couldn't go outside. He had trudged up the steep stairs to the attic and opened the door. Just as he reached for the light switch, he saw standing by the window a man in some kind of old-fashioned uniform with dark stains on the front. Chuck remembered that the man wasn't transparent at all, but looked like a real man. When Chuck asked him who he was, the man turned to look at him, smiled softly, turned back to the window, and then vanished.

Chuck concluded, "Well, I had heard enough ghost stories by then to know I'd just seen one. I stood there and hollered till Mom and Pop came running up the stairs. When I told them what I had seen, I saw them look at each other for a time before they both told me it was probably a trick of the light. It wasn't till I was older that they told me they had seen the same ghost."

Drac and Gabe were silent as they absorbed this new information, and Steele sat absentmindedly stroking his beard as he turned this new information over in his mind. As I glanced around at everyone, I knew that we weren't going to solve this mystery tonight, or even tomorrow for that matter. We were just trying to figure out where to go from here.

Unfortunately, it was going to have to wait. Drac and Gabe had to head back to upstate New York the next day to get ready to head out for a filming commitment. They told Chuck they would be by first thing in the morning to show him the evidence we had gathered during the investigation. I was disappointed that I couldn't be at the reveal, but I had to get back to my life as well, as did Steele. I hoped I would be able to put the Berkeley mansion and its mysteries behind me, even though we hadn't been able to get to the bottom of what was happening there, but I had a nagging feeling that it wouldn't be that easy.

***

I was quiet once more on the way back to the hotel, but this time my silence was more contemplative than moody. It was already dark by the time we pulled into the hotel parking lot. I had checked out of my room earlier in the day and had my car packed up, so as we all got out of the Petery Paranormal van, there was nothing left to do but say goodbye. Although it had only been a few days, I felt like I had known Drac and Gabe for years, and I was reluctant to leave.

Drac cleared his throat and gave me a huge grin. "Well, Kyr, you survived your first investigation. How does it feel?"

I returned his smile and answered, "It feels good. Even though we really didn't get the answers Chuck needed, I feel like we accomplished something." As Drac and Gabe exchanged smirks, I blushed, realizing that my comment suggested that I was part of the Petery Paranormal team. I started to apologize, but Drac laughed, put his arm around me and said, "Don't apologize, Kyr. You really stepped up and did your part, just like a team member would. A little more training and experience, and we'd be proud to have you as part of Petery Paranormal."

Gabe caught my eye and smiled, then hugged me and added, "You're really something, Kyr. I'm impressed—*we're* impressed with your performance. You're a fast learner, and like Drac said, with a little more training and experience, you'd fit right in. I knew we'd make an investigator out of you! Maybe you could even have a second career as a supernatural sleuth."

I couldn't help laughing at his comment. Although I secretly thought that Kyrie Carter, Supernatural Sleuth had a nice ring to it, I really couldn't see myself continuing in paranormal investigation after this case. I just didn't have the nerves for it.

As I turned to head out to my car, I noticed Steele leaning against the van. His expression was somewhat guarded, and he gave me the closest thing to a Mona Lisa smile I'd ever seen in real life. I stopped and returned his look with a guarded look of my own. After a moment, his lips widened into a self-sure smile that made my knees go weak for a second. *Now, what was that all about?* He gave me a curt nod and drawled, "Carter."

I swallowed hard and gave him my best cryptic smile before responding, "Steele." I felt his eyes on me as I made my way to my car and got in. As I pulled out of the parking lot, I glanced one last time at my fellow investigators. Drac and Gabe seemed to be absorbed in conversation as they moved towards the door, but Steele was still leaning against the van, looking in my direction.

As I made the short drive back home, I thought about the experiences I'd had over the past few days. I was still puzzling over the mystery we seemed to have uncovered at the Berkeley mansion and why I felt so compelled to solve that mystery. I wasn't sure what the others thought, but I felt that we had left Chuck with more questions than he started with. *And he's not the only one.* I recalled the question I'd finally given voice to, a question that I was no closer to answering than when I'd started out on this weekend.

I also found myself wondering if Drac and Gabe would return to investigate further, and a small part of me hoped that if they did, I would be able to investigate with them. I chided myself, *What happened to not having the nerve for paranormal investigation?*

I arrived at home and parked in the alley behind my house. Grabbing my bags out of the trunk, I walked slowly up the back sidewalk towards the duplex I rented. As I looked up at the dark windows on my half of the house, wishing to myself that I'd set my lights on a timer or at least plugged in some electric candles, I stopped dead in my tracks, suddenly not wanting to go inside alone. I realized I was being silly, shifted my bags to my other hand, and marched up to the back door, pulling out my keys.

Just as I unlocked the door and pushed it open, Jeremiah Berkeley's cold, cruel face sprang up in my mind. I cursed to myself, wondering why I had to think of that now. I made my way through the house, turning on the lights in every room I entered so that nothing could take me by surprise. By the time I got upstairs to my bedroom, I realized that I was acting like a scared child. Laughing to myself, I went back downstairs and turned off the lights before coming back upstairs to unpack and get ready for bed.

After turning out the light and settling in to go to sleep, I did something I hadn't done in a long time—I said my prayers.

***

I had forgotten to set my alarm, so after oversleeping the next morning, I had to rush to get ready for work. By the time I walked into the library half an hour later than I'd planned, I was already flustered, contemplating how many emails and other tasks I'd have to catch up on before the library opened for the day. I had to finish making preparations for the Halloween costume party coming up the next weekend, as well as getting sign-ups ready for the Book Buddies promotion for three area elementary schools. Those events, in addition to working my regular shifts at the circulation desk in the Children's Library, promised to keep me too busy to think much about Jeremiah Berkeley, or even Drac and Gabe.

Still, throughout that week, in my spare moments, something I had heard or seen during the investigations would come to my mind and I'd spend a moment wondering what it meant or why it was significant. Of course, my coworkers had asked about my ghost hunting weekend, but for the most part I kept my answers vague and general, not wanting to give too many details about events that still had me unnerved. One thing that really bothered me was the fact that throughout the week I'd had recurring dreams about the Berkeley mansion; vague, jumbled dreams about the attic, a floating light by the tree in the cemetery, and Gabe or Steele holding me, protecting me from something.

Just as I felt I was getting back into the swing of things at work, Saturday evening came. The library was decorated with smiling jack o' lanterns, friendly-looking ghosts and monsters, and sweet-faced witches with glittery hats. Snack tables in the children's section were laden with cookies shaped like bats, ghosts, and pumpkins; bowls of candy corn and pretzels; and pitchers of punch and cider. There were stations for games, face painting, and Halloween crafts, and a corner for not-so-spooky stories for the younger children. But what I was most proud of and excited about was the haunted house my colleagues and I had set up in the library basement.

An hour before the party was to begin, I dashed down the stairs, trying not to trip over my long gypsy dress, to make one final check of the setup. I turned on the lights and dimmed them to give the room a spooky atmosphere. Gauzy spider webs hung from the ceiling and on random furnishings throughout the room. Electric candles with orange light bulbs stood on either end of the ancient piano along one wall. A small cemetery scene was in one corner, the grave stones painted with eerie glow-in-the-dark paint. Ghosts made from helium balloons and white sheets hung throughout the room, and a lone skeleton sat in a chair, holding a book. In the very back corner sat a table lit only by a softly glowing crystal ball. I would wait for each child to approach and tell their fortunes. Nothing scary of course, just silly predictions about finding bubble gum in their shoes or dinosaurs in their mailboxes. And for the children I knew well, I would predict that their wildest dreams for the future would come true.

I smiled to myself, thinking my colleagues and I had outdone ourselves with the limited resources we had on hand. For a moment, I almost thought we had done too good of a job, as I looked once more over the room and wished there were some windows in the basement. I shivered as a chill went down my spine, and I raced upstairs.

My momentary fear was soon forgotten as I reentered the brightly-lit main floor where my coworkers still bustled around making sure everything was ready for the children. A little before seven, scores of costumed children and their parents flocked into the library. For the next hour, the usually-quiet library echoed with giggles, delighted squeals, and excited chatter as my coworkers and I guided groups of children through each of the stations. As my group left the craft table and headed for the apple bobbing tubs, I shot an apologetic glance at Rita, who did much of the library's cleaning. She was shaking her head and looking at the orange glitter and paper snippets scattered on the carpet. I almost dreaded to see how much water would be on the kitchenette floor and made a mental note to scratch apple-bobbing at next year's party.

When all the groups had gone through all the stations, we gathered the children together in the middle of the room for the costume judging. As the children were lined up for the judges to make their decisions, I headed downstairs with Maureen to get ready for the children to visit the haunted house.

"Wow!" Maureen exclaimed as she saw the finished haunted house for the first time. "You guys did a fabulous job with this! It looks really spooky!"

I smiled, happy that she was so pleased with it, but I asked nervously, "You don't think it's too spooky, do you?" I certainly didn't want any children having nightmares from anything they saw at our party.

Maureen looked around once more, her hands on her hips. "Oh no, I think you captured just the right amount of spooky for the kids." She donned her witch's hat and took her place by the door. She would walk groups through the haunted house, weaving some scary tales as she pointed out each section. I laughed to myself and tried to remember why I had assigned this particular task to Maureen. She was a hardcore skeptic who scoffed at the very idea of ghosts, UFOs, monsters, or anything else not written in black and white in a science textbook. I briefly wondered what she'd have thought if I'd told her what happened in the back bedroom at the Berkeley mansion.

I shook my head as I heard children's voices in the stairwell. I couldn't think about real ghosts now, not here in this windowless basement. I closed my eyes and tried to get myself into character as Madame Mystique, thinking of silly fortunes I could tell for the children. A moment later, the first group of children entered the room, led by Dan, a college student who volunteered at the library. I listened in delighted surprise as Maureen motioned to each of the scenes in the room and told a story about Franklindale Public Library when it was still a home in the 1800s. She told of old Widow Miller, who lived alone in the house until her death in the late 1890s, how she had apparently died in her favorite chair, reading her favorite book. She told of the piano music that could be heard coming from the basement late at night when only the janitor was in the library. She told of the little graveyard at the back of the house that had been moved to expand the little home into the present library building, which was built in the 1920s. Even though I knew Maureen's story was not the least bit true, each chilling detail made me shiver and forget that it was just a story. I was so enthralled that I almost forgot to get into character when Dan and Maureen led the children over to my corner to have their fortunes told.

The first child was seven-year-old Riley, who came into the library each week to look for racing books. Because I knew him, I was able to have a little fun making up a story for his future. Rubbing my crystal ball, I said in my spookiest voice, "As you, young lad, before me stand, come forward now and take my hand. My crystal ball will tell me true, what the future holds for you."

Even though I was certain that Riley recognized me, he looked a bit apprehensive, so I did my best to keep his fortune on the lighter side. "I foresee many, many treats in your pumpkin on Halloween night," I began. "But beware! Someone—maybe your sneaky big sister—will try to switch your gummy worms for *real* ones!" He giggled, so I continued, "Your favorite teacher will stay home with a sore throat next week, and your substitute will be . . ." I rubbed my crystal ball and looked nervous. ". . .a one-eyed, one-horned, flying purple people eater! I hope there are no purple people in your class!" All the children laughed as I gave Riley a temporary tattoo and a lollipop before sending him over to Dan and calling the next child forward.

Time passed quickly as the rest of the groups made their way through the haunted house. As the last group headed up the stairs, Maureen followed them to be sure all the children who wanted to see the haunted house had had a turn. As I unplugged my glowing crystal ball and waited in my corner, I heard a faint voice say, "Please help me."

I started, looked around, and then said tentatively, "Hello?" When no one answered, I got up and started towards the stairs, thinking Maureen needed help with something. Just as I reached the staircase, Maureen stuck her head in the doorway from the stairwell.

"No more kids. Come on up; some of the kids are getting ready to leave."

"Oh, okay," I responded, a bit flustered. "Hey, Maureen?" I called after her.

Maureen's head appeared at the top of the stairs again. "Yes?"

"You didn't ask me to help you just now, did you?"

She looked at me curiously and replied, "Well, I asked you to come upstairs, if that's what you mean."

"No, I mean before you came back downstairs," I said uneasily. "I thought I heard someone say something."

Maureen shook her head, then laughed. "Kyr, I think your ghost hunting weekend has gone to your brain. Now you're hearing ghosts in the library."

"I guess you're right." I forced a laugh and followed her upstairs. In the back of my mind, I hoped I wouldn't have to tear down the haunted house alone.

***

After Halloween came and went, things slowed down at the library. With my mind less focused on special programs, I had more time to ponder the investigation at the Berkeley mansion. I repeatedly told myself to stop thinking about it, but I just couldn't get it out of my mind. I found myself fighting the urge to pay Chuck a visit to ask him if he'd had any more activity, or wanting to try to contact Drac and Gabe to see if they had any more ideas about what Belle-Anne's journal entries meant. My dreams continued, usually involving just the graveyard and the attic, but occasionally involving the basement as well. The dreams weren't frightening, but they often left me with a sense of urgency and a feeling that there was something I had to do.

For the most part, I kept my concerns to myself, as most of my friends and family didn't believe in ghosts and would have scoffed at what I was experiencing. Many of those who did believe in ghosts were too spooked by anything paranormal to even hear about it. I tried calling JoEllyn, but Brad said she was away on business and would be gone for a week. I was really beginning to feel isolated and scared when one day I got help from an unexpected source. I was visiting with my Aunt Julia one Saturday afternoon, and the topic of my ghost hunting weekend came up. We were sitting in her living room having coffee and her red velvet cake, when she asked, "Kyrie, honey, you haven't told me about your ghost hunting weekend. Did you have fun?"

I almost choked on a bite of cake, and I thought about how much to tell her. I finally answered slowly, "Well . . . it was definitely . . . interesting."

Aunt Julia adjusted her glasses and waited impatiently for me to continue. She finally nudged me and asked, "Well, did you see a ghost?"

A shiver raced down my spine as Jeremiah Berkeley's face sprang up in my mind. "Yes, actually I did. An unfriendly one at that."

Aunt Julia edged closer to me and clapped her hands, making her bracelets jingle. "Details, missy, details! Tell me all about it, and don't leave anything out!"

I smiled in spite of my reluctance to tell Aunt Julia the whole story. We had always been close. Like me, she was the baby of her family and the only daughter, so she often stood up for me when Daddy was overprotective or my brothers picked on me, and more than once she had been the one who comforted me when life was less than kind. She also shared my interest in the paranormal, and she alone believed me when I told her of my experiences. Sometimes it was hard to believe that she and Daddy were sister and brother, so different were their beliefs in the supernatural. Still, I wasn't sure what she'd think about the craziness I'd gotten myself into. I finally decided to stick to telling her just the basics of what had happened.

I told her about Kyle and Andy, and how they had dubbed me "the newbie" and did their fair share of picking on me. She sniffed irritably at the way they'd acted. For reasons I couldn't explain, even to myself, I didn't tell her about Steele. I was still puzzling over the way he'd acted whenever I was around Gabe, and I didn't feel comfortable trying to analyze him with Aunt Julia. I told her about the voices we'd heard, the footsteps and other noises, the light Andy had seen in the tree. I ended by telling her, "And yes, I did see the ghost of Jeremiah Berkeley. He wasn't nice at all, and let's just say he made it very clear that he didn't want me in that room."

After I'd finished, Aunt Julia sat looking at me for a long time, saying nothing. Something in my eyes must have given away that I wasn't telling her the whole story, because she thumped me on the shoulder and admonished, "Kyrie Skye Carter, you should know better than to try to keep something from your auntie! Now what really happened? Something is bothering you about that weekend, so spill it!"

I swallowed hard, not really wanting to draw Aunt Julia into it, but I finally gave in and told her everything. I told her exactly what happened in the back bedroom, how I'd felt that Jeremiah would kill me, and how Gabe had had to carry me out of the room the first night. I saw her smirk at that revelation, and I suspected she'd want more details of that later. I told her about our meeting with Mr. Evans and about the sordid story of Jeremiah's unfaithful wife and his mental decline. I told her about Belle-Anne's hidden journal entries and about my suspicions about the graveyard. I finished by telling her of my recent dreams and about the voice I'd heard in the library basement.

Aunt Julia sat there silently, with her lips pursed, and I wondered what she was thinking. Finally she said, "Kyrie, honey, I've always suspected you were in tune with the spirit world. You've always had a knack for seeing things that others couldn't. I mentioned it once to your folks, but, well, you know how your father felt about all that 'occult' business." I nodded, and she continued, "I think that some unsettled spirit in that house sensed that you can help bring peace, somehow. You just need to figure out who it is and what you're supposed to do."

That's what was worrying me. What could I do? And would it be dangerous? I gave Aunt Julia a sideways glance. "Any ideas about how to do that?"

She chuckled. "Not off the top of my head. But there's something bothering me . . ."

"You and me both," I interjected.

Aunt Julia slapped me on the shoulder. "Now, don't interrupt me; I'm thinking." She set her coffee cup down and looked at me sharply. "What did you say Jeremiah's wife's name was?"

"Rosanna," I replied. "Rosanna Henninger. Why does that matter?"

"Hmm," she muttered. "I don't know, honey. The name just sounded familiar. Maybe it's just because the Henningers were one of Franklindale's founding families, and I heard so much about them growing up."

I sat back, thinking. Of course Aunt Julia would have heard about the Henningers growing up. She'd lived in Franklindale all her life, and she was fascinated with history. I guess I was hoping she'd know a bit more about the scandal, something that would give me a clue on what to do next.

My thoughts were interrupted when she put her hand on mine and asked mischievously, "So, what was it like meeting Gabe Petery? I know you've been sweet on him since you started watching the show. Did you kiss him?"

I felt my face grow red. "Aunt Julia! For heaven's sake, he's married!" I had no intention of telling her about the dream I'd had of him.

Aunt Julia laughed out loud. "*Something* happened with him, young lady. I can tell by the way you're blushing. Come on, you spent a whole weekend in a dark, spooky house with him. I'm sure you jumped into his arms at least once, whether you were scared or not."

I assured her that nothing that exciting happened and that I had tried to hide the fact that I was scared out of my wits because I didn't want Andy and Kyle picking on me. "And anyway," I said. "Gabe and Drac both thought of me as a sister. They picked on me as badly as the boys did when we were growing up."

"You didn't even get a kiss?" Aunt Julia asked, seeming more disappointed than I was.

I sighed and admitted, "Gabe did tell me I'm a special woman and kissed me . . ." I smiled ruefully and finished, " . . . on the forehead."

Aunt Julia scrunched up her face and groaned, "Oh, the forehead kiss. I'm sorry, sweetie!"

I laughed and replied, "Well, like I said, he *is* married. Heaven knows I don't want to get into *that* kind of a mess." Then I laughed again and told Aunt Julia about Rose at the retirement home. "I suppose I could have planted one on him like she did. But I don't think he appreciated that very much."

Aunt Julia laughed too. "You wouldn't have the nerve to do that anyway, Kyrie. No, it's better for you to behave yourself, although it's certainly fun to dream."

I blushed again, thinking, *Oh, Aunt Julia, if you only knew* . . .

CHAPTER THIRTEEN

One day the following week, I was in the Children's Library covering the Preschool Read & Play Day. I had finished reading *The Color Kittens*, one of my favorite childhood books, and the children were sitting around a table mixing finger paints to create different colors. As I watched them trying to remember how to make purple, orange, pink, and green, Maureen stopped to observe the children.

"I see you covered the floor with newspaper," she joked. "You afraid of getting on Rita's bad side?"

I laughed and replied, "Yeah, she really wasn't happy about the Halloween party crafts. I think there's still glitter in the carpet. Oh!" I dashed over to help three-year-old Dylan, who had just put his elbow into his paint. "What color did you make, Dylan?"

"Wexy bof," he answered, looking at me with wide, innocent eyes.

As I wiped a strange-colored mixture of all his paints from his arm, I glanced at his mother for a translation. Gazing at her son as though he were the cleverest boy in the world, she said, "He means Rexy barf. The dog threw up this morning, and . . . that's about what color it was. I'm sorry . . ."

Maureen burst out laughing and headed for her office, and I smiled at Dylan. "Well, Dylan, that's very creative. But let's keep the paint on the paper, okay?"

Dylan looked up at me again and responded sweetly, "Otay!"

An hour later, after the last child had left with a paper full of real and yet-to-be-named colors, I cleaned up the tables and then headed back to my office to have some lunch at my desk and to check my emails. As I quickly ate my turkey sandwich and key lime yogurt, I read through forwarded jokes and photos from friends, work memos, and a notice from my college about an upcoming alumni event.

One email did catch my eye: a message from Aunt Julia entitled, "Exciting news!" I opened it and read, "Kyrie, honey, I have something exciting to show you. It may explain some of your ghost experiences at the Berkeley mansion. Can you come for dinner sometime this week? I'd rather show you what I found in person rather than send it in an email."

I hadn't thought much about that weekend for a few days, so Aunt Julia's email gave me a jolt. I wondered what she had been up to and what she could have found that might tie into the experiences I'd had. I quickly checked my evening schedules for the week and shot her a brief message telling her I'd be there Saturday evening.

For the rest of the week, I could hardly keep from wondering what Aunt Julia had to show me. It was a slow week at the library, with fewer than usual patrons coming in, so my hours at the circulation desk seemed to drag on and on. In my spare moments, or while I was reshelving books, I thought about Jeremiah, Rosanna, Benjamin, Belle-Anne, and Evangeline, and how their lives seemed more suited for a modern reality TV series than for late-nineteenth and early-twentieth century rural Pennsylvania.

As I reshelved some romance novels one afternoon, I glanced momentarily at the suggestive artwork on the covers and thought again about my dream about Gabe. My imagination took over, and I thought about being the heroine of a romance novel, with Gabe as the hero.

A voice suddenly interrupted my reverie. "Excuse me, do you work here?"

I quickly put the novels on the shelf and replied, "Yes, I do. How can I help you?"

An elderly woman with thick-framed glasses and a frail, prim-sounding voice handed me a piece of paper with spidery handwriting on it. "I'm looking for this book. Do you have it here?"

I glanced at the paper, smiled, and guided her to the computer. "Let's take a look." Since our library did not have the particular book she wanted, I spent the next few minutes looking for it on the county database, putting in a hold request, and confirming the woman's contact information. The woman left the library looking satisfied that I had located the book she wanted, and I chuckled, thinking it was indeed a slow week when the exciting moment of the day was helping a patron find a book.

Despite feeling as though it would never arrive, Saturday did come at last. After shutting down the Children's Library computers and making sure everything was in order for opening on Monday, I locked up, left the library, and headed home to change clothes and bake a batch of brownies before heading to Aunt Julia's. As I excitedly ran a brush through my hair and rebraided it, I briefly felt a twinge of emptiness as I realized that the most exciting part of my weekend was going to be spending the evening with my aunt. Although I loved her dearly and enjoyed spending time with her, I thought not for the first time how much I was longing for someone to share my life with.

I was still feeling somewhat sorry for myself when I arrived at Aunt Julia's, and I took a moment to clear my mind before getting out of the car. As I slowly walked up the stairs to the front porch, I wondered how she could live in that big house by herself without being lonely. Uncle Dan had passed away nearly ten years ago, and although she had loved him dearly and had to miss him deeply, she never seemed to show it.

I rang the bell and waited for Aunt Julia to come to the door. Almost right away I heard her quick footsteps coming across the hardwood floor. After greeting me with one of her bear hugs, she took the pan of brownies from me, and we headed out to the kitchen where beef stew was simmering in a crock pot on the counter. She was making noodles and a salad, so I jumped in and began chopping carrots. The homey smell of supper cooking, the bright yellow kitchen walls decorated with Pennsylvania Dutch hex signs, and our cheery conversations improved my mood till I almost forgot I had been feeling so gloomy.

All through our delicious meal, we talked about trivial things: the unusually warm November weather, the latest episodes of our favorite TV shows, the strange hair colors of the newest clerk at the grocery store. Chatting with Aunt Julia was almost like chatting with my best friend from high school.

After supper, we moved outside to sit on the front porch swing and watch the stars winking into sight as the sky darkened.

"Better enjoy the warm weather while we can," she said. "Winter's not far away."

"I know," I replied wistfully. "It's already getting dark early."

Aunt Julia was quiet for a moment, then said with a sigh, "Winter is never easy for me, especially when the weather is bad and I can't get out." I saw the sadness in her eyes. "I miss having Dan to sit by the fire with. It gets so lonely here with no one to talk to."

I patted her hand fondly and replied softly, "I know, Aunt Julia. You know you can call me anytime you need company."

She put her hand over mine and responded, "You're a dear to offer, Kyrie." Then she wagged her finger at me. "But you shouldn't be spending your spare time coddling your old auntie."

Tears welled up in my eyes, and I opened my mouth to protest, but Aunt Julia stopped me. "Kyrie, I know I promised not to meddle in your personal life, but I'm old-fashioned, and I worry about you being alone. I know you're a modern woman, and you don't need a man to take care of you, but I wish you could find someone to make you happy."

I lowered my eyes, once again feeling the emptiness I had felt earlier. This wasn't the first time I'd heard this advice, not only from Aunt Julia, but from married friends, from folks at church, even from the pink-haired cashier at the grocery store. As content as I was with my life, there were times, like today, when I keenly felt the loneliness, and I wished Trevor and I hadn't broken up. My voice was thick as I replied, "I do, too, Aunt Julia."

"Oh, honey," Aunt Julia gushed. "Now I've made you cry. I'm so sorry, love!" She held me as my mother used to when I'd come to her crying over some boy who had broken my heart. I had never been particularly close to my mother, but she had always been extremely supportive when it came to matters of the heart, and I wished she were here now to talk to.

After a few moments, I sat up, wiped my eyes and looked apologetically at Aunt Julia. "I'm sorry. I've just been a little down all evening, just . . . just missing . . ." I almost said Trevor, but I knew it really wasn't him I missed. I threw my hands up and laughed ruefully.

"I understand," Aunt Julia said softly, and I knew she really did. "Well," she said, brightening, "why don't we go inside so I can show you what I found?"

I felt an excited jolt inside as I remembered the reason for my visit. "That would be great," I said eagerly. "I can't wait to see what you've got."

We went inside and sat down in the living room. Aunt Julia turned on some lights and then went back to her bedroom to get something. She came back carrying the family Bible with a stack of papers tucked inside. A sudden chill raced across my scalp and down my back, and I couldn't help glancing over my shoulder at the window behind my chair. I so much expected to see someone peering in at me that I jumped at my reflection in the glass.

Aunt Julia sat down in the other chair, looked at me and asked, "Are you all right, Kyrie?"

I rubbed my arms, still feeling the chill, and answered, "Yeah. I just got a strange feeling when you came in the room." I glanced uneasily at what Aunt Julia had laid on the coffee table.

She stared at me for a moment, then said, "It doesn't surprise me, Kyrie. What I found had me *ferhoodled*, and I wondered how you'd take it."

I smiled at Aunt Julia's choice of words. Her Pennsylvania Dutch background often came out when she was excited or agitated. I swallowed hard and asked, "What did you find?"

Aunt Julia looked at me again and asked in return, "Have you ever looked into your mother's side of the family?"

I shook my head, wondering what dark secret she may have discovered. "I traced Dad's side, and most of what I have is what you gave me from your research, but I never got around to doing Mom's side."

Aunt Julia nodded her head. "That's what I thought." She put her glasses firmly on her nose and said simply, "You'll be surprised to learn you have a family tie to Jeremiah Berkeley."

My hand flew to my chest, and I felt as though lightning had just struck beside me. "What?"

Slowly, Aunt Julia pulled the stack of papers from the family Bible. "This took some digging to find, but I think it may be the answer to why you feel such a connection to what is happening at that mansion." She shuffled through the papers for a moment. "Do you remember when you were telling me about the Berkeleys, and I said the name Rosanna Henninger sounded familiar?"

I nodded, wondering where she was going with this.

She pulled out one of the papers, a roughly drawn family tree, and showed me. "Here's your mother Ellen, and her sister Emma. Their mother was Jocelyn Hollinger; you know that."

"Right. Grandma Hollinger," I said, moving closer.

"Now," she said, pointing to the family tree, "did you ever go back further than that?"

I shook my head, trying to make out the handwriting on the paper.

"Well, Jocelyn's parents were Prestons, John and Pauline. And John's mother…" Aunt Julia pointed to the top of the family tree, ". . . was Evelyn. Evelyn Henninger."

Another chill raced down my spine, and my uneasiness returned. "Evelyn Henninger. Was she related to Rosanna?"

Aunt Julia looked at me for a long moment, then nodded and pulled out another sheet of paper. "This was where I had to get some help. You know my friend Telly over at the Historical Society?" I nodded, and she continued, "Well, the records surrounding Evelyn were marked private in the sites online; I couldn't access any of her family information to see who her parents or siblings were. He was able to do some digging on the Berkeleys and the Henningers, mostly the Henningers. It turns out that your Rosanna had a much older sister."

The pieces were coming together for me. "Evelyn?"

Aunt Julia nodded, looking at me over the top of her glasses. "Evelyn. I had thought maybe Evelyn was an only child since I couldn't find any siblings." She pulled out another family tree. "But this one that I borrowed from your cousin Emerson shows Evelyn and then what looks like a sibling who was scribbled out. Emerson had thought maybe it was because that sibling had died, but I didn't think so. That's why I contacted Telly."

I had a feeling in my gut. "Was Rosanna disowned by her family?"

Aunt Julia sighed and nodded grimly. "Benjamin Holtzman wasn't the only one whose family was disgraced. When Rosanna's parents learned the truth about Evangeline, they cut Rosanna out of their will and never spoke to her or Evangeline again."

"Poor Evangeline!" I said. "She just got kicked around by everyone, didn't she?"

"Yes, she did," Aunt Julia answered. "Things were very different back then, especially for the more upper class folks. Scandals like that were just not acceptable."

I shook my head, glad that things were different now. Even though I had been raised in a very strict family and was always told that having children out of wedlock was wrong, I couldn't bear the unfairness of how Evangeline had been treated. It wasn't her fault, yet she had been branded because of her parents' actions.

Aunt Julia interrupted my thoughts. "And there's something else you should see." She pulled out another sheet, a photocopy of an old picture. "Here's a photograph of Evelyn."

I took the sheet and stared at it, feeling the blood drain from my face. Evelyn and Rosanna could have been twins. *So that explained my resemblance to Rosanna.* "But why do I feel such an urgency to figure out what's going on there?" I asked. "How does this affect me, our family?"

"Well," Aunt Julia said, "Telly said that Evelyn thought it was wrong of her parents to completely disown Rosanna, and he believes she secretly stayed in touch with Rosanna. Apparently Evelyn had her own touch of second sight." She looked sharply at me. "And she had her own suspicions about Rosanna's death and about Benjamin's disappearance. But she wouldn't go against her parents' wishes and pursue those suspicions."

"So maybe Evelyn is the one reaching out to me somehow to put things right?" I was still having trouble grasping why I needed to be the one to get involved in this. What did it matter now, almost one hundred years later?

Aunt Julia seemed to read my thoughts. "I can't say who's reaching out to you, Kyrie, or why they might have chosen you, but this was obviously something that was important to Evelyn, maybe important enough to disrupt her peace. Maybe you winning that contest and investigating the Berkeley mansion wasn't a coincidence."

At Aunt Julia's words, I heard my father's voice in the back of my mind, this time not chastising me over my belief in ghosts, but sharing his belief that there were no coincidences, but that everything happened for a reason. As I thought about everything that had happened over the past month, I wondered not for the first time if he was right. I also wondered if I should try to get in touch with Chuck, or even Drac and Gabe, to tell them of these new developments.

Before I left that evening, Aunt Julia gave me copies of everything she had found about the Henningers and the Berkeleys. I tried not to obsess over the information, but I couldn't stop the questions that came to mind every time I passed the desk in my living room where I had laid the papers. I finally put the papers in a desk drawer, hoping that if I didn't see them every time I walked past the desk, I wouldn't think about the information those papers held.

Still, I found myself puzzling over how my great-great-grandmother played into the activity happening at the Berkeley mansion. Could this family tie, as distant as it was, really have the power to draw me into whatever issues had to be resolved so these spirits could rest? I kept turning over and over in my mind the new information Aunt Julia had given me and my experiences and hunches from our time investigating. I was still thinking about these things as I drifted off to sleep one night, a fact I tried to convince myself led to what happened a few hours later.

In the midst of what started off as a very mundane dream about working in the library, I turned from shelving books to find myself no longer in the library, but standing alone in the graveyard outside the Berkeley mansion. I seemed to be searching for something on the ground among the graves, when suddenly I heard a voice whisper, "Not there—here."

I looked up at the tree and saw a bright ball of bluish light hovering among the branches. I tried to see what the spirit wanted me to find. I stared at the bark on the trunk, now illuminated by the hovering orb, but I saw nothing, no marks on the bark, no visible holes in the tree, nothing that would indicate what I was supposed to find. "What are you trying to show me?" I asked. "Where am I supposed to look?"

The light shone brighter on one spot on the trunk, just above the first large branch where I had sat when we were trying to figure out what Andy had seen. The voice whispered, "Here. You'll find it here." Those words echoed several times, and I woke up in a cold sweat, thinking I had heard the voice in the room with me. I sat up in bed and almost jumped out of my skin when I saw a bluish light reflecting on the wall. I let out a relieved breath when I realized it was just the moonlight shining in the window, but I still had the feeling I wasn't alone.

I fought the urge to turn on the light, trying to convince myself I wasn't afraid. I lay down again and pulled the covers up to my chin, listening for any sound, watching for any movement or out-of-place shadow that would betray the presence of something in the room with me. Though I didn't hear or see anything unusual, I could not relax. This dream was so much more detailed than the others I'd had, and I wondered what it could mean. Sleep eluded me for the next few hours, and it wasn't till the sky was beginning to get light that I finally dozed off.

When my alarm clock went off, I could hardly drag myself out of bed. I showered quickly and made my coffee extra strong, hoping I'd liven up when I got to work. As I grabbed my keys and dashed out the front door, something that didn't look quite right caught my eye, but in my rush and bleary-eyed state, it didn't register right away. It wasn't until almost lunchtime, as I was checking in books at the circulation desk, that I realized what it was.

The papers I had put into the desk drawer were lying on top of the desk that morning.

When that realization hit, I froze with a book in one hand and the scanner in the other. I can only imagine the look that was on my face, because Robin, our new college intern, came over quickly and laid a hand on my shoulder. "Kyr, are you okay?" she asked. "You look like you've seen a ghost."

Her choice of words startled me almost as much as feeling her touch, and I jumped. "Yeah," I said a little too quickly, trying to regain my composure. "Yeah, I just remembered something that...I have to do later."

Robin looked at me skeptically, but she didn't push for details. For the rest of the day, I could see her watching me out of the corner of her eye, and I tried harder to hide my distraction and keep my mind on the tasks at hand.

When it was finally time to head home, I shut down my computer, said a quick good-night to Maureen and dashed out to my car. I wanted to get home to see if I had imagined those papers on the desk or if they were really there. The whole way home I tried to rationalize it, even if the papers were lying on the desk. Maybe I had taken them out to look at them and just forgotten to put them back, or maybe what I saw was just some forgotten junk mail.

My phone rang as I walked in the back door. I tossed everything on the kitchen table and dug it out of my purse. I didn't recognize the number, so I answered cautiously, "Hello?"

A man's voice hesitantly responded, "Hello, uh, am I speaking with Kyrie Carter?"

"Yes," I said, somewhat irritated and hoping this wasn't someone looking for a donation. I walked through the kitchen and into the living room, heading for my desk.

"Hi, Kyrie, I'm sorry to contact you at your home. This is Chuck Evans."

It took me a moment to make the connection. "Chuck Evans? Oh! Yes, hello Chuck. Uh, how are you? Is everything okay?" I thought he was going to tell me that something had happened to his father.

"Well," he began, somewhat hesitantly. "As I said, I'm sorry to contact you at home, but I needed to tell someone . . ."

"Tell someone what?" I prompted.

Chuck was silent for a moment, and then he continued, "Things have really picked up here at the house."

I was standing by my desk, and I lost my train of thought as I looked down and saw that the papers Aunt Julia had given me were indeed lying on top of the desk again. I remembered I was holding the phone to my ear, and I said absent-mindedly, "Really? What kinds of things?"

Chuck blew out a long breath and answered, "Well, a lot more footsteps, voices, more shadows . . . and something came after me."

I sat down quickly, my hand on my chest. "What? Where did that happen? In the back bedroom?"

"No," Chuck replied quickly. "It actually happened in the basement, in the back part where the coal chute comes down. I was moving things around and suddenly felt uneasy . . . threatened. Then something shoved me. *Hard.*"

"Wow," I said. "That's crazy. Have you contacted Drac and Gabe?"

"I left a message at Petery Paranormal," he replied. "I'm waiting for them to get back to me. I just couldn't keep this to myself. I thought since you had had your own unpleasant experiences, you'd understand."

I was silent, trying to decide whether or not to tell him about the dreams I'd had and about the experience I'd had in the library, not to mention what I'd learned from Aunt Julia.

Chuck continued, "And Kyr, there's something else."

"What?" I asked.

Chuck's words made my blood run cold. "I've been having some strange dreams." He described the recurring dream he'd had over the past weeks. His took place in the basement, in the back where he'd been attacked. In his dream, he was standing in the back room of the basement, looking at a small pile of coal that seemed to be out of place. He walked around behind the coal pile and saw that the dirt floor had been dug up and then filled in, as though something had been buried there. "Is my imagination just working overtime, or could there be something to it?" he asked, more to himself than to me. "Maybe there really was something to Belle-Anne's suspicion that Benjamin met with foul play. At Jeremiah's hands. What if he's buried in the basement?"

I shivered at the thought. "That would certainly explain some of the activity at the mansion." I hesitated for a moment then continued, "Chuck, I have to tell you . . . I've been having dreams of my own." I told him about my dreams of being in the graveyard. "Do you think our dreams could be connected?"

"They may be," Chuck answered, sounding relieved that I didn't think he was crazy. "I want to check things out, but honestly, I'm afraid to do anything without Drac and Gabe here. What if I stir up something I can't handle?"

"Oh, of course, I understand." I was holding the papers Aunt Julia had given me, shuffling through them and wondering if I should tell him what I'd learned.

Chuck broke into my thoughts. "Kyr, I was wondering . . . If I can get Drac and Gabe to come back, would you be willing to come too? I mean, since you had such strong personal experiences here."

I thought again about my run-ins with Jeremiah Berkeley and about Chuck's recent experiences, and for a moment I could hardly breathe. I had the feeling that Jeremiah knew he was on the edge of being discovered, and I was certain that he would do everything in his power to prevent that from happening.

***

A couple weeks later, I once again headed out to the Berkeley mansion. The Peterys had set up a follow-up visit to get to the bottom of whatever was happening there. As I drove slowly up the tree-lined driveway, I saw the *Project Boo-Seekers* vans—two of them this time—parked out front. I got out of my car and walked slowly up to the front porch, looking up at the windows as I approached the house. Once again, I had the feeling that I was being watched, but as before, I was relieved to see that the windows remained vacant.

Just as I was about to knock on the door, I heard voices around back, so I headed towards the back of the house where I found Chuck in the graveyard talking to Drac, Gabe, and Rocco, another cast member and investigator with Petery Paranormal. Drac was telling Rocco about the light Andy had seen in the tree when we investigated. As I approached, Chuck spotted me and waved. Drac, Gabe, and Rocco turned to face me, and Gabe smiled and said, "There's the newbie!" He hugged me and asked, "Are you ready to wrestle with Jeremiah Berkeley again?"

My breath caught in my chest as I thought about what might happen this time around, but I replied, "I hope so."

Drac stepped forward and hugged me as well. "Not to worry, Kyr. We brought more reinforcements this time." He introduced me to Rocco and told me that Lynette and Owen were inside setting up cameras and voice recorders in the hotspots. He also mentioned with a gleam in his eye that someone else was on the way there, just in case they needed his help. I knew without asking that he was referring to Steele.

Chuck joked, "It looks like Jeremiah will be up against two red-headed women tonight. I almost feel sorry for him." Everyone laughed, but I could tell he was trying to cover his nervousness.

As I looked at him, I noticed angry red scratches running down his cheek and extending all the way to his shirt. Without thinking, I blurted out, "Oh, Chuck, did Jeremiah do that to you?"

Drac, Gabe, and Rocco looked grimly between Chuck and me, and Chuck answered, "Yes, he did. I'm feeling more and more unwelcome in my own home."

Drac held my gaze and said, "We're not sure if this is the same spirit or not—I suspect that it is—but things have certainly stepped up here since the last time we investigated. We're going to have to play it safer this time."

Gabe added, "I hope you're not too disappointed, Kyr, but we're not going to let you—or Lynette for that matter—investigate alone in there tonight. I don't think anyone should be alone tonight for any reason."

"I'll try to contain my disappointment." He didn't need to warn me; I understood the seriousness of what we were up against.

I saw Rocco looking at me curiously. "What do you have there?"

I had brought along the information that Aunt Julia had given me, still unsure of whether I should share it or not. Now that everyone was staring at me with interest, I guessed I had no choice. I looked at the papers in my hand and then at the others before responding, "Maybe we should all go sit down inside."

As we all sat around the kitchen table, I shared with them what Aunt Julia had told me about my family ties to the Henningers and the Berkeleys, and my questions about whether those ties could be fueling my involvement in this case.

When I finished, Drac was rubbing his chin and looking at Gabe, who had his arms crossed and appeared deep in thought. Chuck was staring at me open-mouthed, obviously shocked to discover we were distantly related. Rocco whistled softly and commented, "Boy, for a newbie, you sure have a way of complicating things, don't you?"

I glanced at him and gave him a tight-lipped smile, then turned back to Drac and Gabe, wondering what they were thinking.

Drac sat back, crossed his arms and looked at me. "My gut reaction is to think it's just a coincidence," he began. "But having actually been here and witnessing the things that happened to you, seeing the hunches you've had, I'm not so sure."

Gabe leaned forward to look more closely at the papers. "The idea does seem far-fetched, Kyr, but I don't think we can completely dismiss it." He raised his eyes to mine. "We're just going to have to see how things play out tonight."

Just then, we heard Lynette and Owen coming downstairs. As they came into the kitchen, Owen exclaimed, "Man, that back bedroom is crazy!" Seeing me, he stopped short, and he and Lynette said hello to me. He continued, "The whole time we were setting up, it was like someone was looking over my shoulder!"

Lynette added, "And the whole time we were up there, I felt like I wanted—no, *needed*—to get out of that room." She looked at me and said, "I can't believe you investigated that room alone *twice*!"

Gabe winked at me and interjected, "Well, Kyr is a gutsy woman. Did you know she's going to start her own supernatural sleuthing business?"

I quickly assured everyone that he was joking, even as I blushed at Lynette and Gabe's praises, but I also felt a jolt of fear as I remembered how dangerous the situation could have been. Then I shuddered as I realized that whatever spirit or spirits we were dealing with seemed to be getting stronger and more aggressive. I found myself dreading what we might encounter in the next few hours.

CHAPTER FOURTEEN

As soon as it got dark, we all got ready to go lights out. Drac said, "Okay, everyone, we're going to focus on the back bedroom, the back part of the basement, and the family graveyard; but if you have any gut feelings about other rooms in the house"—he paused to look at me—"or if anything leads you to another room, go for it. Chuck has given us freedom to investigate wherever we need to."

Gabe continued, "Lynette and Kyr, you need to be especially cautious tonight." He looked at me and then at Lynette. "Kyr already knows that Jeremiah Berkeley hated women, and she has already had a couple run-ins with him. Neither of you should be alone tonight. Really, *no one* should be alone tonight."

Before we started, Drac and Gabe went in to do an EMF sweep of the house. The rest of us waited at Center Command and watched the monitors. Lynette asked me, "So you're sure the spirit we're dealing with is this Jeremiah Berkeley?"

"Pretty sure." I responded, shuddering at the memory of his face. "I got a good look at his face when he materialized in that back bedroom, and then we found a photo of him in the attic—definitely the same guy."

"This could be a crazy night from what the boys said."

Rocco was about to say something when Owen exclaimed, "What the blazes? Is there someone sitting in that chair?"

Rocco, Lynette, and I crowded around the monitor as he pointed at the video feed from the back bedroom. Sure enough, we could see a shadowy figure in the chair by the bed, although we couldn't make out who or what it was. Keeping his eyes fixed on the monitor, Owen radioed for Drac and Gabe.

"Go for Drac," he responded. "What's up?"

"We're all watching the monitors down here. In the back bedroom, we see a figure sitting in that chair by the bed."

After a moment of silence, Drac said, "Copy that. We're in the living room right now, but we'll head up there right away and check it out."

A minute later, the figure in the chair vanished just as Drac and Gabe entered the bedroom. We saw them look around the room, and then walk slowly towards the chair, K-II extended. Drac radioed, "This chair?"

"Yeah, dang it." Owen pounded the table in frustration. "The figure disappeared right before you guys came in the room."

Drac approached the chair with the K-II. At first, we could see the K-II lighting up like crazy as if something were sitting there, but then suddenly the lights went dark. We heard Gabe say, "Man, that was crazy! Like there was something there, and it just—poof!"

Drac chuckled grimly. "Something is definitely already messing with us."

They spent a few minutes asking questions and trying to get the spirit to respond, to no avail. Finally, they came back down to Center Command. "So what's the plan, chief?" Rocco asked.

"Well, except for the K-II spike in the back bedroom, everything measured normally. No cold spots, no hot spots, no responses to our questions upstairs. Just seemed like a typical house."

"We'll just have to see what happens as we start investigating," Gabe said. "Are we ready to break into teams and get started?"

Everyone was anxious to begin. Drac looked at Lynette. "Ordinarily, I'd have you two ladies investigate together, but given the situation tonight, we're going to do things differently. Rocco and Owen, you can pair up as usual. Lynette will come with me, and Kyr can stick with Gabe."

Rocco and Owen headed for the back bedroom, while Drac and Lynette took the basement, and Gabe and I headed for the graveyard. As we walked up the hill in back of the house, Gabe commented, "I haven't actually investigated out here yet." He looked at me and smirked. "I only had the pleasure of pulling a hellhound off of Spook."

"Ha ha, very funny," I said, blushing and narrowing my eyes at him. "I'd rather forget about that, if you don't mind." I looked up at the tree and suddenly remembered the dream I'd had recently.

We stepped carefully among the gravestones, and Gabe asked, "Do you want to sit here and do an EVP session?"

I stood looking up at the tree, shining my light up into the branches, trying to figure out what the voice in my dream was telling me to do. When I didn't answer right away, Gabe came over to stand next to me and asked, "What are you looking at?"

I answered slowly, "Nothing really. Just thinking about . . ." I was going to say "my dream," but instead I finished, "the light Andy saw."

It was Gabe's turn to narrow his eyes at me. He seemed to sense there was something I wasn't telling him. I didn't want to tell him about my dream, even though I was certain it held an important clue. I had pulled Chuck aside before he went to the neighbor's house and asked him if he had told Drac and Gabe about his dreams. Chuck admitted that he too had felt foolish telling them about a dream, so he had kept it hidden. Now, I found myself wondering if maybe Chuck and I should have both come clean.

We sat down beneath the tree and began an EVP session. "Gabe and Kyr at the Berkeley mansion, in the family graveyard," I began. My eyes scanned the moonlit yard and the mansion windows, looking for anything out of the ordinary. "Is there anyone here with us?"

The only sound we heard was a dog barking somewhere in the distance, and I tried not to think about how creepy it sounded. I glanced over at Gabe, and he continued, "Our friend saw a light out here in the graveyard, up in the tree. Was that you? Do you need help?"

The dog stopped barking, and the night became eerily silent once again. Hearing no response to Gabe's question, I was about to pose another when we heard the faintest whisper close beside us.

Gabe and I faced each other and asked simultaneously, "What was that?"

Suddenly there was a bright flash above us. "What the Sam Hill; was that lightning?" Gabe asked, looking around.

"It couldn't be; there isn't a cloud in the sky."

Gabe shone his flashlight all around, trying to find a source for that light. When the flashlight beam illuminated the spot I had seen lit up in my dream, I was suddenly compelled to act. I sprang to my feet, jammed my flashlight into my back pocket, and began climbing the tree.

"Kyr, what are you doing?" As I glanced down at his puzzled face, I thought he looked as though he were trying to decide whether to climb up with me or try to stop me.

"Trust me," I replied. "There's something up here. I can feel it." I climbed easily to the first large branch, and took out my flashlight. Holding it clumsily in my mouth, I began feeling around on the trunk. When I came to a spot where the bark felt somehow different than the rest of the trunk, I began prying it off, a task that was much more difficult than I had anticipated. I laughed to myself, thankful that I wasn't one to spend a lot of time or money on manicures as JoEllyn did.

"Do you need some help?" Gabe asked, still looking puzzled.

"Ouch!" I exclaimed as I split a nail. Glancing at my scraped and bleeding fingers, I called down, "Do you have anything on you that I can use to pry away this bark?"

In the dim light, I could see him fumbling in his jeans pocket. He found what he was searching for and handed a well-worn pocketknife up to me. "Aha, this Boy Scout is prepared!" he quipped.

I opened the knife and began chipping away at the bark. Soon I found a deep depression in the trunk that had been overgrown with bark. "Is this it?" I asked no one in particular, and began feverishly chopping and pulling away the remaining bark.

"What have you got?" Gabe asked, pacing around the base of the tree like a hunting dog.

"There's a hole or something in the trunk," I panted. "I think there's something hidden here." I pulled the bark away till I had a hole big enough to shine my flashlight into. I gasped as I saw the glint of metal in my beam. I had a hunch that I knew what it was, but I couldn't be sure till I got it out.

"What is it?" Gabe asked, concerned. "Are you all right?"

"I'm fine." I snapped the pocketknife shut and handed it back to Gabe. Yanking my bandana out of my hair, I untied it and reached into the hole. My hands were shaking as I grasped the heavy object and pulled it out. I let out a squeal as I realized I was holding a very large knife whose blade was covered with something. My stomach lurched as I wondered if it was decades-old blood.

I felt Gabe's hand on my foot. "Kyr, are you all right? What did you find?"

I couldn't answer him, so I leaned over and handed him the knife wrapped in my bandana. He took it and unwrapped it. "Oh my . . . Are you serious?" Gabe exclaimed. "This is a huge discovery!"

After looking to make sure there was nothing else crammed into the hole, I moved to climb down the tree. Suddenly, right next to my ear, I heard a growl, and then felt a shove that was hard enough to make me lose my balance and start to fall. I tried to grasp the trunk, a branch, anything to keep me from tumbling, but to no avail. I yelled and fell head first from the tree. I put up my hands to try to break my fall, and I felt Gabe trying to catch me. My head hit his as I fell, and we both ended up on the ground beneath the tree.

When I opened my eyes, Gabe was above me checking my arms and legs for broken bones. "Kyr, are you hurt? What happened?"

I sat up shakily and answered, "I'm fine, just shaken." I rubbed my forehead where I had hit Gabe's head and looked into his eyes. "Gabe, something pushed me out of that tree."

Gabe looked back at me, shining his flashlight into my eyes. "Your pupils are even. What do you mean something pushed you? Are you sure you didn't just lose your balance?"

I shoved his hand away to get the light out of my eyes. "*Gabe!* I mean it! Something *pushed* me! I felt it! And before that there was a loud growl right in my ear. You didn't hear that?"

He shook his head. "No, I didn't hear anything."

I threw my hands up in frustration. "I heard it; I know I did," I said. "Wait!" I cried, looking around. "Where's the voice recorder? Maybe we caught it on there."

"Oh snap," Gabe said. "Is that still running?" He felt around the base of the tree till he found it. "Here it is." He rewound it, and we sat and listened to see what we had caught.

We heard our initial questions, the dog in the distance, and then the faint whisper we had both heard. It sounded very close to the microphone. Gabe rewound it and played it a couple times. Gabe said, "I hear 'Find . . . it'? Is that what you hear?" He played it again.

"No," I replied. "Not find *it*. Find *me*. It says, 'Find *me*.'" Suddenly I felt cold, as cold as I had felt after my first run-in with Jeremiah Berkeley. I looked at Gabe, sensing we were on the brink of discovering the key to the Berkeley mansion haunting.

I was about to say something when a flash of headlights in the driveway blinded me. Gabe glanced at me and said, "Not a moment too soon."

CHAPTER FIFTEEN

Gabe helped me stand up, and then stood close to steady me, with one arm around my waist and his other hand grasping my arm. When he was satisfied that I wasn't going to topple over, he released my arm so he could radio the others to meet Steele at Center Command. Gabe kept his arm around me as we walked down the hill towards the driveway, where Steele had just gotten out of his car. My heart started beating double-time as he flipped his hair out of his eyes and looked towards us. As his eyes met mine, the corners of his mouth curved up in a half smile, and I unconsciously bit my lip and reached up to twirl the end of my braid around my finger as I tentatively smiled back at him. *Oh my goodness,* my mind screamed suddenly. *Why am I acting as though I were attracted to Steele?*

Caught off guard by that ludicrous notion, I neglected to watch my footing, and I stumbled over a rock in the dark. As I landed hard on my hands and knees, Steele took a quick step forward to help me, but Gabe was quicker. He knelt down and helped me to my feet, keeping an arm around me. I glanced sheepishly at Steele, embarrassed over my clumsiness and hoping he hadn't read in my eyes the reason for that clumsiness. As my eyes met his, I was taken aback by the smoldering anger I saw in them. After I assured Gabe that I was all right, he went forward quickly to exchange some light-hearted words with Steele, completely unaware of the brief but intense storm that had just passed between us.

I slowly and quietly inched my way over to the van and stood watching the two chat away as though nothing unusual had just happened. The front door opened, and Drac and Lynette, and then Rocco and Owen came out onto the porch and headed out to greet Steele. I tried to hang back inconspicuously, out of Steele's radar, but Gabe would have none of that. He called out, "Hey Kyr, why are you hiding? Come on down and join us." I reluctantly moved towards the others, still feeling the heat of Steele's glare and wondering what had caused his sudden animosity. By the time I reached Gabe, who threw an arm around my shoulders and raised a curious eyebrow at me, Drac had stepped forward and tried to put Steele into a headlock. After they scuffled for a moment, Steele shot me a look of disdain before turning to admire Owen's new tattoo. Then he high-fived Rocco and hugged Lynette before turning back to Drac.

Before Steele could say anything, Gabe propelled me forward and joked, "Spook, don't you want to say hello to Kyr?"

Steele turned to Gabe with irritation in his eyes before shifting his gaze to me and saying curtly, "Carter. Didn't get enough last time?"

I got enough of you last time, I thought irritably, narrowing my eyes at him. "Steele," I replied. "I can handle more than you think I can." I hoped I wouldn't have to prove that.

I stepped backwards to stand behind Lynette, while Drac and Gabe looked at each other with grim resignation. By the way Lynette, Rocco, and Owen were exchanging looks, I assumed they didn't know that Steele and I hadn't exactly hit it off. Drac was the first to recover. He cleared his throat and said, "Okay team, let's regroup and share experiences so far. Rocco, Owen, anything in that back bedroom?"

Rocco responded, "We had a couple random K-II spikes, but nothing in response to our questions." He glanced uneasily at Drac. "Now, you know I don't usually say this, but I honestly don't like that room at all. Something in there just doesn't feel right."

Owen jumped in, "Yeah, just like when Lynette and I set up in there, it just felt uncomfortable, like there was something that didn't want us in there."

"I got the sense something was waiting." Rocco shook his head slightly, crossing his arms in front of him. I shuddered, knowing exactly what it was waiting for.

Lynette jumped in next. "The basement was kind of quiet for a while, but then things suddenly got crazy about fifteen minutes ago."

"What do you mean by crazy?" Steele asked, a spark of interest lighting up his dark eyes.

Lynette replied, "The room started to feel . . . I don't know, charged. Like Rocco said, almost like something was waiting—"

"And whispers," Drac interjected. "We started hearing whispers all around us. We caught them on the voice recorder, but it was hard to make out what they were saying."

Gabe caught my eye and raised an eyebrow at me as if encouraging me to say something. I involuntarily glanced over at Steele before lowering my head. After our tense exchange, I just didn't feel comfortable speaking up. Gabe told Drac, "We caught a whisper too. It said 'Find me.'"

"Find me?" Drac asked, leaning against the hood of Steele's car. "Find who?"

Gabe shrugged and looked back at me, waiting for me to say something. When I again remained silent, he continued, "That's not the craziest thing. Kyr had another one of her hunches, and she climbed up in that tree and found this huge knife hidden inside the tree . . ." He turned abruptly to me and asked, "Kyr, where is that knife?"

"Oh," I answered, suddenly remembering we'd left it in the graveyard when Steele arrived. "I guess it's still by the tree. I'll go get it." I started back towards the graveyard before anyone could say anything else, glad to be away from Steele for the moment. I swore I could feel his eyes on me as I walked away from the others. Having the sudden fear that the knife might mysteriously vanish before I got there, I quickened my pace. To my relief, I found it lying on the ground right where Gabe had dropped it when I landed on top of him. I made sure it was still wrapped tightly in my bandana as I snatched it up and headed back towards the front of the house.

When I got out front, I heard Drac and Steele talking. "Do you really think she was pushed?" Steele said doubtfully. "More likely she lost her damn balance and fell."

Hearing his words, I felt my face grow red. I handed the knife to Gabe, then glared at Steele and said, "No, Steele, I was *pushed*, right after I found that knife hidden in the trunk."

"Oh, I see you finally found your tongue," Steele responded sarcastically. "You know, you ought to—"

Gabe cut in. "Kyr also said she heard a growl right before she was pushed." He thought for a second and said, "Oh snap, that's what we were listening for when we heard that other whisper. I forgot about that." He suggested we all listen to what we had caught on the voice recorder. I got the feeling he was trying to diffuse the tension that had sprung up between Steele and myself.

We all headed back to Center Command, and Gabe set up the computer to play the voice recording. We all gathered around to listen. Drac and Steele moved closer as the whisper came through the speaker. "Right there; that's it!" Gabe said.

Rocco rewound the tape and looped the whisper. "Find me . . . Find me . . . Find me . . . Find me."

Drac stood back and crossed his arms. "That's crazy."

Steele nodded and admitted, "Downright creepy." He ran his fingers through his wavy chestnut brown hair, making it stand up in front, then looked at Gabe. "Did you say you heard a growl? When was that?"

"I didn't hear the growl," Gabe responded, looking at me. "Kyr's the only one who heard it, right before she fell out of the tree."

Steele grunted, then turned to look at me. Out of the corner of my eye I noticed Drac raise an eyebrow at him. "It was right after I handed you the knife," I said to Gabe.

Rocco continued playing the conversation between Gabe and me as I removed the bark and found the hole where the knife had been hidden. We all listened intently for any other sounds or whispers that might suggest there had been a spirit present with us, but no one heard anything unusual. That is, until we got to the point where I was ready to climb down the tree.

"Oh my . . . Are you serious?" Gabe's voice said. "This is a huge discovery!" We heard the rustling sounds of my checking in the hole for other objects and then my moving to climb down. Suddenly on the tape, there was a low guttural sound, followed by my yell and the sound of me falling. The hair on the back of my neck stood up. The sound was chilling, but relief flowed through me that we had caught the sound on tape.

"Is that it?" Drac asked, moving close to the computer.

I nodded, then responded shakily, "It sounded a lot louder when I heard it. It was right by my ear."

Again, Rocco looped the sound, and we all listened, trying to find some reasonable explanation for what might have made that noise. No one could come up with any other options, and Owen spoke for everyone when he said, "Man, that was creepy!"

Lynette added, "If the spirit really did growl at you and then actually pushed you . . . that's crazy!"

Drac said, "Well, that's why we brought Spook back. From what Chuck said, and from what we—especially Kyr—have experienced, this spirit is getting stronger and more malicious."

Steele was standing with his hands on his hips, deep in thought. The slight breeze coming in the back of the van blew his hair into his dark eyes, but he didn't seem to notice. I found myself wondering why I did. At last he looked up, as though he just remembered where he was. "Drac, did you and Lynette say you caught some whispers? Can we listen to those?"

Drac shrugged and handed Rocco the tape from his digital voice recorder. He rewound the tape and then played it from the beginning. Just as Lynette had said, everything was quiet at first; all we heard were Drac and Lynette's questions and the sounds of them moving around in the basement. Almost an hour into their session, we heard Lynette ask, "Wow, did the atmosphere just change in here?"

"You're not kidding," Drac responded. "The air feels charged. EMF readings are going up too."

As we continued listening, we began to hear the whispers Drac and Lynette had mentioned. As they had told us, most of the whispers were unintelligible; we could tell they were voices, but we couldn't make out any words or phrases no matter how many times Rocco replayed them. Finally, one voice stood out. As Rocco replayed that part of the tape, we heard a whisper quite close to the microphone. Steele said, "It sounds like there are definite words there." He looked at Rocco and asked, "Can you clean that one up a bit?"

"Sure can," Rocco replied casually and made some adjustments on the computer. When he finished, he sat back and replayed the tape.

"No way!" Gabe exclaimed. "No friggin' way!"

He and Drac stared at each other in disbelief, Owen let out a low whistle, and Lynette stood shaking her head. A chill had raced down my spine as soon as I heard the words, and my eyes searched all their faces, waiting for someone to say something.

"That's just nuts!" Steele said. "'Find me.' The same words you and . . . Carter . . . heard in the graveyard," he said to Gabe.

I glared at Steele, hearing the tone of his voice as he said my name, but I decided to ignore it. Instead I said to Rocco, "Is there any way we can check time stamps to see if we heard those voices at the same time?"

"I'm on it," Rocco responded, and turned quickly to the computer again. A moment later, he muttered, "Very interesting . . ."

Drac leaned in and asked, "Whatcha got, bro?"

"Good hunch, Kyr," Rocco said, pointing to the computers. "Here's the time stamp for the whisper Kyr and Gabe heard in the graveyard, and here's the time stamp for Drac and Lynette in the basement."

Drac stroked his goatee as he looked at the time stamps. "Exact same time stamp," he said, looking back at Gabe. "You thinking what I'm thinking?"

Gabe was standing with his arms crossed in front of him. His eyes met mine for a moment, and then he looked back at Drac and replied, "Well, we've already got a knife. I'm thinking we need to see what's happening in the basement."

Chuck's dream suddenly came to mind, and I had a sickening feeling that I knew where to look and what they'd find there. Gabe must have noticed, because he touched my shoulder and asked, "Kyr? You okay? You have that look again . . ."

My eyes met his, and I didn't know what to do. I had already had one hunch pay off in finding the knife in the tree, but I was hesitant to tell them about the dreams Chuck and I had had. But what if those dreams were significant? My dream had provided an important clue; what if Chuck's held one as well?

Steele made a sound as though he were going to say something, but I saw Drac put a hand on his shoulder and shake his head to discourage him. Steele pursed his lips and said nothing, although I could see the impatience burning in his eyes.

I closed my eyes for a second and then let out a breath. Steele already had a low opinion of me, so whatever I said wouldn't make a difference one way or the other for him. I had already told Drac about the other dream I'd had; would he think I was crazy or making it up if I told him about this dream? I finally decided to come clean. My eyes met Drac's, and I began, "Well, you remember back at the first investigation, I told you about that dream I had?"

Drac nodded then briefly glanced at Gabe and barely managed to suppress a grin. My eyes quickly went to Gabe's face; his expression was a mixture of amusement and embarrassment, and he avoided my gaze. I tried to will away the flush I felt creeping into my cheeks as I continued, "I've had a few more since then; that's how I knew about the knife." I briefly told them about the dreams I had after the first investigation and the vivid one I'd had after Aunt Julia gave me the genealogical information. I finished by telling them, "Chuck told me he had a dream about the basement, that there may be something . . . or someone . . . buried under the coal heap. He suspects it may be Benjamin Holtzman."

After I finished, the silence was deafening. Everyone was looking at everyone else with skeptical curiosity. Rocco was first to speak. "Wow, Kyr, those are some crazy claims," he said, crossing his arms and leaning back in his chair.

"I know," I answered shakily. "That's why neither Chuck nor I wanted to say anything. It just seems unbelievable."

"Well," Drac said, "crazy and unbelievable or not, it seems we need to check out the basement more carefully." He was about to split us up into teams and begin investigating again when Steele spoke up.

"Drac, Gabe, could I speak to you? Privately?" he asked, glaring in my direction.

Drac and Gabe looked at each other as though they'd been expecting this, and then Drac motioned for Steele to lead the way. The three of them walked back towards the graveyard, and the rest of us watched as they had a rather heated discussion. The few snatches of conversation that made their way to us confirmed my suspicion that the conversation was about me. Steele was saying, ". . . imagination running away with her . . . just a groupie wanting attention . . . can't believe you're buying her BS . . . Gabe, you can't be that blind . . ."

Drac and Gabe responded to his arguments, and it was obvious that they were also becoming increasingly agitated. ". . . need to adjust your attitude . . . your own imagination is running away . . . you're not the only one . . . you should know me better than that . . ."

I turned and walked to the front porch, where I sank down on the bottom step and buried my head in my hands. I heard footsteps coming towards me and felt a hand on my shoulder. Lynette sat down on the step next to me and asked, "Are you all right, Kyr?"

I nodded and looked up at her. "What is his problem anyway?" I asked tensely. "I never asked for any of this."

Lynette laughed and replied, "Spook does have an attitude till you get to know him." She craned her neck towards the graveyard and continued, "He prides himself on being skeptical and detached. Sometimes he takes it a bit too far."

I'd like to detach his head from his shoulders. I raised my head to look at her. "Be honest, Lynette. What do you think? Am I crazy? Is it all in my head?"

She turned her eyes back to me. "I don't think you're crazy, and I don't think you're making it up. I have no idea what's going on; even Drac and Gabe are stumped. They want to debunk all this stuff, but . . ." She threw up her hands and shook her head.

I stood up and started pacing back and forth. I was about to say something when I noticed Drac, Gabe, and Steele heading back towards Center Command. Lynette got up and started in that direction, and after a moment's hesitation, I followed.

Back at Center Command, the tension was obvious. There was a lingering uneasiness between Steele, Drac, and Gabe, and Rocco and Owen seemed to not know where to look. Drac glanced at Steele and then back at me; then he cleared his throat and said almost forcefully, "Okay guys, let's get back to business. Rocco and Owen, I want you in the basement. Focus on the area around the coal pile. I'm going to touch base with Chuck to see what he wants done if we find anything. Gabe and Kyr, I want you in the back bedroom; it seems something is just waiting to happen up there. Be sure to stay together. No one—especially Kyr—is to be alone in that room. I'll stay at Center Command with Lynette and Spook to monitor things. We'll move in if anyone needs help."

Everyone nodded as Drac gave the assignments, and we quickly moved to begin investigating again. As we made our way to the house, Rocco joked, "Off to the basement we go. Spiders and snakes and bugs, oh my."

Owen and Gabe laughed out loud, but I rolled my eyes. I admired Rocco's bravery when dealing with ghosts, but I was in just as much awe of his fear of creepy-crawlers, especially considering that he worked in pest control.

Gabe and I headed up the stairs to the second floor. As I looked into the darkness, I had a feeling that the darkness in the back hallway was even darker. About halfway up the stairs, I hesitated, grabbing the railing and trying to see if anything was standing at the top of the staircase. The air felt colder to me, and I released the banister and flexed my cold fingers.

"You okay?" Gabe asked, coming up beside me.

"Yeah," I responded. "It just feels different in here already. Definitely *not* friendly." I was glad he was standing right beside me, and I fought the urge to lean into him.

Gabe pulled out his thermometer and walked slowly down the stairs and back up again. "The temperature drops almost eight degrees between the bottom of the stairs and where you're standing," he said. "Shall we keep going?"

I gave myself a little shake and said, "Let's do this."

We reached the top of the stairs and headed back the hallway towards the back bedroom. Just as I had the day we went to the attic to find Belle-Anne's journal, I felt as though something waited at the end of that hallway, something evil. As we got to the bedroom door, I stepped aside to let Gabe go ahead of me. He passed in front of me, then turned, smirked, and asked, "A little nervous?"

"Not really," I lied. "You've got the thermometer; I thought you'd want a reading before I went into the room."

Gabe stifled a laugh and responded, "If you say so." He made his way into the room and paused, moving the thermometer around in front of him. "Whoa!" he said suddenly, making me take a quick step backwards.

"What?" I asked. "What happened?"

Gabe moved further into the room before answering, "The temperature drops another four or five degrees in here."

I came into the room and instantly felt on edge. I knew without a doubt that something was going to happen tonight, something significant, and I shivered at the thought. "Well, should we do some EVP work?" I asked Gabe.

He was fumbling in his pocket, and he replied, "Hang on a sec. I want to get some EMF readings. Go ahead and get the digital voice recorder set up." While I did that, Gabe moved around the room with the EMF meter. "Huh," he muttered.

"What?" I asked again, turning towards him.

"This room is buzzing," he said. "It was almost flat when we were in here before the investigation. Now it's crazy all over the room."

After looking over his shoulder at the EMF meter, I sat down on the bed where I had sat when I did the other EVP sessions. "Hello? Is there anyone here with us?" I asked. "I'm sure you remember us; that's Gabe, and I'm Kyr."

The room remained quiet and cold, and the EMF readings stayed solidly high. I still felt as though someone or something was waiting, and I kept fighting the urge to look over my shoulder. A faint buzzing began in my ears, and I shook my head, unsuccessfully trying to get rid of it. Gabe shook his head as well and poked his finger in his ear; obviously he was feeling the same thing. Even in the dim moonlight coming through the window and the glow coming from our equipment, I could see tension around his dark eyes.

"Come on, now," Gabe said, coming over to sit next to me on the bed. "If you've got something to say, say it. Don't let me stop you."

"Why won't you show yourself when Gabe is here?" I challenged. "Are you afraid of him?" I got up and walked towards the door.

Gabe noticed where I was moving and called out, "You've shown us you can slam that door. Can you do that for us now?"

The door didn't move, and aside from the high EMFs and the uncomfortable atmosphere in that room, everything stayed eerily quiet. After a few more minutes of futile questioning, I looked over at Gabe and sighed in frustration. He chuckled. "Welcome to ghost hunting."

I laughed shortly, remembering what JoEllyn had always told me. Suddenly, Drac's voice crackled over the walkie. "Drac for Gabe and Kyr."

"Go for Gabe and Kyr," Gabe responded.

"It seems kind of quiet up there," Drac replied. "You two sleeping?"

Gabe joked, "So tell us something we don't know. Except for a temperature drop and high EMFs all over this room, it's been dead. How are things in the basement?"

Owen's voice came over the walkie, "We've had some bangs and whispers. EMFs are really spiking around the coal bin. We're in the process of trying to move the bin out of the way to see if there's anything under it. Good thing there's not a lot of coal in here."

"Copy that," Drac said. "Chuck is on his way down here. He wants to hang out in case we find something significant."

"That's cool," Owen responded.

"Hey Gabe?" Drac called.

"Go for Gabe," he replied, reclining on the bed.

"Keep trying to make contact. Tell Kyr not to hesitate to provoke the spirit. She's had some luck with that before."

"Copy that," Gabe responded. He glanced over at me with a smirk. "Should I come down to Center Command and leave her alone in the room?"

I leaned over and thumped him hard in the ribs. "You wouldn't dare!"

Drac laughed over the walkie and replied, "Nah, we may need her for bait later."

"Kyr, you know I wouldn't do that to you again." Gabe sat up, and his eyes met mine as he teased, "Not here anyway."

"Don't even joke about that," I responded, shaking. I made a face at him and mimicked his last comment. "Not here anyway."

Gabe laughed and gave me a playful shove. He was just about to say something when Owen's excited voice came over the walkie again. "Owen to Drac."

We heard Drac respond, "Go for Drac."

"You're not going to believe this," Owen said quickly. "We managed to move the coal bin about a foot, and the EMF readings are off the charts. What are the chances that something is buried here?"

I didn't know if the room got even colder or if a chill raced down my spine at his words, but I sat frozen as I stared open-mouthed at Gabe. He returned my stare and was about to radio back to Owen when all hell broke loose.

CHAPTER SIXTEEN

Without warning, the door slammed shut, and a deep growl filled the room. I ran to the door, knowing even as I did that it would be locked. I fumbled with the doorknob, trying to get it open, but to no avail. Gabe hurried to my side and tried the door too. When he couldn't open it either, he turned to me to say something. I didn't even wait for him to speak; I just threw myself into his arms and hid my face in his shoulder. He put his arms around me for a moment, whispering softly into my hair, trying to calm me. The walkie suddenly crackled, and Drac's voice boomed out, "Gabe! Owen! Rocco! What's happening? We just lost video in both the bedroom and the basement!"

Gabe let go of me and grabbed his walkie. "Drac, something's happening up here. As soon as Owen said they found something, the door slammed shut and we heard a loud growl."

Owen's voice confirmed, "Dude, we heard that too, down here!"

I opened my eyes and looked hesitantly around the room. While nothing tangible had changed, the atmosphere had gone from uncomfortable to downright threatening, and I couldn't help thinking it felt as though we were in a trap. I edged away from Gabe towards the corner; I felt somewhat safer there. I kept staring at the furniture, trying to suppress the childish nightmare fear of the furniture coming to life and attacking.

Owen's voice came over the walkie again. "Hey guys, something is happening down here too. Temperatures are dropping fast—"

Suddenly we heard Rocco's voice in the background. "What the Sam Hill?"

"Rocco, Owen, what's going on?" Drac asked.

"Man, we're getting pelted with chunks of coal," Owen responded. "Something really doesn't--Ouch, dammit!—want us here."

Steele's urgent voice suddenly broke in, "Okay, everyone out of the house, *now*! I need to get in there and deal with this thing."

"Copy that," Owen answered. "We're outta here."

Gabe moved towards the corner and stood with me. "Well, Spook, we've got a problem with that—we're locked in."

"Sit tight; we'll get you out," Drac radioed. "Hey Kyr, stay cool, at least you're not alone this time."

Small comfort. I looked at Gabe, studying his face as his eyes darted around the room. I could still see the tension around his eyes; he was definitely concerned, but he didn't seem to be frightened. At that moment, I didn't know if I thought he was brave or just crazy. He turned to me and saw me staring at him. He gave me a curious half smile. "What's that look for?"

I stared at him a second more, then glanced around the room again. "Aren't you afraid? Even a little?"

His eyes followed mine around the room before he responded, "I'm honestly not real comfortable in this room right now, but I'm not actually scared."

I shook my head in disbelief and crossed my arms in front of me to stop my trembling. In the back of my mind I heard my father and my childhood pastor both telling me that all spirits were demons in disguise. The way I felt right now, I was almost convinced they were correct. "I'm glad *you're* not."

As if he read my thoughts, he moved closer to me and put his hand on my shoulder. "Come on, Kyr, it'll be all right. Remember, this spirit is just a person without a body." He gave a short laugh. "An *angry* person, but a person just the same."

I gave him a tight-lipped smile and tried to joke, "It's the angry part that scares me."

Gabe chuckled then said to me, seriously, "You've got to overcome that. This spirit can feed off your fear. You've stood up to Jeremiah before, and he backed off. Just keep standing up to your fear; don't let it beat you."

I knew Gabe was giving me good advice, but it was hard not being afraid when we were locked in a room with an angry, unfriendly spirit. Without thinking, I voiced my biggest fear about the situation. "He knows we know the truth about what happened, and he wants to make sure no one finds the proof."

Gabe turned towards me again, and his dark eyes met mine. He grasped my shoulders firmly and said, "Come on, Kyr. Get a hold of yourself. Nothing's going to—"

A large ceramic decorative stein that had been sitting on top of the dresser suddenly flew across the room towards us. Just in time, I screamed, "Gabe, look out!" and shoved him out of the way. Ceramic shards exploded around us as the stein hit the wall right next to where Gabe's head had been.

"Holy crap!" Gabe exclaimed, brushing ceramic pieces and dust off his shirt. "This is getting personal."

"Ya think?" I edged my way out of the corner, no longer feeling safe there, but I wasn't sure where to go. I couldn't silence the idea that we were trapped with a very angry, very vengeful spirit who had no qualms about hurting one of us.

"Come on, Jeremiah, why won't you talk to us?" Gabe coaxed, shining his flashlight around the room. "Throwing things at us isn't going to solve anything."

I was just about to say something when another growl filled the room. At that moment, a loud knock sounded on the door. I let out a startled cry, not knowing whether I was more startled by the growl or the knock. We heard Steele's voice on the other side of the door, "Gabe, Carter, you okay?"

"Yeah, we're having a blast," Gabe responded jokingly. "Come on in and join the party."

Another angry growl filled the room as Steele tried the door. "What the hell is going on in there?" he asked.

"Jeremiah didn't like my joke," Gabe said, grasping the doorknob and trying the door again.

"Yeah, he doesn't have much of a sense of humor," I added, moving back towards the door. The hair on the back of my neck stood up, and I sensed we were in for more than a few growls. "Not to mention he's pretty antisocial."

The sound of the vanity shaking made both Gabe and me turn quickly. Just as Gabe aimed his flashlight in that direction, the mirror detached itself from the vanity and fell over, shattering all over the floor.

"This is not good," Gabe muttered. I turned to him, definitely hearing the edge of fear in his voice. He turned back towards the door and redoubled his efforts to open it.

Steele pounded on the door again and asked anxiously, "What was that? Gabe, what the hell is going on?"

Still trying to open the door, Gabe grunted, "The mirror on the vanity just came off and shattered all over the floor. We gotta get out of here; Jeremiah means business!"

We heard Steele radio to Drac. "Hey, Drac, is everyone out of the basement?"

"Yeah," he responded. "Rocco and Owen are at Center Command with me and Lynette. What's going on?"

I screamed as a picture flew off the opposite wall and across the room to smash against the door. "Geez!" Gabe exclaimed, throwing his arms up in front of him. "He really does mean business!"

"Drac, you need to get up here," Steele said tensely. We could hear him trying to force the door open. "We've got to get them out of that room."

We heard Drac respond, "I'm on my way," before our walkie went dead.

The air in the room seemed to get thicker. I thought I could see a darkness forming in the corner by the dresser, and I wondered if Jeremiah was about to show himself. As I peered in that direction, I noticed the dresser begin to shake. My breath caught in my throat and I couldn't speak, so I grabbed Gabe's arm and gestured towards the dresser. Just as Gabe turned to see what I was pointing at, the drawers flew out of the dresser, one by one, aimed right at us. We both yelled and dove towards the corner, but we were unable to avoid being hit by the drawers.

"Oh man, that's going to leave a mark," Gabe grunted, straightening up and shoving the drawers out of the way. "You all right?" he asked, laying a hand on my arm.

I looked up at him, still unable to speak, and nodded. My eyes widened as I looked towards the frame of the dresser and saw it moving. I screamed and ducked, pulling Gabe down with me as the dresser frame flew across the room. At the last second, Gabe threw himself on top of me to shield me, just as the dresser hit the wall and crashed down on top of us.

I felt the weight of Gabe's body on top of me and opened my eyes to look at him. His face was only inches from mine, and he was straddling me beneath the heavy piece of furniture. "Sorry, Kyr, didn't mean to get fresh with you," he joked, trying to turn himself to push the dresser off of him so he could get up.

I finally found my voice. "Yeah, well, I'll forgive you this time." Even as frightened as I was I laughed to myself over the irony of the situation. I had dreamed of being this close to Gabe Petery for years, but I never thought it would be like this.

Gabe managed to shove the dresser off of him and get himself into a kneeling position. I sat up slowly too, pushing away pieces of drawers and scattered clothes. Gabe stood up and extended his hand to help me up. It was then that we realized Drac and Rocco were on the other side of the door with Steele, and they were pounding on the door and calling to us. "Gabe! Kyr! Answer me, are you okay?"

"Yeah," Gabe responded shakily. "Yeah, we're okay. Shook-up, but okay." He was trying to move the dresser frame and drawers away from the door.

Drac shouted, "What the hell is going on in there, bro?"

Gabe called back, "Stuff is flying all over the room, Drac." He looked over his shoulder and continued, "That loud crash was the dresser attacking us."

The door began to rattle again as they tried to get inside the room. Drac's voice came through the door. "Gabe, you and Kyr need to stand back. I didn't want to have to do this but we're going to break down the door."

"Hang on, Drac," Gabe called back. "We've got to move this stuff away from the door. It's like Jeremiah is trying to barricade us in here."

Gabe and I both began moving things away from the door. The drawers and piles of clothes weren't hard to move, but the dresser frame was heavier than it looked, and we knew it would take both of us to move it across the carpeted floor. I kept glancing over my shoulder, sensing that Jeremiah wasn't done with us yet.

As we began moving the dresser frame across the floor, I said low, "So, do you still think nothing's going to happen?"

Gabe let out a long breath and was about to answer when we heard a sudden sound behind us. In the seconds that followed, so many things happened at once. I heard simultaneously another loud growl fill the room and Gabe yelling behind me. I felt the sharp pain of something hitting my head, and just before I lost consciousness, the sharp smell of coal oil filled my nostrils.

The next few hours were a blur of sounds and images, none of which was very clear, even days afterwards. I heard shouts from Gabe, Drac, Steele, and Rocco. I saw faces illuminated by flames. I smelled smoke and burning cloth and flesh. I had the sensation of being carried, and I was aware that both my arm and my head hurt. Everything went black again, and when I awoke, I saw flashing red lights and heard sirens.

***

When I finally came around, I was in a hospital bed. I squinted at the lights, which seemed to be too bright, and looked around. A thin, light blue curtain was drawn around the bed. I was hooked up to an EKG machine and a blood pressure monitor, and a rough blanket was pulled up to my waist. I looked down at my arm, which was bandaged from my wrist all the way to my shoulder. I was suddenly aware that it hurt badly, and I wondered what had happened. Suddenly realizing that I was in the ER and I was alone, I tried to sit up, but quickly lay back down and groaned as my head began to throb and the room began to spin.

A stern-faced nurse peeked in the doors and said a bit too loudly, "Oh good, you're awake. How are you feeling?"

I considered the question for a moment before responding, "I feel like I got hit by a truck. What happened? I don't remember how I got here."

"Well, honey, you were in a fire; that's how your arm got burned," the nurse explained, checking the EKG and the blood pressure monitor. "And you took a pretty nasty hit to the head. The doctor will probably keep you overnight to monitor you and run some tests. I'll get you something for the pain and let your friends know you're awake."

She exited the room before I could say anything more. I closed my eyes and let my head fall back on the pillow. I tried unsuccessfully to remember what had taken place and how I had gotten to the hospital. I recalled being at the Berkeley mansion and being trapped in the back bedroom while things flew around the room. I also remembered that Gabe had been with me, but I didn't know if he was all right. I barely had time to worry, before there was a tap on the sliding glass door.

Drac peeked around the curtain. "Hey, sweetheart," he said softly, coming into the room. "How are you feeling?"

Gabe came in right behind him and added, "Hey, Kyr. Man, did you give us a scare."

They sat down next to me. "How are you doing?" Drac repeated.

"I feel like I got hit by a truck," I answered slowly. "Or a dresser," I added, looking at Gabe and suddenly remembering that bit of information. I noticed that Gabe's face and clothes were smudged with smoke, and he had a cut on his forehead. "What happened?" I asked. "I can't remember much."

Drac and Gabe both grinned at my joke, then exchanged a serious look as though they weren't sure how much to tell me. Finally Gabe asked, "How much do you remember?"

I closed my eyes for a moment, then opened them and looked at Gabe again. "We were in that bedroom. Stuff flying everywhere . . . hitting us. Someone . . . Steele . . . trying to get us out." I paused, trying to remember. I shook my head, then wished I hadn't, gritting my teeth against the pain. "Something hit me on the head. All I have after that are flashes of images . . . flames . . . smoke . . . faces . . . "

I looked at Drac and Gabe, pleading with my eyes for them to give me answers.

They exchanged a look again, as though they were uncertain how much I could handle hearing. Gabe finally said, "Well, the kerosene lantern that was on the desk was what hit you on the head. Kerosene went everywhere, mostly on you, and somehow a fire started. Your shirt caught fire, and I grabbed a blanket to smother it. You were on the floor unconscious before I could get the fire out."

I stared at Gabe as he spoke, then looked down at my arm, realizing how lucky I was that I hadn't been burned much worse. My fear must have shown on my face because Drac grasped Gabe's arm, and he said low, "Gabe, maybe that's enough for now."

"No!" I said quickly. "Gabe, please, I need to know what else happened. How bad was the fire? Was anyone else hurt? What about Jeremiah?"

Gabe reached out to grasp my arm, but stopped himself just in time and stroked my cheek with his thumb. "Shhh, take it easy. Rocco and Spook managed to break down the door; then Drac and I got the fire out. Spook carried you outside and tended to you till the ambulance came. No one else was hurt."

I looked at Gabe, confused. "Steele . . . did that . . . for me?" My brow furrowed, and my lower lip quivered with emotion. "He hates me."

Drac and Gabe both laughed, and Drac assured me, "He doesn't hate you, Kyr. He was just convinced you were . . . an overzealous fan—"

"A groupie," I interrupted irritably, remembering Steele's words as he talked to Drac and Gabe.

Drac winced, realizing for the first time how much of their conversation with Steele I had overheard. "A groupie," he conceded. "Looking for attention or instant fame or . . ." The sudden flush that tinged Gabe's cheeks suggested that Steele knew of my feelings towards him and had said something about it.

"Why would he say something like that?" I demanded, ignoring the throbbing in my head as my anger flared. "Why would he think that when he doesn't even know me?"

Glancing nervously at the blood pressure monitor, Drac soothed, "Calm down, Kyr. Don't set off any alarms; I don't want that nurse on my ass."

Gabe laughed and continued, "Spook can be a little overzealous himself—"

"A little?" I interrupted, raising an eyebrow.

"Okay, maybe a lot," Gabe admitted. "Look, Spook has come in contact with more than his share of fakes and nutcases, and he's been the one to deal with some of the rabid fans who sometimes show up at the locations we investigate. Something just made him think you might be one of them." Gabe looked at me and grimaced apologetically. "I'm sorry. That sounded . . ."

"It's all right," I said. "I guess I understand. I was kind of acting like a starry-eyed fangirl . . . " I felt my face turn red as I realized what I had just said. I saw Drac and Gabe exchange a look and try to hide their smiles.

Thankfully, at that moment the nurse came in with some pills and a cup of water. I took them from her and swallowed the pills. "The doctor is doing his rounds," she told me. "He'll be in shortly to see you. He wants to run some tests to make sure your injuries aren't more serious than they look." She turned to Drac, narrowed her eyes and warned, "Don't you be getting her agitated or tire her out too much."

Drac smiled sheepishly and responded, "Yes ma'am. We won't."

Gabe avoided looking at Drac's face so he wouldn't laugh out loud as the nurse raised her eyebrow at Drac. She grunted, glared at him and left the room.

I looked back to Drac and Gabe and asked, "Jeremiah? What happened with Jeremiah?"

Gabe answered, "Spook stayed back at the mansion with Rocco, Owen, and Lynette. He's going to try to get rid of the spirit. He's hoping Chuck can go in with him so he can take back his house once and for all."

This still wasn't answering my question, so I asked outright, "What about the basement? Did you find anything?"

Drac shook his head. "No one can do anything in that basement until Jeremiah is gone. Spook is hoping to convince Jeremiah that it will be all right. The truth needs to come out; maybe that will help him rest."

Despite my less-than-favorable opinion of Steele at that moment, I found myself concerned for his safety, as well as Chuck's. I hoped he knew what he was doing.

CHAPTER SEVENTEEN

After visiting me in the ER that night, Drac called Aunt Julia to tell her what had happened. She was so upset that she rushed down to the hospital and gave Drac what-for right there in the ER waiting room. I laughed myself silly when one of the nurses told me that Aunt Julia was so angry that she had Drac cowering in one of the waiting room chairs as she yelled at him and hit him with her purse for not keeping me safe. Of course, she also gave me a stern lecture when she got to my room, and I hoped she wasn't going to become overprotective and forbid me to go on any more ghost hunts. I needn't have worried, however; once she got it out of her system, she calmed down and wanted to hear my side of what happened at the mansion.

It was quite late by the time Aunt Julia left and I was settled into a room for overnight observation. Of course, I got very little sleep as one nurse or another kept coming in to check on me.

First thing the next the next morning, Aunt Julia came bustling into my room; she wanted to be there to talk to the doctor before I was discharged. A few hours later, after the doctor had looked over my test results and given me the all-clear, I began to get ready to go home. Aunt Julia helped me get into my clothes, since I was still having trouble maneuvering my burned arm. As she pulled a black hoodie sweatshirt out of the closet and handed it to me, I realized it wasn't mine. "Hold on," I said to Aunt Julia. "Where did this come from? This isn't mine."

Aunt Julia held it up and looked at it, then looked back at me and asked, "You mean you've never seen this? Is everything else yours?"

I acknowledged that everything else was mine and looked back at her, confused. She examined the sweatshirt again, looking at the tags, and commented, "Well, it's definitely a man's sweatshirt." She suddenly grinned playfully and then winked at me before asking, "Is it Gabe's?"

I wrinkled my nose at her and replied, "No! Don't be silly. It's too big for Gabe anyway." I continued examining the sweatshirt and tried to think if I had seen it before. It suddenly dawned on me where I had seen that shirt before, and I felt my face growing red as I wondered how it had come into my possession.

Aunt Julia cocked her head curiously and said simply, "Kyr?"

I turned to her and said incredulously, "This is Steele's hoodie! He was wearing it when he arrived at the mansion." I tried unsuccessfully to recall how I had come into possession of Steele's hoodie, and I searched through the closet for my shirt and my bra. I turned again to Aunt Julia and stood shaking my head.

She looked back at me for a moment and then said with a twinkle in her eye, "So this Mr. Steele gave you his sweatshirt. That was sweet of him."

"Oh please," I snorted. "There is nothing sweet about that man at all! I told you, he's rude, arrogant . . . as big of a jerk as I have ever met. He made it quite clear that he can't stand me."

"Oh, come on, Kyr." Aunt Julia laughed, sounding like Drac and Gabe the previous night. "I'm sure he doesn't hate you. He did carry you down the stairs and out of the mansion. And he loaned you his sweatshirt."

I made a face at Aunt Julia and replied irritably, "He just didn't want it on his conscience if I died in a fire on an investigation on his watch." A sudden realization hit me as I pulled the hoodie clumsily over my head—What exactly had happened to my shirt and bra? Obviously someone had removed them. I had Steele's hoodie; had he partially undressed me at the mansion? The sudden thought of Steele seeing me half-naked made me shudder and then turn crimson with mortification.

Aunt Julia clucked her tongue at me, put her hands on her hips, and said, "Honestly, Kyr, he may not be the nicest person in the world, but you make him sound like a monster! He did save your life, so he can't be *that* bad!" She shook her head as she turned and began folding my hospital gown and pulling the sheets up neatly on the bed. "Sometimes you're so much like your father, seeing the worst in people!"

"Well, if you'd been there last night—through this whole investigation—and seen what he was like, you'd change your mind," I replied stubbornly. I watched Aunt Julia for a moment as she tightly tucked in the sheet and the blanket on the bed. "I may be like Daddy, but you're just like Grandma Carter, folding dirty laundry before it goes to the wash and making up a bed that's just going to be changed anyway!"

Aunt Julia stopped abruptly and looked down at the perfectly-made bed before turning to me sheepishly. Suddenly seeing the humor in the situation, we both laughed at our argument. "At least we come by our quirks honestly," Aunt Julia said.

Just as we finished gathering the rest of my things, there was a knock at the door. Thinking it was a nurse, I called, "Come in."

The door opened and Drac stuck his head in. "Hey, Kyr, we didn't wake you, did we?"

"Not at all; I'm awake," I responded as he and Gabe came in the room. "We're just waiting to sign the discharge papers and head home."

"That's good. I'm glad we didn't miss you," Drac said. Then he noticed Aunt Julia standing by the bed eyeing him sternly. He cleared his throat and greeted her uneasily, "Ms. Carter."

Aunt Julia's expression softened, and she laughed. "Good morning, Drac. Good morning, Gabe. Don't worry; I'm not going to bite your head off again."

Gabe laughed. "Not much scares Drac, but you had him shaking in his shoes last night." He looked at me and asked, "How are you feeling, Kyr?"

Still smirking at Drac's unease, I replied, "I've still got a nasty headache, and I need to figure out how to move my mummy arm, but I'll survive."

He smiled and answered, "Good. I . . . we all . . . feel terrible about what happened." He looked pleadingly at Aunt Julia and added, "Honestly, we have never had something like this happen, and for something like this to happen on Kyr's first investigation . . ." His voice trailed off as he glanced at me apologetically.

I smiled, punched him on the shoulder, and joked, "Nothing like a trial by fire, right?"

Drac and Gabe laughed uneasily, and Aunt Julia exclaimed, "Honestly, Kyrie! What a thing to joke about!"

I was about to respond to her when a stifled laugh at the door made me turn quickly. I stopped laughing and felt the color drain from my face as I saw Steele standing there in the doorway, looking much less arrogant than he had last night.

"Spook, we forgot you were waiting," Drac said quickly. "Come on in and join the party."

Gabe added, "You don't even have to break down the door to get in."

Steele inched his way into the room, slouched over and hands in his pockets, looking uncomfortable and sheepish. If we hadn't had such a rough start and I hadn't heard the things he had said about me, I might have felt sorry for him. As it was, I stood there staring at him, not knowing what to say. Drac and Gabe were silent too, glancing back and forth between Steele and me.

At last, Aunt Julia stepped forward, extended her hand and said graciously, "Mr. Steele, I am Julia Carter, Kyrie's aunt. I want to thank you for keeping an eye on her last night."

Steele shook Aunt Julia's hand and replied uneasily, "Nice to meet you, ma'am. Um . . . really . . . I didn't do that much . . ."

He avoided looking my way, but I noticed that he cast a helpless glance at Drac and Gabe, who didn't step in to help him at all.

"Nonsense, Mr. Steele!" Aunt Julia contradicted. "You were the one who carried my niece to safety and tended to her till the ambulance arrived, and we are indebted to you." I stared incredulously at her, wondering why she was being so melodramatic. She caught my eye and prompted, "Isn't that right, Kyrie?"

I glanced at Steele, who was looking at the floor and actually blushing, then at Drac and Gabe who were also looking at Steele and trying not to laugh, and back at Aunt Julia, who raised an eyebrow, crossed her arms and repeated, "Right, Kyrie?"

Suddenly feeling cornered, I muttered, "Okay. Right, Aunt Julia." Feeling like a preschooler who was being chastised for being ill-mannered, I faced Steele but looked down at his feet—was he wearing orange Converse high-tops?—and said, "Thanks for watching my back."

Steele grunted in acknowledgement and shifted uncomfortably, glancing over at Drac and Gabe, who were obviously enjoying this exchange. Somehow keeping a straight face, Gabe fixed his gaze on Steele and said meaningfully, "We're *all* just glad that Kyr is all right. Right, Spook?"

Steele cleared his throat, glared briefly at Gabe, and answered shortly, "Yeah, I'm glad she's okay, too."

Thankfully, at that moment the nurse came in with my discharge papers. Drac, Gabe and Steele waited in the hallway while the nurse went over my follow up information with Aunt Julia and me and had me sign the paperwork.

After the nurse left, we all headed out of the hospital. I had to shade my eyes from the bright sunshine, which made my head throb for a minute. Then while Aunt Julia went out to bring the car around to the front of the building, Drac, Gabe, and Steele filled me in on what had happened at the mansion the night before. Drac began, "When we broke down that door, it just looked like a freakin' bomb had gone off in that room, stuff everywhere, furniture overturned, the fire—"

Gabe snorted before interrupting, "You should have been in there while it was happening." He shook his head, crossed his arms and glanced my way.

I shuddered at the memory of the objects flying across the room, aiming right for us. It had been unnerving enough just seeing things like curtains moving during the investigation, but to have objects—especially large pieces of furniture—hurling across the room with the obvious intention of hitting us was downright terrifying, and I hoped I would never have to experience it again.

"Like we told you," Drac continued, "Gabe and I got the fire out while Spook carried you out of the mansion and tended to you while Lynette called for help. We managed to keep the fire contained to that one small area of the room."

A strange expression came over Gabe's face as he added, "The crazy thing is that it seemed like everything calmed down after we got you out of that room. That fire all but extinguished itself." He looked meaningfully at Drac, then continued, "And the EMFs went back to normal shortly afterward."

I leaned against the wall, looked pointedly at Gabe and said, "To hell with getting the Hollywood scary movie images out of my head; I say that bastard Jeremiah was out to get me."

Running his fingers through his hair, Gabe seemed to search for the words to say. Finally, with a quick glance at Drac, he admitted, "In this case I have to admit you may be right. But I still say this is an exception."

I rubbed my aching head, still trying to take in everything that had happened. I had seen enough episodes of *Project Boo-Seekers* and done enough reading about other investigations to know that Gabe was probably right. Still, I had a hard time wrapping my brain around the fact that I had somehow managed to stumble into investigating the one place with the one spirit that would make my experience that exception, and I wondered again if Jeremiah would have caused this much trouble for another female investigator, or if his venom was the result of my familial ties with Rosanna.

Suddenly remembering that Steele had said he was going to try to get rid of Jeremiah's spirit, I cast a furtive glance his way, still not wanting to talk to him. Seeing Aunt Julia's car approaching from the far end of the parking lot, I finally gave in to my curiosity and turned to Steele. "So . . . did you get rid of that demon Jeremiah?"

My breath caught in my throat for a second as my eyes met his, and I realized that he had been watching me. He looked away quickly and crossed his arms tightly in front of him before responding, "He wasn't a demon, Carter, just a very angry, very unsettled spirit." He narrowed his eyes at Drac and Gabe, who seemed to be sharing some silent joke.

I focused my attention on Steele, trying to ignore Drac and Gabe's antics. "Okay, so how did you get rid of that 'very angry, very unsettled' Jeremiah?"

For a moment, Steele's lips twitched as though fighting a smile. To my irritation, I had to suck in my lip and bite down on it to fight a smile of my own. Looking away quickly, he cleared his throat and swallowed hard before attempting to recover the previous night's aloofness. "After the ambulance took you away and I got the all-clear from the firefighters said it was clear, I tossed the knife you found in the tree and a few other things into my backpack and made a beeline upstairs to confront Jeremiah. That back bedroom looked like a war zone. There was still shattered glass and kerosene on the floor where you were attacked, and the carpet was scorched from the fire." He pursed his lips and shook his head as though deciding how much to tell me. Finally, he met my eyes and said gravely, "Given the amount of kerosene on the floor, it's odd that the fire was contained only to the spot where you were standing." I swallowed hard, thinking about the implications of his words. Before I could speak, he continued his story. "Someone had opened the windows a bit to air out the room, but it was still smoky as hell, and the atmosphere was very heavy. There was an energy in that room. A dark, negative energy. "

"A dark energy?" My eyes widened at his words. Hadn't he just told me that Jeremiah wasn't a demon? What else could that mean?

Reading the questions in my eyes, he quickly explained, "Not dark as in evil or demonic, Carter. Dark in the sense of negative emotions—anger, hate, guilt, fear. For a dead guy, Jeremiah was a mess."

I swallowed a chuckle at his joke, but then turned serious. "So how did you get rid of him?"

His eyes were grim as he looked at me and then launched into his account, reminding me of Cherry Pit's storytelling prowess.

***

"Jeremiah Berkeley," Steele called out. "I know you're here, so why don't you show yourself?"

He waited, his sharp eyes darting around the room as he slowly paced, watching for any sign that the angry spirit was about to make his presence known. Now that he knew what Jeremiah was capable of, there was no way he was letting his guard down even for a second. Unnatural silence filled the room, but he wasn't fooled; he knew he was being watched. "Come on, you bastard. Come out and fight like a man."

The air was thick with tension, and Steele's pulse pounded in his ears. He stopped pacing and just stood with his eyes closed, waiting for Jeremiah to make a move. Slowly, he became aware that the atmosphere seemed lighter. The darkness was seeping out of the room. A glance at the EMF meter confirmed his suspicions. "Oh no, you're not," he blazed, his eyes flashing fire. "You're not going to skulk out of here and hide."

He unzipped his backpack, pulled out the knife, and held it up high. Immediately, the EMF meter spiked. "You recognize this, don't you, Jeremiah? You thought you could hide what you did, but you were wrong." The air grew thicker once more, and the temperature dropped noticeably, making him shiver. "You used this knife to kill someone. Someone besides your wife."

The accusation hung in the air, fueling the menacing hatred that permeated the room. The darkness gathered together into a swirling mass that never quite manifested into a recognizable personage. Still, Steele knew it was Jeremiah. Looking squarely at the gathering form, he challenged, "You can kill your wife while she's on her sickbed. You can kill someone else in cold blood. You can bully a woman who comes here to try to help you, but you can't show yourself to me?" His breath condensed before him as he took a step towards the figure. "You're not a man. You're a coward. You hear me? A coward!"

A wordless growl filled the room as without warning the figure darted forward and lashed out. Steele cried out and fell to the floor. As he lay on the ground with blood flowing from a long gash across his cheek, the dark mass overtook him, enveloped him. Before he could get his bearings, everything went black.

***

Steele ran a hand through his hair. He was sweating, and all the color had drained from his face. Afraid he might collapse, I took a step towards him and laid a hand on his arm to steady him. Drac and Gabe looked ready to move towards him as well.

He turned to me with haunted eyes, reliving what had happened at the mansion. "When I came to my senses, I tried to get up, but I felt as though I were frozen. It was so cold, and the sense of hatred and hostility emanating from Jeremiah's spirit was like a weight holding me down. Before I knew what was happening, my mind filled with thoughts of my own wife's unfaithfulness. Rage, stronger than I've ever felt, rose up in me, and then humiliation, grief, and hatred, till all I wanted to do was go find Erin and . . ." He brought his hands up and fisted them. "Strangle her with my bare hands. And then I wanted to find the scumbag she'd been sleeping with, slit his throat with the knife I was holding, and watch him bleed to death."

I drew back in horror at his words. I knew he had a temper—I had seen evidence of that—but this was different; this was frightening. Drac and Gabe watched him warily as well, and I got the impression that this was the first time they heard this part of the story. He lowered his eyes to the pavement, taking labored breaths. He looked so tortured, so pained, that I hurt for him. Reaching out to touch his arm once more, I swallowed hard and asked softly, "What happened next?"

At first it seemed he hadn't heard me, but then he looked at me. The haunted look in his eyes was replaced by determination. "I knew those thoughts weren't mine, at least not all of them. *I* didn't want to kill anyone; I'd never wanted to kill anyone. That realization gave me the upper hand, and I knew what I needed to do."

***

"It's over, Jeremiah," Steele said. "It's not a secret anymore. We know you killed Rosanna, and you killed her lover, Benjamin Holtzman." His eyes darted around the room. The dark mass had disappeared, at least for now, and the atmosphere wasn't as heavy, but he knew that Jeremiah was still present, gathering strength for another attack. He needed to act now, before the spirit could come at him again.

Like a boxer returning to his corner of the ring in between rounds, Steele scrambled over to his backpack and dumped the contents, a small pouch tied with a thin leather cord and a smudge stick of white sage, on the floor. Still keeping a wary eye on the room, he snatched up the pouch. Clutching it tightly for a moment, he closed his eyes and visualized its contents—several polished stones—as he mentally grounded himself, preparing for the next round of this psychic battle.

A moment later, the heaviness began pressing in once more. Steele slipped the pouch around his neck and quickly palmed the bundle of herbs before fishing in his pants pocket for his lighter and lighting it. The scent of burning sage filled his nostrils and slowly spread through the room. Darkness began gathering in the corner of the room, and Jeremiah's emotions invaded his mind once more. The intense anger, malice, and humiliation were still there, but now he also sensed fear and guilt. Again, he saw his ex-wife's face, and the desire to harm her began rising within him. He got to his feet and waved the burning sage, surrounding himself with the smoke and steeling his mind against the attack. "It's not going to work this time, Jeremiah," he said. "I dealt with my anger long ago."

Deserved to be punished. Steele froze for a moment. The words hadn't been spoken aloud, but he heard them clearly in his mind. That was the first time Jeremiah had clearly communicated with him. At first it seemed obvious that Jeremiah was arguing that his unfaithful wife and her lover were deserving of punishment, but as the words sank in, he sensed that Jeremiah was also saying that he deserved punishment.

Still wary, but feeling some sympathy for the unhappy spirit, Steele slowly made his way around the room, making sure the smoke from the smoldering herbs penetrated every corner, combating the negative energy. "You had every right to be angry at Rosanna and Benjamin. They were wrong to do what they did, and they should have suffered the consequences. But taking justice into your own hands was wrong too, and you know that. You've been punishing yourself for a hundred years. A hundred years of tormenting yourself! Your anger, your guilt, your fear of being discovered have held you here, and you've held Rosanna and

Benjamin here." He gave the smudge stick a final decisive wave. "You've suffered long enough, Jeremiah Berkeley. It's time to let the truth be told so you can all move on."

At his words, the energy in the room shifted, and it felt as though a weight had lifted from his chest. The air still pulsed with emotion, but instead of anger and malice, there was a sense of sadness and regret, but also release.

***

As Steele concluded his account, his shoulders sagged as if from exhaustion, but he also seemed satisfied with his accomplishment. "After I was sure Jeremiah no longer posed a threat, I brought Chuck in to reclaim his home. He told Jeremiah that he owned the home now, and that Jeremiah was no longer welcome there." He gave Drac and Gabe a wry smile. "You know how soft-spoken Chuck is. It took some coaching to get him to sound like he meant it, but he put his foot down and closed the deal." He and Gabe bumped fists as though everything was hunky-dory.

I hated to rain on their parade, but there was one important piece of unfinished business. "But what about . . .?"

Steele turned to me as though he had just remembered I was there. My breath caught for a moment as our eyes met. My heart began racing, and I felt light-headed as his dark eyes held me entranced. As I quickly looked away, my gaze was drawn to the angry red scratches on his face, and I shuddered recalling who had given them to him. A long gash just below his right eye was deeper than the rest; I unconsciously reached up and gently caressed it.

Steele started at my touch, and his hand came up quickly to grasp mine. "Battle scars . . ." He gave me a crooked smile and cleared his throat before addressing my unanswered question. "No, Carter, I didn't forget about Benjamin Holtzman's body. While I was wrestling with Jeremiah, I got a very strong impression that there was something in the basement. Judging by the emotions that went along with that suspicion, I suppose it is possible that Benjamin's body is buried in the basement."

I stared at him indignantly, somewhat justified by the look of chagrin that accompanied his words. After all his snide comments about my wild imagination, he was now admitting that my hunch may have been correct after all.

He caught the look in my eye and cautioned, "Although we still haven't actually proven that hunch by finding something in the basement."

For a second time, my pulse quickened as we held each other's gaze, and I was relieved to see out of the corner of my eye Aunt Julia's car slowly approaching the patient pick-up area.

She rolled down the passenger-side window and peered out. "Are you ready, Kyrie darling?"

"Um . . . yeah," I stammered, unsure of what was going through my head. I glanced at Drac and Gabe and shrugged. "So . . . what's next? Is Chuck going to look into the suspicion that there's . . . something in the basement?"

Drac returned my gaze and then looked at Steele. "Well, yes. He knows he needs to find out once and for all what, if anything, is down there. Of course, he's not going to do it alone."

Gabe crossed his arms in front of him. "We—Drac, Spook, and I—agreed to back him up on this." He looked towards Steele. "Just in case anything happens."

Conflicting emotions surged through me at that point. After the previous night, really after all my experiences in that house, I wanted so much to be done with it, and I was ready to wish them all well and walk away. But something wouldn't let me. I opened my mouth to speak, then closed it uncertainly. I glanced at Aunt Julia, who was listening and watching through the open car window, then at Steele, who raised an eyebrow, and finally at Drac and Gabe, who looked quickly at each other.

"Kyr," Drac began, putting his hand on my shoulder. He seemed to have read my thoughts. "I know you've gotten really wrapped up in this case, especially after finding out you've got family ties to Chuck, but I really think you've been through enough."

Gabe added, "I'm with Drac on this one, Kyr. You've more than proven yourself. You need to let this go now and let us finish the job."

I knew they were both right, and I nodded in resignation, feeling tears welling up in my eyes as I stepped towards the car. It was no use to argue with them. Just as I grabbed the door handle, Steele suddenly spoke. "I can't believe I'm saying this, but I have to disagree. I think Carter should be there when we go into that basement."

Drac, Gabe, and Aunt Julia simultaneously cried, "What?!"

I swung my head around—far too quickly—to face him, and I stumbled slightly at the wave of dizziness that washed over me. I managed to stay upright by leaning against the car. "What did you say?"

With one hand on his hip and the other rubbing his head as though someone had hit him with a two-by-four, Steele responded, "Like I said, I can't believe I'm saying this, but I think Carter should be there. For whatever reason, she is tangled up in this case, and I think she should be there—just to watch, not in the way—for her own closure. So even though it's against my better judgment . . ."

As I turned to face Drac and Gabe, I felt like a puppy begging for a treat. I was silent as they stood staring at each other, seemingly communicating telepathically. Finally, Gabe raised an eyebrow and shrugged, and Drac let out a long sigh. He turned to me, looking somewhat defeated. "Are you sure you're up for this?"

I glanced at Steele, then back at Drac and Gabe. I avoided looking at Aunt Julia; I'd deal with her later. "Well, no," I admitted. "I want to just wash my hands of this whole thing right now, but I just can't." Glancing at Steele, I grudgingly said, "As much as it pains me to agree with him, I think he's right. I need to find out what's there, for closure, so I can let this go and move on. I need to know the truth."

Drac rolled his eyes up towards the sky and groaned. "Oh, I can't believe I'm saying this. As long as you're physically up for this, all right; you can be there when we go into the basement. As long as it's okay with Chuck, that is."

I turned to Steele with a timid smile, which he hesitantly returned. Seeing him smile at me that way, I suddenly had the urge to throw my arms around him for sticking up for me. The thought of being in his arms made my head spin with excitement. Would our tentative truce last through the next part of this adventure?

CHAPTER EIGHTEEN

Aunt Julia and I were both quiet as we started home. Each of us seemed to be waiting for the other to speak. At last she glanced my way and began, "Kyr, are you sure you want to go back to that house? Like Drac said, haven't you been through enough?"

I sighed, relieved that we were broaching the subject right away, but unsure of how to convey what I was feeling. I shifted in my seat and responded, "Well, like I told Drac, I'd like nothing more than to forget it and be done, but I just can't. I don't know how to explain it, but I need to do this."

Aunt Julia gave me a wry smile. "That's always been one of your strengths, Kyr, not wanting to leave something unfinished." She sighed resignedly. "I'd rather you stay away, but you're a grown woman and you need to make your own decision and do what feels right for you."

I smiled to myself, thinking how different Aunt Julia was from my parents. They would have pressured me to drop this whole thing long ago, that is, if I would have even begun this adventure at all. Even though Aunt Julia was obviously concerned and didn't want to see me hurt, she was willing to let me do my own thing without trying to lay a guilt trip on me. As I stared out the window at the cows in the fields, I thought about how liberating it was to me to finally be doing something I wanted to do without worrying about my parents' disapproval.

Aunt Julia interrupted my thoughts. "Well, it seems you and Mr. Steele are getting along now."

I glanced at her and saw the smile tugging at the corner of her mouth. I considered her remark, wondering about the tentative truce Steele and I seemed to have reached. Yes, we'd finally had a fairly civil conversation, and miracle of miracles, he had actually taken my side about returning to the mansion, but his arrogance and his obvious dislike of me were always just under the surface. I wasn't sure I was ready to say we were getting along.

When I didn't respond, Aunt Julia joked, "I brought the car around as slowly as I could to give you two a chance to talk." She gave me another wry smile. "I was hoping Drac and Gabe would take the hint and skedaddle too, but they didn't. Typical men."

I shifted in my seat again and sighed. "Oh, Aunt Julia, forget the matchmaking. Steele is married . . . or was . . . I don't know which, although what woman could live with him, I don't know." I didn't mention what he had said about his wife cheating on him. As much as I wanted to say he probably deserved it for being impossible, the truth was I felt sorry for him, having been in a similar position myself. I just didn't want Aunt Julia taking his side. "And Drac and Gabe probably stuck around to make sure we didn't kill each other."

Aunt Julia said no more, but I could tell she was watching me out of the corner of her eye. I couldn't tell if she was worried about me or still plotting ways to get Steele and me together. Even trying to think of Steele in a romantic way made me shudder, and I wanted to tell her again to forget it, but I decided that the less I said, the better. Even if Steele and I were interested in each other, the last thing I wanted or needed was a man with the kind of baggage he had; I had enough of my own to deal with. I wanted to find someone who was dependable and uncomplicated, yet sweet and playful. Someone like Gabe.

The drive from the hospital seemed to take longer than the half hour it actually took, mostly because I felt it in my throbbing head every time we hit a pothole. I let out a contented sigh when we finally pulled up in the alley behind my house. It seemed as though I had been gone a week instead of the couple days it had been.

Aunt Julia grabbed some things out of the trunk before we headed to the back door. I fumbled with my keys as I unlocked the door and went in. I was a bit irritated with myself when I felt a sense of relief that it was the middle of the day instead of nighttime, and that I wasn't alone. I hoped my experiences weren't going to turn me into a person who was afraid to be alone in the house.

At Aunt Julia's prompting, I sat down in the living room while she busied herself with putting my things away and preparing a light lunch for us. I hated being idle, and I wondered how I would get through the next few days of being babied. I picked up the book lying on the lamp table next to me and tried to read, but focusing on the words and trying to make sense of what I was reading made my head hurt, so I gave up. Then I attempted to work on the afghan I was crocheting, but it was too difficult to work with the yarn with my stiff mummy arm, so I gave that up as well.

Thankfully at that moment, Aunt Julia came in with a tray. We settled in and enjoyed a lunch of ham and cheese sandwiches and canned vegetable soup. Aunt Julia joked, "My homemade soup is much better, but canned will do in a pinch."

I smiled and agreed with her. "Maybe you should teach me how to make homemade soup while you're here. That is, if it's not a secret recipe."

Laughing through a bite of sandwich, she responded, "Oh, don't be silly. Nothing secret about my recipes." She glanced fondly at me. "And even if they were, I'd have no trouble sharing them with my favorite niece."

I smiled again, thinking how glad I was to have Aunt Julia nearby and wishing once more that I could have shared this kind of closeness with my mother.

After lunch I settled back down in the living room and tried to find something on TV to occupy my mind. I smiled wryly to myself, remembering my dad's complaint that he had over 200 cable channels, but there was never anything on worth watching. *Some things never change.* I finally settled on a tornado documentary on the Weather Channel.

Aunt Julia came in a few minutes later. "Do you need anything before I make a run to my place to pick up a few things?" She was planning to stay with me for the next few days till my arm healed a bit and to make sure my concussion didn't cause me any problems. I had tried to convince her that I would be all right alone, but she would have none of it. She insisted that she knew I could take care of myself, but right now I needed to have someone there to lean on. When I told her I could have friends check in from time to time, she protested, "Most of your friends are married with families of their own to worry about. I'm alone; I have the time to spare, and I am *your* family." I eventually gave in, knowing how important it was for her to stay busy and to feel useful.

"I'll be fine," I insisted now. "You won't be gone long, and I promise not to take on any home improvement projects while you're gone."

"Hm," she said suspiciously. "You'd better behave, or I'll . . ."

I smirked at her hesitation; Aunt Julia was really no good at making threats. "You'll what?"

She waved her hand at me. "Oh, just you behave!" She gave me a quick hug and headed out the door.

A few minutes later I turned the TV off. I had seen the documentary before and really wasn't interested in watching it again. I found myself wondering how things were going at the library and thought about calling Maureen. After picking up the phone and starting to dial the number, I thought the better of it. If I heard what everyone was doing, I'd just want to rush down there and do some work myself or at least get online and catch up on some things.

I laid my head back and closed my eyes. I was tired, but unused to napping during the day, so I knew I wouldn't fall asleep, but at least I could rest. Almost right away, I heard a strange noise in the house. I sat up straight, holding my breath, thinking right away of Jeremiah. What if he'd left Berkeley mansion only to follow me home?

Taking a deep breath, I calmed myself aloud. "Okay, Kyr, come on. Get the scary movie images out of your mind; not everything is a ghost . . ." I sat motionless, listening for the sound again. Even though I was expecting it, when it came again, I jumped. Suddenly recognizing the sound, I relaxed and sat back. Just the dogwood tree hitting the siding in the wind. Another sound caught my attention, and I identified that one as the heat pump kicking on. As much as I tried to rest, I seemed to hear every little sound inside and outside the house and mentally debunked each one. Usually when I was at home alone during the day, I was busy, so I either didn't hear many ambient noises, or if I did, I ignored them. But now that I was forced to be inactive, I heard everything.

When Aunt Julia returned a little while later, she was surprised to find me still wide awake. I laughed ruefully and told her, "Well, I guess I didn't realize how much noise a house makes during the day."

She raised an eyebrow at me and joked, "Too much *Project Boo-Seekers*, or too much ghost hunting?"

I shook my head. "Neither. Just not used to being here and being still during the day." Giving Aunt Julia a mischievous look, I joked back, "It's a good thing I pay close attention to their debunking techniques. At least I can tell the difference between a ghost and the house settling."

Aunt Julia laughed out loud. "You're a scamp just like your uncle."

The rest of the day seemed to drag on since Aunt Julia wouldn't let me do most of the things I liked to do when I was home, and since I couldn't read or crochet. I was thankful for her company, however, as I at least had someone to talk to. I was surprised at how tired I was at bedtime, and I was glad to make my way upstairs earlier than I likely would have any other time.

I clumsily got myself out of my clothes and into my nightshirt. As I folded Steele's hoodie, making a mental note to remember to take it along when I returned to the mansion, I caught a whiff of something. I brought the hoodie close to my nose and inhaled. There was a slight smell of smoke, but I also noticed the scent of cologne or aftershave. I couldn't identify what kind it was, but it smelled like leather, spice, and woods, and the scent reminded me of someone dashing and adventurous. I closed my eyes and thought about what kind of man would wear cologne like that. I thought about Gabe; the glint in his dark eyes, his short dark hair, and his sweet playful smile that just made my knees go weak when I saw him on TV, and even more so in person. But this scent just didn't seem to go with his personality.

Of course not, dolt. This is Steele's hoodie, so it's his cologne. Suddenly, Steele's face came to mind, and I found myself thinking about his brown eyes, and his long, wavy, almost-black hair. I recalled how that one lock of hair always fell into his face, making me want to brush it back. Then I thought of his stubbly beard and wondered what it would be like to touch it, or to kiss him.

My eyes flew open, and I tossed the hoodie onto my bed. What on earth was I doing? I must have hit my head harder than I realized if I was having those kinds of thoughts about Steele. That, or Aunt Julia was downstairs chanting love spells. I turned and flounced to the bathroom to brush my teeth. When I came back into the bedroom, I picked up the hoodie and hung it on my door knob before climbing into bed and turning out the light.

My sleep that night was broken by Aunt Julia coming in every couple of hours to make sure she could awaken me. Still, I knew I had some crazy dreams, as I remembered bits and pieces for the next few days. But there was one that was quite vivid and that I remembered in detail for quite a long time.

I was once again trapped in the back bedroom of the Berkeley mansion. Jeremiah was there, taunting me and telling me I'd pay for meddling and revealing his secrets. He locked the door and sealed the windows, then set fire to the room before vanishing with a maniacal laugh that echoed long after he was gone. As thick smoke and flames surrounded me, I tried to scream but couldn't. Suddenly, strong arms wrapped around me and pulled me out of the room. Out on the lawn, in bright moonlight, I saw it was Gabe. He touched my face and stroked my hair. He closed his eyes and pulled me close in a sweet, tender kiss. When I pulled back to catch my breath, I looked into his eyes, but it wasn't Gabe who was holding me; it was Steele. Somehow I wasn't shocked by this; in fact, I was quite pleased. I reached up and gently touched the scratches on his face, then stood on tiptoe and tenderly kissed each one. His arms went around me, and he pushed me to the grass. His lips claimed mine in a passionate kiss that I returned willingly. The scent of his cologne filled my head, and I felt myself becoming dizzy with desire.

When I awoke, sunlight was streaming through my window. I realized I had my pillow locked in an embrace, and I was tangled in the sheets. I sat up, puzzling over the details of my dream. Pulling my nightshirt closer around me, I realized that Steele's hoodie was wrapped around my shoulders. "What in the world . . ." I muttered.

Just then, Aunt Julia came into the room. She stopped short, seeing me sitting up, looking confused, with Steele's hoodie wrapped around me. Giving me a questioning look, she said, "I was just coming in to wake you. Did you have a bad dream?"

I shoved aside the hoodie, brushed my hair back out of my face and said, "Not a bad dream . . . I guess . . . just . . . strange." I glanced down at the hoodie and continued, "I hung that hoodie on the door knob last night. How . . .?"

Aunt Julia cocked her head and offered, "Well, the doctor did say you might have a little trouble sleeping. Maybe you got cold in the night and walked over to the door in your sleep."

That didn't make much sense to me, as there was a blanket folded up on the end of my bed that I could have grabbed if I were cold, but since I had no other explanation, I decided that that's what must have happened.

***

A couple days later, we were all back at the Berkeley mansion. There was a distinctly different atmosphere about the whole property; I noticed it even as we drove up the driveway. The house looked as stately and impressive as before, but gone was the shadowy, menacing aura that I had sensed on my previous visits. Even Chuck seemed almost a different person, more relaxed and at ease, and he looked several years younger. After shaking hands with Drac, Gabe, and Steele, Chuck came over to where I was standing and hugged me carefully. "Kyrie, I'm so glad you're all right. I feel terrible for everything you've been through here."

I smiled up at him, touched by his concern. "Thank you, Chuck. None of this is your fault. Jeremiah was just . . ." I faltered, not wanting to say anything too harsh. "He was just being Jeremiah. I just hope his spirit can rest."

Chuck led us into the house, and we prepared to head to the basement. As we slowly descended the rickety stairs, Chuck said, "Whatever you said to Jeremiah, Spook, it seemed to work. There hasn't been any negative activity in the house since then. The whole place seems different. Watch your heads."

Drac, Gabe, and Steele ducked beneath a low-hanging beam near the bottom of the stairs. Steele replied, "I'm glad he kept his word and left." He swung at a cobweb that was dangling in front of his face. "Let's hope he stays away."

Drac turned to Chuck. "Any idea what you're going to do if we find . . . anything down here?" He obviously still doubted we'd find a body.

Chuck scratched his head and responded, "Well, I have a friend, Bill McCardle, who's a police officer with the county. I mentioned the whole situation to him, to get his take on it. He and I grew up together, so he's heard all the stories about this place. He doesn't really believe in ghosts and things—doesn't *not* believe either. Anyway, when I told him what we suspected about the basement, he kind of laughed it off, figuring it was a lot of imagination and nonsense." I felt Steele's eyes on me, but I resisted the urge to look at him. Chuck shrugged and concluded, "He said to give him a call if anything turns up."

Drac and Gabe looked at each other for a moment, and Gabe said half-jokingly, "I wonder what he'll say if we present him with a body?"

Chuck laughed uneasily and led us to the back part of the basement by the coal pile. While the rest of the house seemed calmer and even friendly now, this part of the basement still felt heavy to me. In the light from the single bulb hanging from the ceiling, shadows seemed to move out of the corner of my eye. I stole a glance at Steele, wondering if he felt anything, but his face was unreadable.

Three shovels leaned against the wall near the entrance to the small coal room. The large, nearly-empty coal bin had been moved out in front of the furnace. Drac stepped into the eight-by-ten-foot room, followed by Chuck. Gabe and I peered in the doorway, while Steele leaned against the coal bin. Drac scuffed his foot on the dirt floor where the bin had stood for almost a hundred years and looked pointedly at Chuck. "Time to see if we can solve this mystery once and for all." Chuck's eyes betrayed his uncertainty, but he nodded in agreement. "Judging by the entries from Belle-Anne's diary, and the dreams both you and Kyr had . . ." A low grunt from Steele made me turn towards him for a moment.

He didn't speak or even raise his eyes to mine, just stared intently at the floor. "There's a good chance that there's more than coal in this room."

Chuck hooked his thumbs in his belt loops and shook his head. "I never would have guessed that this room held something as gruesome as a murder victim, let alone someone from my own family." A jolt went through me as I realized that Benjamin Holtzman was more than just the victim of Jeremiah's jealous rage; he was also Chuck's great-grandfather. I looked at him with new respect, wondering how I would feel if it were my own relative who was believed to be buried there.

Ever the voice of reason and skepticism, Steele straightened up and reached over to grab the shovels. "Well, we have yet to prove there really is anything"—he gave me a hard look—"or any*one* buried here. That's what we're here to find out."

Steele handed shovels to Drac and Gabe, while Chuck grabbed a trowel from a pile of gardening tools. They all crowded into the coal room and began digging. Feeling like a slacker, I began looking around me for something I could use to dig. Gabe caught my eye and stopped digging. "Don't even think about it, Kyr!"

Steele glared up at me for a second and ordered, "You stay back out of the way. I don't want to have to carry you out of this house again."

My face reddening, I opened my mouth to say something, but he turned away and began digging again, ending the conversation. Gabe was still looking at me, and he raised an eyebrow. Drac was watching me too, so with a final glare at Steele, I crossed my arms and leaned against one of the supports to watch.

They dug for quite a while, seeming to make little progress. "Good ol' clay and shale," Chuck joked. "Imagine trying to garden in this kind of soil."

I laughed shortly, recalling the struggle my mother had had trying to grow vegetables in our back yard. I continued to watch as they dug. When Gabe shifted to get a better angle with his shovel, I noticed the K-II in his pocket flashing like crazy. "Gabe, why is your K-II going off?"

They all stopped digging, and Gabe grabbed the K-II from his pocket. It ceased flashing as soon as he had it in his hands. We all watched it for a moment, but the lights remained dark. He shook his head and looked at Drac. "I don't know. Maybe it's picking up EMFs from something." He took the K-II and moved it slowly around the area they were working, but the lights did not change. He shook his head again and handed me the K-II. "Why don't you keep a hold of this? See if anything happens, maybe ask a few questions."

I took the K-II from him, and the others went back to digging. Oddly enough, as soon as they all started digging again, the K-II lit up. When they stopped digging, the K-II ceased flashing, but as soon as they started up again, so did the flashing lights. Tired of staying in one spot, I began pacing around, asking questions. "Is anyone down here with us?"

The lights flashed. *Yes*.

"Are you trapped here?" *Yes* again.

"Are you the one frightening women in the back bedroom?" My voice trembled as I asked that one; thankfully the lights stayed dark.

"Will what the men are doing help you leave?" There was a second's hesitation, and the lights lit up and stayed lit for several seconds. Drac, Gabe, and Steele all witnessed it, then glanced over at Chuck, who had stopped to mop the perspiration from his brow.

"I guess that means we should keep digging," Chuck said, smiling.

I soon ran out of questions and again stood alternately watching the dig and eyeing the K-II, which continued to flash as they dug deeper into the ground. After what seemed like a long time, Gabe stood up and stretched his back, then handed his shovel to Chuck and hauled himself out of the hole to come and stand next to me. He crossed his arms and looked down at me. "I know you're just itching to get in there and help."

I crossed my arms too and gave him a half smile. "Yeah," I admitted. "I feel like I'm just in the way standing here and watching."

Gabe chuckled and replied, "No one thinks you're in the way, Kyr."

My eyes involuntarily went to Steele. He had stopped digging to take off his sweatshirt. I couldn't help noticing the way his muscles strained against his T-shirt, and I watched as his strong arms pushed the shovel almost effortlessly into the stubborn ground and tossed huge chunks of clay and shale out of the hole. I could see the bottom of a tattoo peeking from beneath his short sleeve, and I wondered what the design was. Realizing I was staring—at Steele, no less—I shook my head and turned back to Gabe, who was watching me curiously. I felt my face flush, and he quickly hid a smile and said, low, "Spook doesn't think you're in the way either. Remember, he's the one who wanted you here."

I let my breath out in a huff and was about to respond when Steele suddenly knelt down and shouted, "Hang on; I think I got something here."

Drac and Chuck stopped digging, and Gabe and I both crowded in the doorway while Steele quickly yet carefully shoved dirt and stone out of the way, first with the trowel and then with his bare hands. He had found a huge, flat chunk of rock that somehow seemed out of place. He and Drac scrambled to push more dirt and rock away to uncover it. Finally, he and Drac were able to pry the rock loose and haul it out of the hole.

"Holy . . . ! I don't believe it!" Drac and Steele said at the same time.

My eyes flew wide with horror at the sight that greeted us. There, staring up at us from the hole, was a human skull. Bits of hair still stuck to the top, and dirt filled the eye sockets. I dropped the K-II as my hand flew up to my mouth; a pill bug skittered from between the teeth and down the lower jawbone. Suddenly feeling as though I had walked into a horror movie, I wailed, "Oh, my God . . . ," and began trembling and breathing heavily, trying not to scream. I wanted to look away, but I was hypnotized by the morbid scene in front of me. I vaguely felt hands on my shoulders and heard voices calling my name, but they seemed far off. Someone roughly turned my head away from the scene; I blinked a few times and found myself looking into Gabe's concerned eyes. "Kyr, snap out of it."

"Get her out of here!" My eyes sought out whoever had spoken, and I met Steele's glare. I didn't even have a chance to feel irritation towards him as my eyes were again drawn to the skull leering from the hole. I began whimpering again and cowered closer to Gabe. Steele grabbed his sweatshirt, covered up the skull, and repeated, "Get her *out* of here! *Now!*"

Gabe gently but firmly guided me up the basement stairs and out of the house into the frigid evening. He opened up the back of the Petery Paranormal van and helped me inside, where I put my head in my hands and burst into tears. Gabe said nothing, but sat next to me with his hand on my shoulder till I got hold of myself and was able to stop sobbing. Ashamed of my reaction, I kept my head down, not wanting to face him. *I can just imagine what Steele thinks of me now.* I didn't wonder at the time why it mattered what he thought.

After a few moments of silence, Gabe asked quietly, "Are you all right?"

Still not looking up at him, I nodded. "What is wrong with me?" I asked angrily. "For God's sake, I've seen skeletons before. Why am I freaking out like an idiot?"

Gabe gave me a shake and replied, "Kyr, this isn't some anonymous skeleton on display in a classroom; you're a little wrapped up in this. You know, or think you know, whose skeleton it is, and you may know how it ended up there. That puts a different spin on things."

What Gabe was saying made sense to me, but it didn't help the way I was seeing things. "But the last thing I needed was to freak out in front of . . ." I was going to say Steele. "In front of everyone. I feel like . . ." I couldn't even finish the sentence.

"Come on, Kyr, stop beating yourself up." I thought I could hear a smile in Gabe's voice, and I wondered if he knew I was thinking about Steele and thought I was worried about impressing him. "This is why Drac and I were hesitant to have you down here; we were afraid if we found anything it would be too much for you."

"I couldn't stay away," I argued, finally looking up at him. "I had to know what was hidden here."

Gabe smiled and handed me a handkerchief. "It's clean, I promise." He laughed as I snatched it from him and made a face, remembering the last time this had happened, with Steele. "I know you wanted to see this through," he said, serious again. "We've said it before, Kyr, you've got a lot of guts. You could have just bailed out a long time ago, but you keep facing your fears and fighting through to the end. You should be proud of yourself."

I snorted, not feeling very brave or very proud at the moment. I found myself thinking again about Steele, wondering how much further I had fallen in his eyes. I couldn't figure out why it was so important for me to prove to him that I wasn't a loser, but I wanted to redeem myself yet again. I had no idea how I could do that.

I didn't have long to wallow in my self-pity, however. Drac and Steele emerged from the house a few minutes later and came out to the van. "Well, there's no doubt about it," Drac began. "There's a full skeleton buried in that basement. You can clearly see what we assume are bloodstains on what's left of the clothes. Chuck is going to put in a call to his friend Bill to see what the next step is."

I shuddered, thankful I wasn't Chuck and didn't have to spend the night in a house with a skeleton buried in the basement. Drac glanced at me, then winced slightly at the look on my face. "Sorry, Kyr. I guess I should have saved you the details . . ."

I lowered my eyes again, wishing I could get the images out of my mind, but not wanting to let on that it still bothered me. "I'm fine," I responded, hoping I sounded convincing. "How is Chuck taking it?"

"Well, he's pretty shook-up—" Drac began.

"Though not as much as you were, Carter," Steele interrupted. I glared at him, ready to utter a nasty remark, but as I looked at him, I realized he was just teasing me. I tried to come up with a clever retort, but the playful glint in his eye made my breath catch in my chest, and I couldn't think of anything to say. Drac and Gabe both laughed, and Gabe nudged my shoulder as if to assure me that Steele didn't think I was a loser. I glanced at him and then back at Steele, whose face had gone back to being as unreadable as ever. I wondered if I had imagined what I had seen in his eyes just a second ago.

Drac continued, "Finding a body buried in your basement would freak anyone out, but given the things that have been happening here, I think it's almost a relief to him. Maybe now things will calm down once and for all." He looked at Steele and raised an eyebrow. "At least, let's hope so."

A couple hours later, after we had all talked to Chuck's police friend who had come right over after Chuck phoned him, we got ready to leave the mansion, hopefully for the last time. Bill said he'd have to call in a forensics team to investigate the basement just to be sure it couldn't be considered a crime scene. However, he assured Chuck that by the looks of the skeleton the case would likely be quickly dismissed.

For what seemed like the hundredth time, I said good-byes to Drac and Gabe, although I wondered this time if it would really be the last time. My parents might have been rolling in their graves at the thought, but I was hooked on ghost hunting, and I had a feeling I would be getting in touch with JoEllyn about joining her group in the near future. Drac and Gabe exchanged a look when I told them that, and Gabe joked, "Look out, spirit world. Kyrie Carter, Supernatural Sleuth is on the case."

As they finished loading up the van, Steele and I were left standing together in an uncomfortable silence. I tried to read his expression, but it was closed as always, although I couldn't help thinking he still had an air of disdain around him. He finally cleared his throat and said, "You sure you won't have nightmares tonight?"

I sensed he may have been teasing me again, but his remark had a slight edge to it, so I wasn't sure. I responded, with the same edge in my voice, "No, I won't have nightmares tonight. I'm not a baby, you know." As soon as I made that last remark I mentally kicked myself. *Oh, why did I say something that stupid?*

"I didn't mean that I thought you were a baby," he replied, with even more of an edge to his voice. "But you are a little overly *sensitive*." Recalling Drac's suggestion that I might be an empath, I wondered if his choice of words was deliberate. "And you sometimes act like you're afraid of your own shadow."

I felt my face turning red at his words. He wasn't the first person in my life who had said those words to me, but for some reason it made me angry to hear them coming from him. I shot back with the first words that came to mind. "Well, I'd rather be overly sensitive and afraid of my own shadow than a . . . stuck-up, arrogant . . . jerk." My eyes met his, and without thinking about how horrible it sounded, I muttered, "No wonder your wife left you." As soon as I said those hateful words, I regretted them, as more than a momentary spark of hurt flashed in his eyes. I had gone too far, and I knew it. "I'm sorry . . ." I whispered. "That was . . ."

"Forget it," he growled, low. He turned quickly and stomped to the van; he got in the back seat and slammed the door.

Gabe came over to where I was standing and shook his head at me. "Kyr, that was way out of line."

I looked up at him with tears in my eyes. "I know . . . Oh, God, why did I say that?"

Gabe stood looking reproachfully at me for a moment. "There's a lot more to him than you can see on the surface. He comes off as arrogant, but he's hiding a lot of hurt. You've got to realize that."

I hung my head, wishing I could undo the last few minutes. He may have been arrogant towards me, but what I had just done was unforgiveable, especially after he had carried me out of the house and tended to my burns just days before. Suddenly I remembered his hoodie. I ran to my car and grabbed it, holding it to my face for a second to breathe in the scent of his cologne. I walked slowly towards the van, then thought the better of it and walked back to where Gabe was standing. "This is Steele's . . . Could you . . . ?"

Gabe shook his head, smiling mischievously at me. "I'm not doing your dirty work, Kyr. You need to face the music and give it back to him yourself . . . or else keep it as a souvenir."

My eyes widened and I felt myself blushing. Had he seen me holding the hoodie close to me and read something into it? I hoped not; it was enough having Aunt Julia on my back. Gabe walked away from me, and I could hear him laughing. I swallowed hard and headed towards the van. I knocked on the window and when Steele looked at me, I held up his hoodie. He glared at me and turned away, then rolled down the window and reached for the hoodie. "Um, thanks for . . . lending me this," I said softly. Part of me still wanted to know how I had come to have it, but I obviously wasn't going to get that answer now.

Steele nodded tersely at me and started to roll up the window. I reached out and stopped him. "Steele? I really am sorry. What I said . . . It was unforgivable . . ."

"I said forget it," he replied and rolled the window up the rest of the way.

Drac and Gabe were standing by the front of the van watching our exchange. I felt miserable that this was going to be my last memory of this investigation. Drac came over and hugged me. "He'll come around, Kyr. You wounded his pride, but he'll be back to his not-so-sweet self in no time."

I tried to smile at his joke, but I couldn't. I was trying too hard to fight back the tears. Gabe came over next and hugged me. "Drac's right, Kyr. He'll be mad for a day or so, and then he'll let it roll off his back. I think he knows he's been pushing your buttons this whole investigation. You went too far, but so did he." I looked up at him, wanting to say something, but not knowing what. Gabe grinned and teased, "Who knows, maybe you two will end up being the best of friends."

Knowing what he was hinting at, I thumped him on the shoulder. "Gabe you're so . . ." To my chagrin, I couldn't come up with a good-natured insult quickly enough.

Drac laughed. "Ooh, good comeback, Kyr."

I made a face at him and threatened playfully, "I'll get Aunt Julia after you!"

His eyes widened in mock fear, and he ran over to the driver's side and jumped in. As I turned to head back to my car, I glanced at Steele once more. I thought I saw the glimmer of a smile, but as soon as he caught my eye, the hardness returned to his face, and he looked away. With my head down, I trudged back to my car and got in. As I drove cautiously home, I tried not to think about the way things had ended with Steele, instead trying to remember everything else about my first investigation.

***

Not surprisingly, the police forensics team had judged that the skeleton was close to a hundred years old, so Chuck's house wasn't considered a crime scene. He was unable to find any descendants of the Holtzman family who wanted to claim the remains, so he had them buried in the small family graveyard behind the house. I thought it was sad that even after so many years the family's pride wouldn't let them forgive Benjamin's indiscretion.

The last I'd heard regarding the Berkeley mansion, Chuck reported that he still had activity in the house, but what remained was friendly and even at times playful, and he accepted it and decided to live peaceably with whoever had chosen to remain there. He also related that one day, not long after the skeleton had been buried in the family graveyard, he had gone up to the attic for something and had come face-to-face with the same male spirit he had seen there as a child. As their eyes met, the spirit smiled and nodded at him, then turned towards the window and vanished. He hadn't seen the apparition since then.

As for me, with Chuck's permission of course, I wrote about my experiences as a newbie ghost hunter. I wrote about the things that had happened during our investigations, the dramatic family history Chuck had discovered in the journal in the attic, and finally about the skeleton in the basement. It was quite the piece of writing, and it was published as a series in our local newspaper, thanks to an editor friend who pulled a few strings for me. And thanks to the publication of that story, I began doing some freelance writing for the newspaper, mostly focusing on local legends, mysteries, and of course ghost stories.

I kept my promise to Cherry Pit and visited him several times before he passed away a few months later, the day after his ninety-first birthday. He seemed to find peace in having the mysteries of his family home settled once and for all, and he was tickled pink that my story had been published in the paper. The nurses at the home said he never stopped bragging about his home being made famous by Petery Paranormal and *Project Boo-Seekers*, and by his new favorite author, Kyrie Carter. *Author.* I liked the sound of that.

For a long time after the investigation ended, I basked in the sense of accomplishment I'd felt over helping to solve the Berkeley mansion mystery, despite being an inexperienced newbie who was afraid of her own shadow. The pure gratitude I'd seen on Chuck's face over having his home back again made my heart swell with pride that I'd played an integral part in his happiness. Before going on this investigation, I'd thought that the lure of paranormal investigation was the thrill of the chase, the chance to capture the elusive evidence that would prove to all that ghosts were real, but I was wrong. I realized that the real thrill, at least for me, and for people like Drac, Gabe, and even Steele, was in helping people get answers to questions they were often afraid to ask.

Still, despite helping Chuck find the answers he sought, my own burning question—the one I'd shared with Drac, Gabe, and Steele after our first night of investigation—went unanswered. I recalled Steele's comment that he didn't think there was a definitive answer to my question, but that didn't mean I wouldn't keep trying to find it. And I knew what my next step would be.

Just before Christmas, I rethought my earlier declaration that I didn't have the nerve to take up paranormal investigating as a hobby, and I approached JoEllyn and Brad about becoming a full-fledged member of Ghosts and Beyond, as an investigator, and not just their behind-the-scenes researcher. JoEllyn expressed her elation over having me on the team by presenting me with a personalized T-shirt a couple weeks later at Christmas; it read simply *Supernatural Sleuth*.

THE END

ABOUT THE AUTHOR

Leta Hawk had her first encounter with a ghost at four years of age. Since then, she has been fascinated with ghoulies and ghosties and all things that go bump in the night, and now she writes about them. She lives vicariously as a supernatural sleuth through her *Kyrie Carter* series.

When Leta isn't penning spooky stories, she can be found rounding up dust bunnies or tackling Mt. Dishmore and Laundrypile Peak in her Central Pennsylvania home, which she shares with husband Mike, sons Wesley and Wayde, and black lab Raven (but no ghosts).

61072164R00142

Made in the USA
Middletown, DE
17 August 2019